An American Story

An American Story

CHRISTOPHER PRIEST

GOLLANCZ

LONDON

First published in Great Britain in 2018 by Gollancz
an imprint of the Orion Publishing Group Ltd
Carmelite House, 50 Victoria Embankment
London EC4Y 0DZ

An Hachette UK Company

1 3 5 7 9 10 8 6 4 2

A CIP catalogue record for this book is
available from the British Library.

ISBN (Hardback) 978 1 473 20057 9
ISBN (Export Trade Paperback) 978 1 473 20058 6
ISBN (eBook) 978 1 473 20060 9

Typeset by Input Data Services Ltd, Somerset

Printed and bound in Great Britain by Clays Ltd, Elcograf S.p.A.

MIX
Paper from
responsible sources
FSC® C104740

www.gollancz.co.uk

To Don Greenberg

In the rare cases when a historical event, especially a traumatic event, stirs emotions on a massive scale, touching many millions of people, it enters popular culture. Great numbers of people soon form beliefs about what happened and why – creating a historical narrative. It is difficult to overstate the significance of these narrative beliefs. People will try to make sense of the events that fit their prior understanding of how the world works.

Philip Zelikow

ONE

then: 2000

NYC – the story

She said to me: 'Here's the story. It's probably not what you expect. You want me to read it to you?'

She was holding an information sheet she had just retrieved from her mailbox in the lobby of the apartment building. It had been mailed from the office of a heritage organization in Edinburgh, Scotland.

'OK,' I said. I was still on my first cup of coffee. It was too early in the day for a story, but she was sitting across from me, looking pleased, wanting to make me hear it.

'I'll leave out some of the ordinary stuff. Here goes: "It began as a Victorian house, built in 1855 for a man named John Smith." Would that *really* be his name? John Smith? That's like John Doe, right? "The house was then called Swanstonhill. It had an extensive estate, including woodland and meadows, situated on high ground overlooking the village of Port Bannatyne, on the Isle of Bute. It commanded panoramic north-facing views over the narrow stretch of sea called the Kyles, which separates the island from the Cowal peninsula."'

We were a world away from Scotland, sitting in her cosily untidy apartment on the thirteenth floor of E 104 St in New York City. The only window in the room looked out on to other

1

windows at the same height in the apartment building opposite. Sunlight reached her room once a day, around five in the afternoon, for about twenty minutes.

'"In the early 1870s a natural spring was discovered at the western end of the property. The water was high in minerals and health-inducing salts."' She peered closely at a small map included in the text. She continued, putting on a terrible imitation of an English accent which she almost immediately changed to an even worse Scottish one: '"Building work began on an immense extension to the original house, running along the high ground towards the west. Extra wings were added, notably the one at the west end, which was built to contain the spring. During this period hydropathic hotels were popular throughout Europe. The wealthy flocked to them to refresh bodily energy and gain all-round healthful feelings, by drinking the water or bathing themselves in it."'

She briefly held up the page for me to see a photograph. It was black and white, slightly out of focus, a reproduction of an ancient picture postcard. It showed a row of small cottages fronting a long hillside. The building she was talking about loomed up on the hill behind them, a Victorian pile, with steep roofs, gables and spires, picture windows. Trees grew everywhere.

'"The new building extension,"' she went on, abandoning the embarrassing fake accents, '"included a pump room, an immersion pool, steam baths and exercise and massage areas. The central part of the extension was created as an eighty-eight-room luxury hotel, with many saloons and drawing rooms. All the main bedrooms faced the view towards the north – lesser rooms were situated at the rear of the hotel, and this was where the guests' servants stayed."' She lowered the sheet of paper. 'Do you Brits still take your servants with you on vacations?'

'I used to,' I said. 'But I've had to let most of mine go. I now

only have a couple of manservants and a housemaid. And the chef, of course.'

She carried on.

'"In June 1879 the building reopened as the Kyles Hydropathic Hotel, and was soon functioning successfully as a luxury resort for factory owners, eminent lawyers, wealthy retailers and so on, from the prosperous industrial belt of Central Scotland, as well as attracting a steady stream of important guests from England and parts of Europe." Why don't I like the sound of these people?'

'You don't have to like them,' I said. 'They're all dead now.'

'"When not taking the waters the guests had many other diversions open to them. There were tennis courts, a croquet lawn, a nine-hole golf course, a swimming pool, and extensive planned gardens. Walks and pony rides in the surrounding wild terrain, the interior of the island, could be arranged. Top chefs from Europe were in charge of the kitchens, and the service of the general staff throughout the rest of the hotel was rated as excellent."

'OK, this is where it gets more interesting. "The hydro operated until the outbreak of the First World War, when it had to close. It reopened after the war, but at a much reduced level. Although the mineral springs remained available, the hotel now operated on a more conventional, modern basis.

'"When the Second World War began in 1939 the hotel was again forced to close. It was requisitioned by the Royal Navy, and the building became officially known as HMS *Varbel*." They turned a hotel into a *ship*?'

'That's a convention of the Navy,' I said. 'They designate their land-based establishments as ships.'

'"Operating from *Varbel*, men of the Royal Navy served throughout the war with distinction and bravery. They were mostly assigned to mini-submarines and two-man steerable

torpedoes. Their most notable success was the immobilization of the German battleship *Tirpitz*, in Alta Fjord in Norway".'

She turned the sheet. She skimmed a few lines.

Then she read: '"At the end of the war the Navy returned the hotel building to the owners. They left it immaculately clean and undamaged, but because of the building's great age, and the fact that during the war it was impossible to carry out building repairs, the hydro was unsuitable for use as a hotel. The cost of renovation was so high that the building remained unused. That is its present condition. It remains standing but for now is unused." Great! We can use it.'

'What's great about that? And how did you get hold of this information?'

'I sent off for it. We're looking for a spooky old place to hold next year's convention. We thought a Scottish castle would be ideal, but this sounds even better.'

'Oh yes,' I said.

Her name was Lil, and I was in love with her. She was in her early thirties, working for a large book publishing corporation in New York City, but when she let her hair down she and some of her friends would spend long weekends at conventions. I knew exactly what kind of conventions she liked to go to. She wanted me to be at the next one with her.

It was not to happen – in under a year's time Lil would be dead.

TWO

now

Two people I had known

There came unexpected memories of two people I had once known. One of them was from the margins of my life, one from my heart. There was no direct connection between them, or none that I knew of apart from my knowing them both, yet the news that one of them had died reminded me inexplicably of the death of the other.

I had woken up to a feeling of peacefulness. I was alone in my bed – my life partner Jeanne was away and would not be back for another three days. The house was quiet because Jeanne had taken our two young sons with her. There was none of the normal background domestic chaos of making the boys get out of bed, urging them to put on their clothes, the clatter of breakfast and rushing around and forgetting things and occasional shouts and doors closed noisily.

Whenever Jeanne was away I slept with the room's curtains open, because of the view of the firth. Jeanne said that daylight made her wake up too soon, but I liked to turn over and look out across the calm waters, glimpse the first ferry setting out for the mainland. This morning the sun was shining, and across the firth the mountains of Argyll were dark and green.

The radio had been on all night at a low volume, but I turned

it up to hear the news. Halfway through the headlines the death was announced of Kyril Alexeyevich Tatarov, the Russian-born mathematician. I was unexpectedly moved by the news, because although I had met Tatarov only a couple of times, he was a great man and I had in fact actually met him at a time when any kind of meeting was almost impossible to arrange. He was a complex and contradictory man, intelligent off the scale because no scale existed for his sort of mind, but odd and with many human foibles. Twice he had shown me small and unsought kindnesses.

I waited for the full story to follow the headline, thinking about him. The reporter came on and spoke well and accurately of Tatarov: he was a brilliant theoretician, a geometrist and topologist, winner of the Fields Medal, the Clay Millennium Prize, born in the Soviet Union in 1932 and exiled with his family to the USA when still a small child. His father was a statistician, his mother a teacher. Tatarov had spent most of his adult life working in an American university, his unique career and achievements largely unrecognized outside the closed intellectual world in which he thrived.

Tatarov's sensational and unexplained disappearance in 2006 was mentioned of course – it was completely out of character and one of the few events of his life that had become known in the wider world. At the time the mystery had been reported and followed in news media on both sides of the Atlantic. Much of the speculation about him was salacious and inappropriate: rumours of a *femme fatale*, an exchange of secrets with a former KGB agent, a plot to kidnap him back to Russia, and so on. None of this was remotely true, but his disappearance was never explained.

The alarm was raised one day when he failed to appear for a seminar at the Courant Institute in New York. He had said nothing about travel plans, his university apartment was locked, he

left no note or explanation. Because of political upheavals in Russia at the time there was speculation he had been abducted by the KGB or FSB – no denial came from Moscow, which for a time seemed to support the idea, but he was not produced or paraded for the press as a refugee from the West. If this had happened it seemed like an odd time for it, so long after the collapse of the Soviet Union. Confusing everything, the FBI released a computerized airline ticket for a flight on the day he disappeared – on the ticket he was identified as taking a journey from New York's JFK to London Heathrow, with an onward flight to Glasgow. That particular part of the mystery was never definitely resolved, although a reporter on the *New York Times* later traced the ticket code to another passenger booked on the same flight, someone who was not connected in any way but who had not checked in on the day.

After a few weeks Tatarov quietly reappeared at the Courant, saying or explaining nothing, and returned to his work.

The incident inspired a feature film not long after. It was not a good film and it was soon forgotten, but it did have a starring role for a great actor and it had made me some extra money. Because I wrote the screenplay I was partly, not entirely, responsible for the film's mediocrity. I had never written for the screen before, and have not done so since. I was hired to write the screenplay because I had published a couple of magazine features about Tatarov, which constituted most of the information about him that was on record. The producer was not to know, and I intended that he should never find out, that I knew the true story of Tatarov's disappearance. I was, however, bound by a promise of confidentiality.

The first time I met Kyril Tatarov was for a meeting which lasted less than an hour, one afternoon when I was granted an interview with him. It took place in 1996. I was a young journalist and Tatarov was a tenured professor at the Courant

Institute in New York. He was then in his mid sixties.

It turned out to be a difficult meeting — how do you prepare for an interview with a genius? I did not do well. He assumed I knew more about mathematics than I really did. His manner of speaking was discursive and full of references to matters I knew nothing about. He spoke quickly, leaning back in his chair with his eyes closed or half-closed, the flow coming unstoppably for several minutes, but then halting without warning. He expected my next question to follow at once. He was absorbed in establishing the proof of something called the Pèlerin Conjecture, a topological knot theory, which had remained unproven since the postulate was developed by the great French mathematician Jean-Louis Pèlerin in the early twentieth century.

I was not a mathematician but a journalist working as a freelance for a general interest science magazine. I had done what preliminary research I could into the conjecture, but I was ill-equipped to engage with Tatarov on any serious level. The Pèlerin was an arcane problem within a discipline that was itself a deep enigma to most people. Professor Tatarov, to give him credit, quickly sensed this, and in his own way he tried to simplify and explain what he was saying, but his own way was not even close to mine. At the end of the interview he offered me a few notes which one of his students had written, in the hope they might elucidate a little more. I went away from the Courant embarrassed and humbled, but also feeling rather fond of Professor Tatarov.

Afterwards I managed to transcribe the recording of what Tatarov had said with sufficient accuracy for the interview to make sense, perhaps seeming facile to other mathematicians but comprehensible to ordinary readers. After the piece appeared Professor Tatarov himself made no complaint about errors, but to judge by some adverse comments he made during the course of the interview about the magazine I worked for I assumed

8

he would probably not read the article. However, my career as a science correspondent did gain a little credibility from the interview, and a few weeks later a nationally distributed magazine offered me a contract for regular work. I felt indebted to Professor Tatarov for this.

The brief radio obituary also mentioned the one other time Tatarov came to public awareness. He had been nominated for the Fields Medal and tried to decline it, but then changed his mind after persuasion and pressure from his colleagues. A year or so later he won the Clay Millennium Prize – again he tried to refuse it, and once again gave way to the friendly persuasion of those around him. Then he was rumoured to be in line for a Nobel, although there was no separate Nobel for mathematicians. He was interviewed on television. The first questions were about his disappearance in 2006, but he refused to answer. He was asked why he kept trying to decline the most prestigious awards in his academic calling. He was repeatedly urged to say if he would accept the Nobel, if awarded.

Professor Tatarov was enraged by the persistent questioning, and became incoherent in his answers. His general physical appearance, his chaotic hair, staring blue eyes and untamed eyebrows, uneven teeth, florid countenance, briefly made him notorious as an archetype of a certain kind of reclusive academic. His behaviour made him seem erratic, brilliant, engaging, monstrous, slightly mad.

The interview was cut short, but almost immediately afterwards it went viral on the internet. This was where I saw it, and it made me feel sorry for him. He was unworldly, highly specialized, preoccupied with many complex ideas and concepts, and totally ill equipped to deal with lighthearted banter from a television presenter.

That was Kyril Tatarov, who had just died. He was in his early nineties.

The other

But then there was the other. Why Tatarov's death at a great age should remind me once again of Lil, of Lilian Viklund, was not immediately clear. As people they could hardly be less alike, their deaths were now more than two decades apart, and in my heart and memory they occupied completely different places.

At the end of the news bulletin I switched off the radio and I continued to lie in bed with memories of Lil sweeping in on me, pushing aside my thoughts of Tatarov.

I had not thought about Lil for a long time, at least for many months, but I had been profoundly upset at the time of her death.

She was my girlfriend, she died, I was bereaved, but I moved on and built a life without her. Stating it as coldly as that is a true way to describe what happened, but in reality everything to do with her death was traumatic and shocking. Lil was my lover, my friend, my intimate, and until the day she died I assumed she was to be my future. Then she was taken from me with violence and cruelty.

The years following her death drifted by, the shock of the news and the upset of the loss diminishing, but slowly, so agonizingly slowly. Gradually I began to think of her less obsessively. I started to reshape my life without her. When one's lover is murdered so young I suspect it is never possible to recover fully. You are not able to forget completely, never able to throw off an infinitesimal grain of hope. Because although I did eventually manage to bury my feelings of terrible loss, the grief, the loneliness, I was never allowed closure. I knew she was dead, I knew she had been killed, but I never had proof. The people responsible were not taken before a court, her body was not found. That tiny, always unsettling, grain of hope remained.

A few years after Lil was murdered, I met Jeanne and she shortly became my partner. Although we never married, Jeanne and I had been living together for years. We were raising two sons, Seth and Louis, who were of school age. Jeanne and I both followed our careers in the context of a busy and absorbing family life. Like every other long-established couple we shared many things – a home, holidays, books, paintings, music, memories, the children above all.

Lily Viklund, and my long affair with her, moved further away into my personal past. I could never forget Lil entirely, but in the press of contented life with my family and the turning cycle of the years she became increasingly a figure from before.

Even so – I vividly remembered how she looked, and somewhere in my study there were dozens of photographs of her, stashed in an old box. I could never forget her voice, her American accent, the way she stood and moved and dressed, the political matters that aggravated her, the passions of her beliefs and, oddly, her love of trivia, old TV programmes and homemade jewellery. She was a subtle and complicated woman, often mercurial in her moods, sometimes annoying and frustrating, but always loyal and loving. And of course her sudden death at the hands of others, when still so young, gave all memories of her a painful, unignorable impact.

Boats and islands

Jeanne and I lived on a small island in an inland sea: the Firth of Clyde. The island was called Bute, or *Eilean Bhòid* in its Gaelic original. The only town on the island, formerly called Rothesay, reverted to its Gaelic name: *Baile Bhòid*. After the Scottish UDI many of the western isles, and the smaller settlements in the Highlands, had chosen to revert to their Gaelic names, a kind of folk reaction against the technocratic and progressively

modern industrial society that was transforming the country. After a short but difficult transition period, Scotland rejoined the EU as a separate nation. The old forced union with England, to the disadvantage of the Scottish, was over.

For Jeanne and me it was the best of many options: Jeanne was born in Edinburgh but had spent most of her adult life in England. For her it was a return. I was English, born in London, but my maternal grandparents were Scottish. For me it was an exploration of my personal heritage. Our migration to the north meant we were able to bring up our boys as Scots, as full Europeans. So far the plan was working well.

That morning I was alone in the house, free to laze in the bed a little longer than usual. Jeanne had taken the children to visit her mother, who lived in Morningside, a district of Edinburgh. I had slipped into a harmless, temporary routine of sleeping with a radio at my bedside, curtains open all night so I could enjoy the light on the bay in the morning, sometimes listening to music as I fell asleep, always turning it off once I was fully awake. I liked the sound of quiet voices in the night, the classical music, news reports from around the world. I slept through most of it but it was a comfort to have it there. The radio helped fend off, equalize, the feeling of being alone. The house was too static, too full of silence, whenever Jeanne and the kids were away.

I missed Jeanne every time she made one of these trips, which since her mother's health began to decline the previous year had become a regular duty for her. An undercurrent to our lives at present was the growing awareness that Lucinda, Jeanne's mother, should no longer be alone, that she might have to move to Bhòid to be with us.

Overnight, the two car ferries that connected with the mainland were moored at the pier a short distance from our bedroom window. At six o'clock the first of them was brought

back to mechanical life by the crew. The starter motor of the vessel's main generator began turning somewhere deep inside the engine room. It sometimes woke me up, but often I was already awake, waiting for the signal sound. The steering engines would start soon after. The ferries were equipped with azimuthal rudder propellers for navigation in the shallow harbours, and whenever the ship was taking on passengers and vehicles these engines were turned towards the beam, holding the hull firmly against the quay wall. They emitted a quiet but insistent noise, reaching me across the harbour waters like the contented mumbling of a large resting animal.

The generator brought life to the workings of the ship. I imagined it recharging batteries, starting the pumps, waking instruments, booting the navigation computers, turning the radar antennae, sending a flow of electrical power to the saloon and cabins, ventilating the vehicle deck and cargo holds.

The first crossing to the mainland was scheduled at six twenty-five, by which time the waiting cars and trucks had driven across the ramp and into the vehicle deck. The foot passengers tramped at the same time across the companionway, a climbing zigzag of sloping metal passages above the space between the ferry terminal and the upper saloon of the ship. The dark shapes of these people crossed behind the translucent windows, enigmatically lit from above. They were almost certainly people I knew, or at least would recognize from seeing them about the streets of Baile Bhòid. Soon I would be clambering up the same sloping passages when I caught a later ship.

It was pleasant to lie there, feeling the town slowly come alive, thinking about Lil again, remembering her not as dead but as she had been when alive. The distance in time removed any sense of guilt about doing so. Such memories were pleasant, but the way she came to an end always loomed over them.

Jeanne knew about Lil. She knew about our intense

relationship, the plans and hopes we had – she knew how Lil had died, the traumatic impact her death had had on me. Jeanne and I were in love from our first few days together, and I could never have kept these things from her. Almost straight away she sensed I was harbouring something from the past. I wanted to unburden myself, but knew it was an imposition, so I tried to hold it back. It did not take Jeanne long to make it possible to let go and in the end I told her everything I could about Lil. I left nothing out: what had attracted me to her, the plans we had made, the problems we had tried to overcome. I tried to be objective, calm, practical, true, sensitive to Jeanne's feelings, not self-pitying. Inevitably, there came a release of the emotion which I had been suppressing and could no longer control. Jeanne said nothing, advised nothing, held me close.

Why, though, had the news of Tatarov's death brought this reminder? He had had a long life and a great life – he died two days ago. Lil was thirty-one when she died, might have had a long or a great life had she been given the choice, but she died young, more than two decades ago.

Crossing the border

I needed to catch the ferry at eight o'clock, so I soon climbed out of bed, showered, shaved, dressed, took a quick breakfast of a sweet pastry I had bought the previous evening, washed it down with lukewarm instant coffee. I checked the house was secured, then walked the short distance to the harbour and went to the ferry terminal.

While the ship sailed smoothly across the firth I made a call to Jeanne in Edinburgh, confirmed I was leaving as planned and that nothing had come up to change my plans. I would be home the next day, before her. She put Seth on the phone, the older of my two boys. He wanted to be home, he said, Gran was ill and making him depressed. His voice was hushed – I sensed

him turning away, holding the phone hard against his ear. He was on a school break and naturally felt he was losing valuable free time. Jeanne came back on and said she would probably stay for another night, perhaps two. Lucinda had developed a troublesome cough and was breathing with difficulty.

An hour and a half later, after the train ride from the mainland ferry port, I was at Glasgow Airport, queuing with hundreds of other people to pass through the English border. There was a treaty border post of this sort at every Scottish airport where there were flights to the south. When my turn came I showed my Caledonian passport, hoping the English police officer would not notice that I had been born south of the border and ask me the questions I had been asked several times before on earlier flights. This time he did not – an immense line of other passengers was behind me. The officer went slowly through my papers, finally making me touch the fingerprint scanner. He spoke with flat, deliberate Yorkshire vowels. After my fingerprint was scanned he stared at the computer screen for several seconds, not blinking. He typed some letters, maybe words, maybe a code, waited again for a response. I heard my flight being announced while I stood there.

Then I was through, technically across the English border and no longer in Scotland, onward to the second delay. A maze of roped walkways had been set up across the hall, making the long line of us snake to and fro, shuffling past each other again and again. Everyone seemed tense. We came at last to the checking of the passport and the boarding pass, then the security machines and searches, the retinal scan, residence identity check, jackets and shoes off, belt removed, cabin luggage weighed and x-rayed, phones, laptops and tablets examined or searched separately. This time I was not requested to boot my laptop, but I saw several other passengers standing impatiently

beside their machines as the monitors displayed the familiar logos.

I hurried away to the gate, where I was one of the last to board the plane.

Shortly after midday I was in the webzine office in London, being talked through the editorial plans for a special feature in the issue after next. These meetings, once a regular happening in the office, were now fairly infrequent. All contributors, salaried or freelance, were expected to be present. The introductory overview from the managing editor set a tone of apprehension. The magazine was suffering a shortfall in advertising revenue, he said, and more redundancies were becoming inevitable. As a freelance I was immune from the threat of redundancy, but I knew all too well that they could save money by no longer commissioning work from me.

They moved on to specifics. The planned feature was going to be concerned with developments in cosmology and particle physics, neither of them my favourite subject. I made myself look attentive, but I was barely connecting mentally, my thoughts elsewhere.

'So, Ben – will you do that?'

I swivelled around, realizing that Miranda Hamid, the features editor, had addressed me.

'Sorry, Miranda – will I do what?'

'The in-depth profile of Sandy Bellow. She has a new season starting at the end of the month. We should cover it. We haven't published anything about her series yet.'

'OK,' I said.

It would be a soft option for me, a commission I could complete in under a day. I did not think, though, that I should say how negative I felt about Ms Bellow's television work and contributed little to the discussion that followed. We had already been provided with a programme-by-programme synopsis of

the whole season. I would not look forward to interviewing her. I was therefore quietly relieved when around the table a change of mind slowly emerged from others there. Ms Bellow had been written about too often in other media, someone else said, given too much publicity. She was a presenter who rarely showed much depth of understanding about the subjects of her programmes. Although I agreed with this I felt it was unfair, so I found myself arguing unconvincingly in Ms Bellow's favour – I was not the only science journalist who sometimes felt out of depth when taking on certain subjects. I knew from social media that she was an intelligent and well educated woman, probably underestimated because of the medium she worked in and the level of the audience at which her programmes were aimed. But soon the idea of a profile of her was anyway dropped, and I let it go. Other ideas were being aired.

Miranda remembered that I had once interviewed Kyril Tatarov, and she asked me if I had anything I wanted to write about him now. I said no. She said they had already posted a stock obituary online, but felt that something longer might be appropriate. I said no again, and after a moment we moved on to the next subject.

Towards the end of the meeting another project was suggested to me. It would mean a trip to Paris the following week. I remembered that Jeanne and the boys would be back at home by then and I did not want to be away. I thought about it, then agreed. There were several non-stop flights between Glasgow and Paris every day. I could probably do the trip with only a single overnight stay in Paris. Someone else wanted to do the story instead of me, a new writer called Karl Wilson – we all discussed that, but in the end they agreed it should be me who went. I was relieved – I had turned down a lot of other work during the meeting.

That was my working day.

I went for a drink afterwards with Karl Wilson and two of the staff writers, then took the Underground to Southwark, just across the Thames.

It was by this time too late to catch a flight back to Glasgow, one that would definitely connect me with the island ferry. I had learned that when flying between England and Scotland I could run into delay at airports, and I had missed the last ferry a couple of times in the past. Recently, whenever I was in London overnight, I had started sleeping at the two-room apartment owned by the magazine's management company. It was not ideal because other people who worked for one or another of the companies in the group were able to use the place, so there was no guarantee of clean bedding or supplies of food. It was small and fairly squalid, on the ground floor and close to a road, with traffic noise penetrating the old windows for most of the night. The place felt dirtier and more unwelcoming every time I went there. It was, however, free of charge.

A woman from one of the video channels operated by the company was already staying in the apartment, and although she was not there when I arrived she had claimed the only bed. Something like this often happened – there was always some issue about using the flat. I thought about moving to a hotel for the night, but then also thought about the extra cost. There was a couch, and I kept a sleeping bag in one of the closets. I had used them both before.

I called Jeanne again when I arrived in the apartment, and afterwards went out for a meal. I had forgotten to convert some of my euros into pounds before leaving Bhòid, so I knew the English bank would add a steep currency conversion surcharge to my credit card.

I was on my own for too long that day. There had been too much travelling, too many delays, too much introspection during the meeting, then an evening spent in an uncomfortable

place. I should have been at home with my family or arranged to meet colleagues or friends in the evening. Instead, I walked around the London streets near the apartment, thinking how alien it felt. Many shops were boarded up, and several of the houses or apartment blocks I passed had high security gates. A police car went by slowly: it was a heavy SUV with anti-impact shields on the main windscreens and powerful spotlights mounted on the roof. The words Immigrant Advisory Service were printed on the side, with a free hotline telephone number for people wishing to report unauthorized or illegal residents.

Everywhere there were signs I understood but did not recognize, and in general there was a feeling in the city I found disorienting. It was like this whenever I visited the English capital, and it was slightly worse every time. I had the uneasy sensation that I no longer spoke the language, as if I was abroad. I was a native Londoner, born in Kentish Town, but London was beginning to feel like a foreign capital to me.

My mood was low. I was still remembering Lil. I wanted to be back on my island off the Scottish coast, waiting to see Jeanne and the kids, staring across the calm waters of the firth at the steep hills and high moors of the Cowal peninsula.

When I returned to the flat the woman who was staying there had already gone into the bedroom and closed the door. She had left the television on, so I opened a can of beer and sat on the couch until the news came on.

Kyril Tatarov's death was no longer mentioned. The main story was news from the USA, and what I heard began unexpectedly to make sense of what had been preoccupying me all day.

Wreckage

It was the headline story, with reporters already on the scene. The remains of a crashed aircraft had been discovered in the

Atlantic, about one hundred miles off the coast of Delaware. The wreckage was in deep water. The two or three fragments already raised to the surface had been identified as coming from a large jet. No pieces of wreckage with serial numbers had yet been found and no clear markings were visible. There was no clue as to the make of aircraft, which airline it belonged to if it was a civil aircraft, nor did anyone know if it was a military plane, or even to which nationality it might belong.

The bulletin went on to cover other current news stories, but at the end a specially extended news report returned to the Atlantic crash site.

There was an aura of secrecy and urgency about the find, a sense remarked on by reporters that more was probably known than they were being briefed about. The wreck had been discovered by a US Navy vessel more than a week ago, and only when a heavy lifting barge was requisitioned from a civilian oil drilling company did the story start to emerge and the press begin to gather. As reporters and TV crews hurried to the scene, chartering many boats, the area of sea was cordoned off by the US Coast Guard. Several large ships of the US Navy were moving to the area. The location of the wreckage was beneath a regular transatlantic route and scheduled flights were being diverted north and south.

One of the reporters, working for an independent cable channel in Boston, claimed on camera that the CIA and Homeland Security were controlling the search. This was immediately denied by a spokesperson for the National Transportation Safety Board, the body responsible for the investigation of every civil aircraft accident in the USA. Their involvement indicated the crashed jet was a commercial one. Meanwhile, none of the main airlines who flew the Atlantic route were aware of any aircraft that had gone missing, and there were no unexplained historical accidents.

After Lil's death at the hands of terrorists I developed a compulsive interest in air crashes. If a terrorist involvement was suspected I invariably suffered a feeling of sick dread, of sorrow, of fear, of morbid curiosity, but rage and frustration if the terrorism was confirmed. There was nothing I could do about it. I was not frightened for myself – I flew regularly. But when someone you love is killed in a hijacked plane a complex array of feelings and emotions is aroused by any major air incident.

I switched channels, finding other news bulletins, hoping for more information, but for now much of the reporting I could find was speculative. There was talk of attempts to find the black box, the flight data recorder, even though it was obvious to me, as it would be to professionals working in the flight industry, that if the wreckage had been submerged in deep seawater for as long as seemed likely no readable data would remain.

From one of the reports I learned that the media had found out about the discovery the evening before, Eastern time. That would make it the early hours of the morning, Scottish time. News broadcasts would therefore have been mentioning it all day, but because I was travelling I had not been aware of them. As I sat on the uncomfortable old couch, sipping my can of beer, I slowly realized that this incident must have been described in the same bulletin that was on the radio when I woke up. Because I was suddenly preoccupied with my thoughts about Tatarov I had probably taken in the information subliminally. It might explain why my thoughts circled inexplicably around both Tatarov and Lil.

'Are you intending to watch that all night?'

The woman's voice startled me, and I turned in surprise. She had entered the room and was standing behind the couch. In the semi-darkness I could only just make her out. She looked

tall and angular, clutching a robe or a blanket about her body. She had earphones around her neck.

'You left it on,' I said. 'I was watching the news.'

'I left it on because I forgot to turn it off. You've been switching channels for half an hour. I can't get to sleep with that noise going on.'

'I'm sorry. I didn't realize you could hear it.'

'Even through these,' she said, indicating the headphones. She leaned forward, peering at the screen. 'Have they identified the plane yet?'

'I don't think so.'

She stepped across and squatted down on the carpet in front of the TV.

'The story has been coming through on the agency channels all day,' she said. 'We were following it in the office. It began as the discovery of the plane, but now it's about access, about whose plane it was, and who is now responsible for the investigation. They're not going to say yet, but it must be an American aircraft.'

'How do you know that?'

'Because the CIA are involved. The Coast Guard, the Navy, the Homeland Security people. They wouldn't turn out like this if they thought it was someone else's. They obviously know something about it they're not letting on.'

'So it could have been a military aircraft? Would it have been carrying weapons? A nuclear device?'

'We thought that at first, but then one of the NTSB guys they interviewed on CNN said they had found a civilian airliner. He came back on a few minutes later and corrected that. They weren't sure yet, he said, they couldn't confirm anything about the plane. It looked to us as if he'd been told to keep his trap shut.'

She sat there a few minutes longer, staring at the screen. Then the broadcast ended, and she climbed to her feet again.

I said: 'I'll turn it off now.'

'Thanks. I know you, don't I? You're Ben Matson.'

'Yes.' We nodded formally to each other.

'I'm Jaye Hume,' she said. 'I work for EcoMo, the video company. Same group, same building, two or three floors below your office.'

I did not recall seeing her before, but there was only a dim table-lamp on in the room and she was a dark shape from where I was sitting. A lot of people worked for the magazine group. I did not know them all.

'It's not my office,' I said. 'I go in there sometimes. I only work for them now and then.'

'You're an editor?'

'A writer. A freelance journalist. I have a contract with them, but I work for myself.'

'I'm in the production office.' She backed away towards the door. 'OK, I'm going to bed. See you.'

She pulled her earphones over her head and closed the door. If she said anything more I did not hear it.

'Goodnight,' I said quietly, to the door.

I found my sleeping bag in the closet where I kept it, and spread it out on the couch. In the kitchen I brushed my teeth, then pulled off my trousers and shirt and started to wriggle down into the bag.

The door suddenly opened again. She was still holding the blanket or towel about her body.

'Look, Ben – I feel bad about grabbing the bedroom before you arrived. I'm not as tall as you. I'd fit on the couch a bit better – would you like to swap with me?'

'No – you had the bed first. I don't mind.'

'I've been on that couch myself. It's hard and lumpy.'

'It's only one night,' I said. 'I'll survive.'

'Then –' She continued to stand in the doorway. 'Why don't

you —? I mean, it's a large bed in here. If you'd like to come in and —'

'No, Jaye — thank you.'

'It's not what you might think.'

'I'm not thinking anything. Thanks again, but no thanks. No offence.'

'None taken.'

She was gone in the morning, before I woke up.

THREE

then: 2000–2001

Lily Viklund and me

This is what happened to Lil and me.

Lil was born in the American Midwest, two sisters and a brother, father running a lucrative motor vehicle spares franchise, her mother a teacher at the high school. One of Lil's sisters was her twin, but they were not identical. Lil went to Michigan University in Ann Arbor, then after graduation moved east to find a job. She returned home to see her family at regular intervals. In New York City she was an intern at an advertising agency for a while, then worked in television, but by the time I met her she had been in publishing for several years and had become promotions executive for one of the big New York firms. She was high flying and well paid, but soon after I met her I realized that the image she projected was a workplace role she close to play. She liked the money and she liked the lifestyle it allowed her. She said she was good at what she did and loved doing it, but out of office hours she dropped the mask.

The evening I met her I was at a launch event for a book her company was about to publish. I can no longer remember why I was there – maybe someone had handed me an invitation they did not want to use. I was alone in New York on a writing

assignment, profiling some prominent New York IT executives. It was well paid but dull, and I was left to kick my heels in the evenings. A publisher's launch party was better than another long evening alone in a hotel room.

I did not in fact find Lil at all attractive when I met her: she was playing her role, playing it well, and seemed to be super-efficient in a mechanical, corporate sort of way. I knew it was a façade, but I still found it repellent.

When she approached me I was cool towards her, and she reacted accordingly. It was not a good start. She had come up to me, clearly not knowing who I was or why I was there. She was holding a copy of the book they were promoting. It was a newly indexed and academically annotated edition of Bram Stoker's *Dracula*. The book's editor, who was of course present at the event, was a well known English professor from a university in the Midwest. Lil launched into an obviously rehearsed descriptive spiel, handed me a copy of her press kit, asked me where I would be reviewing the book. Before I could answer she urged me to obtain a commission for a solus review and to contact her office for reproduction of the cover image. Her business card was attached to the press kit. I felt overwhelmed by her full-on publicity barrage.

As soon as it was over she was obviously about to move on and find some other likely contact to try to network, but something made me want to break, or at least slightly damage, the hard shell of her manner. Making small talk I mentioned in a semi-serious sort of way that a few years earlier I had stayed for a time in Purfleet. I expected the reference to drop into a black hole of non-recognition, but I was mistaken.

To my amazement she whirled around and came directly back to me.

She said: 'Did you say Purfleet? You were in *Purfleet*?'

'Yes. I was there.'

26

'Why did you say that? Do you know Purfleet?'

'I was staying there for a while. Not long. A couple of weeks, when I was on a training course. It's not –'

'Purfleet is where Carfax was! Count Dracula's house near London!'

'Well, I know the novel, and I thought –'

'You know the book? I *love* the book!'

Still somewhat daunted by her glossy image, I imagined even then that she must have picked up the reference from the book they were publishing, so I tried to make a joke of it. She was in earnest, though.

It quickly turned out that she was a genuine fan of the original novel, had read it several times and had repeatedly watched most of the movies. Earlier in the year she had been to a Dracula convention in New York, and said she could show me photos of herself in her vampire robe. Knowledge of Purfleet, an obscure Thameside port town in the dullest part of Essex, was deeply embedded in her, as of course was so much else about the novel.

She impulsively showed me the bangle she wore on her arm, which I had noticed, but not closely.

'I put this on for tonight,' she said. 'I don't normally wear it to the office.'

It had several discs and charms swinging from the gold band. She held some of them up for me to see. They were just about the last thing I imagined a dynamic New York publicist might be wearing. One of the discs had on it a tiny enamelled image of Dracula as played by Christopher Lee. Another was a picture of Bela Lugosi. There was one with a stylized gothic castle and one of the charms was in the shape of a crescent moon. Several more. Her professional façade had vanished. She in fact knew Stoker's novel and a host of details from it far better than I did, because I had read the novel only once, long ago when I was still a teenager.

This completely unexpected conversation continued for a couple more minutes. Then she said: 'We've got to talk, but right now I have to work. Stay there.'

She headed off to deliver her spiel to someone else. When the event ended she made sure we left together. She took me to a bar on Third Avenue, and it was there, while we drank wine late into the night, that she showed me the convention photos on her laptop: death-white make-up, thick eye shadow and heavy lip gloss, a black wig and a long skintight dress she had made herself, shimmering in the light.

It was by no means everything about her, but it was enough to reverse forever the glassily professional image I had glimpsed for the first minute or two.

There was another kind of dark

Lil was thirty when we met. She was well travelled, spoke French and Spanish, and some German. She belonged to two different women's groups, and when she was twenty-two she had been briefly arrested at a demo. She loved sport and was an active supporter of the New York Mets, she worked out four days a week, liked the theatre and movies, and she read books. Not the books the company normally published, she said, although she had plenty of those at home. She loved gothic fiction, fantasy, some biographies, novelizations of films. Nothing unusual about her therefore, apart from the vampires, and anyway they did not matter.

The big problem emerged the second time I saw her. It was the next day, I was still in New York, due to fly home a couple of days later, and both Lil and I wanted to spend as much time together as possible before then. We were completely new to each other, but we were already making tentative plans: when would I be able to get back to New York, would she be able to visit London sometime soon?

She took me for a walk in Central Park: a warm afternoon, tourists, people jogging, families out and about.

I asked her about her surname. 'Viklund – that's a Scandinavian name, isn't it?'

'Swedish.'

'You've lived in the US a long time?'

'I was born here. In Michigan. My parents are Americans, three generations back. Viklund is my husband's name.'

That silenced me for about ten seconds. Then I said: 'Your ex husband's name, presumably?'

'No – we are still married.'

The city, the whole world, seemed to go quiet around me as this sunk in. Lil said: 'I'm sorry. There's no good way to say it. It's probably better you should find out now –'

'I know how the rest of it goes. Are you getting a divorce?'

'We're separated. The marriage is over. The divorce will come later.'

Her story came out. The park and all the activity in it receded temporarily from my awareness. Her husband's name was Martin Viklund – a Swedish name and a heritage from his Swedish great-grandparents who had moved to the USA when young, but he was an uncomplicated American. ('Uncomplicated is part of the problem with Martin,' Lil said. 'Subtlety is not his strong suit.') He worked for the government at some kind of high level. She didn't specify what he did, but said he was a senior official, close to the White House administration. He was nominally employed by the Department of Defense and worked from the Pentagon in Washington, but he moved around a lot. She described him as a fixer, an operator. He was a civilian, not in the military, but he hung out with senior officers and defence strategists. She could tell me little about his work, partly because he was secretive about it but mostly because from the beginning they were forced to spend a lot of the time apart. She

had her own life, her job and her circle of friends here in New York City. She and Martin had commuted to see each other every week or so, but only at first. She said the marriage had been heading for the rocks from the outset, but it took them both a long time to accept that. They had been married for about three years – a terrible mistake, she said.

I agreed.

More was to come. There were no children, but there were property issues – about who owned what and to what extent and how it would be split. She said she owned her apartment free and clear, but with a bank loan. Martin disputed that and wanted half the value. ('It's a lot of dough,' she said. 'Property values here are sky high. I'd have to sell and I don't want to.') Meanwhile, there were two other properties that had to be divided, or sold and shared: an apartment in DC and a house in Los Angeles. She said she was not interested in those and just wanted out, the same as he did, but her lawyer said she had to fight for them or risk losing everything of hers. So they both had attorneys working for them and against each other, but nothing was settled, nothing would be resolved for at least a few more weeks, probably months.

'Anything else I need to know about you?' I said.

'Martin's a gun freak,' she said. 'I said he was uncomplicated – that's how he is. He has a lot of guns.' I was still English, in the year 2000, a citizen of a country that was then more or less gun free. I reacted predictably and unoriginally. She smiled. 'Martin goes hunting every summer with some of the people he works with. They go out into the boonies and kill things. But he won't come after you. He thinks of himself as a nice guy. The only thing wrong with him is me and being married to me.'

Two days later I flew back to London. I was totally infatuated with her. We ran up expensive phone bills that week, and the

next weekend I flew back to see her again. This time I stayed with her in her apartment.

'Martin's a civil servant,' she said, and showed me photographs of them together. Martin was smiling in all the pictures, looking civilized and relatively harmless. He had short-cropped hair and noticeably white and straight teeth. 'He has two college degrees,' she went on. 'He works for the federal government, he wears expensive suits. He's kind of important, a power administrator who controls a shitload of federal spending. He has someone drive him to and from the office. He has aides and consultants. He meets with the President – I was with him at one fund-raising dinner and was introduced to the President and the First Lady. He reads official papers and watches a lot of stupid TV when he's home and slumping in a chair. He has one strong drink in the evening when he gets in from work, and his friends are all like him. Yes, he loves guns, but this is America.'

I did not meet or even see Martin, and as I spent more and more time with Lil he seemed to become an increasingly distant presence. Lil and he often spoke on the phone, but rarely when I was around. Their conversations were, she told me, long and sometimes difficult, but never angry. They were in dispute over property, but they were modern, affluent Americans. The lawyers took care of all that. Martin's lawyer was an attorney on permanent retainer to the Defense Department – Lil's lawyer was a woman committed to equal rights and women's self determination in law, property and career. It was going to be expensive.

Lil and I were soon a regular item. At that time I was making enough money to be able to fly across to New York every two or three weeks, and when a vacancy propitiously appeared at work, Lil chose to take it. In addition to her regular work Lil would become vice president of their European rights office in London, making a trip across to the UK every month. This

meant that we were able to see each other regularly in London almost as often as we did in New York.

The black dog

On Lil's second visit to see me in London I arranged a surprise trip for her. We had four clear days ahead of us, and I told her I'd like to drive her around and show her something of Britain. We set off to the north and spent the first night in a hotel in Harrogate. In the morning I drove east, crossing the North York Moors, the higher levels of which were already sprinkled with snow, then down into the Victorian seaside town of Scarborough. After lunch we headed northwards along the coast. Lil, holding the road atlas on her lap, suddenly looked up from the map and said, 'Oh my God, you're taking me to Whitby! I don't *believe* it!'

Since our first meeting we had found much more to talk about than Lil's almost obsessive interest in *Dracula*, but now that our first turbulent days of revelation and personal discovery were behind us I thought it was time to start enjoying ourselves. In Chapter VII of Stoker's novel, a reporter from the (fictitious) newspaper *The Dailygraph* describes how the little North Yorkshire fishing port of Whitby is the scene of a sudden violent storm. At the height of the storm a Russian schooner named the *Demeter* comes into view riding the tempest full-sail. She collides with a sandbank just outside the harbour. At the wheel stands a decaying corpse, lashed to the helm. As the ship comes to a crashing halt a huge dog leaps from the prow, gallops ashore and disappears into the graveyard of a nearby church. The dog is, of course, Count Dracula himself in one of his shape-shifting forms, a fact which becomes clear as the novel goes on.

Directly because of this memorable scene Whitby in the present day had become a sort of Mecca for all admirers of vampire

folklore, and following from that various other alternative beliefs. The town became a tourist spot where it was not at all unusual to see people wandering around the streets dressed as zombies, or as Druids, werewolves, wizards, medievalists, black-art celebrants, steampunks, and much else. Every April and October the Whitby Goth Weekend was held in the town, and most other weekends during the summer months saw a fan convention of one sort or another.

Lil was as excited as a small child to be there.

Because it was winter the town was not busy with tourists or convention goers. I found a place to park along the river front and we set off to explore on foot. Most of all this involved a strenuous climb up the famous stone steps of the cliff, one hundred and ninety-nine of them, to the ruined Abbey that loomed over Whitby. The gaunt ruin is rumoured to be haunted, but anyway is so craggy and dark that no alleged ghost would be required to convey the right mood of despair and foreboding. We struggled around the remains, slowly recovering our breath, then went to the northern defile where there was a view of the estuary of the River Esk, and a wide panorama over the North Sea. An icy wind was gusting in from the general direction of Norway and Russia, freezing our faces and hands. Lil remained content!

Later, when we were back at sea level, walking through the narrow lanes of the old part of the town, we came across a workshop where craftsmen fashioned pieces of jewellery from deposits of jet lignite, found along the coast close to the town. We went in, glad to be out of the cold wind for a while, and had a long look at the ancient grindstones, brush wheels, polishers, chisels and hammers used by the lapidaries during the nineteenth century. Jet jewellery when polished and mounted was for a time the most coveted of gemstones in fashionable salons and at society events. It was still a lovely jewel, but was

no longer all the rage. Next to the reconstruction of the past was the modern workshop, where two young craftsmen were working.

Lil and I looked at the many pieces of jewellery on show – pendants, necklaces, brooches, earrings, bracelets, and so on – reacting with pleasure at the beautiful and intricate work that was there. After Lil had said how much she loved the look of jet, I decided to put my plan into action.

I said to one of the craftsmen: 'Could you make something for me to a special design?'

'Depends what it might be, how much you want to spend.'

I handed him a sheet of paper, where I had earlier drawn a crude sketch of my idea, and written down a detailed description, the size, the design, and so on. He looked at it closely, showed it to his colleague.

'I think I know what you're wanting,' he said.

Lil's curiosity was getting to her, and she reached forward to try to see what I had written down.

'Have you done anything like it before?' I said, as the man gamely moved the paper out of her sight and reach.

'Not exactly – but I know the sort of thing you have in mind.' He gave Lil a friendly look, and smiled at us both. He named a price for it, which I accepted. 'I can't get it done today,' he said. 'But towards lunchtime tomorrow we should have something to show you.'

Lil and I were anyway intending to stay the night in Whitby, so that was no problem. I don't know if Lil was able to guess in advance what I had planned for her, but as soon as we were out on the street again she took my hand tightly, and whispered her thanks.

We drove to Robin Hood's Bay the next morning, a few miles down the coast, walked around the pretty village for about an hour, then returned to Whitby.

They were ready for us in the workshop and had laid the piece of jewellery on a silk pad for Lil to examine it. It was a charm for her bangle, etched with a design and brought to a highly polished finish. They handed her a loupe so she could easily see the detail. She leaned over it, suddenly laughing. I too bent over it, curious to see what they had made of my instructions.

They had worked the piece almost exactly as I imagined and described it. The centre of the design on the tiny charm was the enlarged head of a great hound: its jaw was open, the fangs showing, ears erect. Behind, in deep perspective to give emphasis to the size of the animal, was its back and a hint of a tail stump. Beyond that was an image of a sailing ship, masts broken, sails in tatters, hull stoved in, a wreck. On the back they had engraved: *Whitby, January 2001*. It was a miracle of miniature art.

Lil took off her bangle and handed it to the craftsman. He swiftly mounted the charm on the bracelet. She slipped it back on her wrist, dangled it to see the new charm, then hugged me, kissed me, said thank you again.

The other man said, 'We wondered if you might like to see another version of the same image? There are after all two of us here.' They were both grinning at us. 'No extra charge.'

He put a second polished jet charm on the silk pad. Through the loupe we saw a reverse engraving of the same image. Dominated by the back of the hound's head, ears eagerly erect, was a view of the cliff at Whitby, a glimpse of the gaunt ruined Abbey. A minute crescent moon hovered beyond. *Whitby, January 2001* was also engraved on the back.

'You must have it, Ben,' Lil said. 'Put it on your key ring.'

'No – it's a non-identical twin, like you. It's yours.'

'Ben – I want you to have it!'

So it ended up on my key ring, where it has stayed ever since.

We later drove around the Yorkshire Dales, made a detour through the Lake District, then eventually returned to London. Two days later, Lil flew back to New York. I planned to follow her within a month.

FOUR

then: 2001

Beginnings

At the time I met Lil I thought of myself as English, and in those days being English meant being British, and being British meant being European. All that changed later.

As a contracted freelance I was making regular money but I also had plenty of opportunities to travel, often underwritten by expenses refunds. I had no ongoing relationship with anyone else at the time Lil and I met.

I was born in 1966, in a terraced house in north London. I had a younger brother, Saul. I went to a local primary school, then to an Inner London comprehensive. After a slow start, because I did not take school seriously until I was about twelve, I discovered a love of science, an admiration for mathematics, a joy in the discovery of problems and the deep satisfaction of being able to solve them. When I was eighteen I went to Sussex University, close to Brighton, and after three years came away with a first class honours degree in Neuroscience and Cognitive Science. All this was nearly frittered away while I went on an extended backpacking tour of central and east Asia, ending up in a gloriously unfocused summer of heat, casual sex, laziness and illicit substances in a beach resort in Queensland, Australia. When I returned to London I was suntanned,

worldly in outlook, determined never to use drugs again, and also deeply broke and in need of a job.

I started journalism more or less by accident. I found a lowly position as a trainee assistant at a biochemical research laboratory, making little use of my degree, but then one day my boss needed someone to write a description of one of their programmes of test results. I found I could express well what needed to be expressed, could write in a way non-specialists were able to follow, and moreover enjoyed doing it. I began a tentative freelance career not long after that, at first mostly writing press releases for a pharmaceutical company I was in contact with.

My interview in 1996 with Kyril Tatarov was one of the first genuine commissions I received from a magazine, and after that my career as a journalist began growing and consolidating.

I went to New York City two or three times towards the end of the 1990s, once as part of a vacation but usually because I had been sent there on a story. It was during one of these trips that I met Lil at her publisher's event, and after that nothing was ever the same for me again.

Travel plans ruined by journeys

After our trip to Whitby, Lil and I settled into our happy but expensive way of life, constantly on the phone to each other or flying across the Atlantic.

At the end of the summer we knew that would change because we were going to have to make a couple of long flights to the west coast, probably separately, but together if we could arrange it. I had been staying with Lil in her apartment for nearly two weeks, sweltering in the gasoline-tainted New York street canyons, freezing in the air-conditioned stores, restaurants, theatres, and so on. Because it was the beginning of September Lil now needed to spend some time in the London

office, dealing with the sale of European rights in several of her publisher's fall titles. I would fly back to London with her.

Before that, though, there was a problem with her husband, Martin. He was in California, staying at his house in Venice Beach, and he told Lil he wanted her to go out there so that she could meet with his attorney and sign some papers. He also wanted to discuss an inventory of whatever property she had in the house that she claimed as her own.

'Couldn't you discuss and agree that on the phone?' I said. 'Or by email? It's just a list. You don't need to see the things that are yours.'

'Yes, but that's not the way Martin is. He only works face to face, and that includes me. It's a habit he picked up from the staff generals. Anyway, I have clothes in California and I want to go through them and pick out what I want to keep. And there are tapes and videos and books. A lot of stuff.'

'Do you need them all? Really?'

'Perhaps.' Then she said: 'I guess not. I'll probably end up taking a lot of it to Goodwill.'

'He could do that for you,' I said.

'He could – but he won't. He wants me there to decide. I suggested he get some house clearers in and ship everything that's not his back here. But that wouldn't work either. He wants me there.'

'So you're going to go.'

'Yes.'

'And what's this about you having to meet his attorney? You told me the Defense Department was supplying the lawyer. They're in Washington, surely?'

'I think it's something about Californian law. There has to be a local attorney for out-of-state divorces.'

Lil had assured me from the start that Martin was out of her

life, out of our way, and that was in many respects true. I never had to see him, or avoid him, or even take his needs into account. But in spite of that he still somehow found the means to manipulate Lil, in ways I never understood, and never was able to discuss with her. Whenever she had been on the phone with him, or once or twice after she met with him, and often after we met up again after a short period apart, she would be mercurial in her moods, stubborn, evasive, annoying. We rowed a couple of times, and both times it was indirectly related to Martin's continued presence in her life. I urged her to get the divorce concluded quickly, and sometimes she agreed and sometimes she said it had to take its course.

'We must wait,' she would say.

Or: 'OK, I'll call him.'

Or: 'You're pressuring me. Don't do that!'

So we agreed: she would fly out to California, get it over with as soon as possible.

My objections started to fade away when I heard from Nick Hatterton, an editor in London, that there were reports of a breakthrough in stem cell research in a lab at UCLA, and I should if possible get across to Los Angeles to meet with the team and write an account of what they were doing. Expenses would be paid. I asked for a stay in a good hotel, and a meals and drinks allowance in addition to travel, New York to LA, then LA to London. Nick agreed.

What I did not mention to Nick was that I was already planning to follow up another commission, one for a magazine he would probably think of as a competitor to his. Contract or not, I considered myself still to be a freelance, and whenever the occasion arose I would accept other work and publish it under a different byline. I had done this for several years. I never found out if Nick or anyone else on the magazine knew about it – if they did, no one said anything and no one tried to stop me.

I knew other writers who sometimes doubled up their work in this way.

The other job would involve a stay in Charlotte, North Carolina, two overnights. This was where a retired government scientist, who had worked in environmental resources, was now living. His name was Barrett C. Dornan and he had written his memoirs, due to be published in a few months' time. A profile of him was needed. This would be printed to coincide with the book, and would be the basis for a possible TV film about his work. I had heard about the job through my own contacts, and was eager to take it on. The fee was attractive.

It would make no practical difference to Nick Hatterton. He would get the article he wanted, and I would only claim from him the actual expenses I ran up on the Los Angeles portion of the trip. The extra cost of the detour to Charlotte would be easily covered by the fee for that story.

Lil, though, was disappointed and annoyed, irrationally to my way of thinking. Our original plan had been that she would stay in New York while I flew down to Charlotte, and once I was back we would fly to London together. The sudden trip to California had been sprung on us both, or at least on me.

I said: 'We're both now going to Los Angeles. We'll fly there separately, meet up, then fly from there to London together.'

It seemed so simple, but Lil said, and her voice suddenly sounded evasive: 'Why don't you do the trip to Charlotte, then come back here? I'll go see Martin on my own.'

'You don't want me around when you're with him?' I said. 'Anyway, I've already bought my ticket from Charlotte to LA.'

'You could change it.'

'Why should I? You know I need to go to LA. What's the problem, Lil? Why is this suddenly something we can't do?'

'No problem.'

'Yes, there is. It's Martin, isn't it? You just don't want me around.'

'I won't be *with* him.'

'It's something.'

'Martin's not something. He's sitting on valuable real estate I have a legal share in, and I need to keep him at least friendly. I'll go out to the coast, clear my stuff out of the house, sign the papers he wants me to sign, then get the next flight back to New York.'

'But I'll be in Los Angeles by then.'

'Then go and come back. We'll meet back here.'

I said: 'Why do I never get to meet Martin? What's going on, Lil?'

'You don't need to meet him, and I don't want you to meet him. The thought of that creeps me out. All he is to me now is a divorce settlement.'

'You've never told him about me, have you?'

'Sure I have.'

But there was a momentary pause before she said that.

Perhaps she thought that if Martin learnt she had a new lover it would delay the divorce, or would affect the size of the settlement. He must have known that an attractive woman like Lil would not stay single for long after he walked out on her – or had she walked out on him? I was never sure what had happened between them, and Lil was always vague about it. She said as she often did that nothing about Martin mattered any more, except she needed to close down the marriage and get on with her life. It suited me not to have to involve myself any more than I already was, but it made me a recipient of their decisions without having any real influence on them. It was part of the convenient pattern our relationship had formed around us: I was happy with Lil, loved her sincerely and passionately, but that was in the context of my knowing only half of her life. So

long as I accepted that, all went well. Martin remained the part of her life I was not allowed to see. Suddenly, his insistence that she should fly out to Los Angeles on a meaningless errand, aggravated by Lil's own insistence that she must go through with it, and finally that I should take no part in it – it all brought tensions to the surface that normally we kept buried.

Martin had some kind of continuing hold over her, but she denied it or minimized it. The idea made me uncomfortable – I began to wonder how well I really knew her or understood her background.

We were still trying to decide what to do, although it was obvious to me what we should, when Martin called her. She went to the phone in the next room, closing the door. This was not a long call – she came back after about five minutes.

'I have to go to LA,' she said. 'He's really insistent.'

'I thought this was already decided.'

'When are you going to be in Charlotte?'

'I'm flying there on Sunday, staying two nights. I'm talking to the guy all day Monday, then I have a plane out of Charlotte at nine on Tuesday morning.'

'That's to Los Angeles?'

'I couldn't get a through flight from Charlotte. I have to go to Detroit and connect there. But I should be in LA by the evening.'

'OK, now listen. Martin wants me there by Monday evening at the latest. That's OK, because you'll be arriving the next evening. He told me not to fly on Tuesday.'

'Did he say why? Tuesday is a good day to take internal flights. You can always get a seat.'

'Getting a seat is never a problem for Martin. He says he might have to return to DC and wants the house sorted out before then.'

'But if he's going to DC why don't you see him there?'

'He wants me at the house in Venice.'

'So what's all this about you not flying on Tuesday?'

'He didn't say.'

We returned to our vexing combination of argument/ agreement, basically accepting the same plans for travel after the weekend but never quite concurring on why or how. It continued to bother me that Martin, allegedly out of her life entirely but for the attorneys' deals and settlements, had this ability to influence her decisions. She tried to reassure me but she got me wrong. There was nothing, she said, that I did not know about Martin and her – that she was still sleeping with him, perhaps? – but this only revealed the misunderstanding that existed between us.

Later that day she booked a one-way flight from JFK to LAX, departing New York in the early morning of the Monday, landing in Los Angeles in the afternoon. We agreed that we would make contact soon after I landed on Tuesday afternoon, on my flight from Charlotte, via Detroit, and plan to meet later, the Wednesday or even the Thursday, depending on how long my work lasted, how long it took Lil to work out whatever had to be worked out with Martin. Soon after that we would meet up and book an overnight flight to London.

I flew to Charlotte on the Sunday afternoon, checked into the Hilton Garden Inn at the airport, then called Lil from the room. Suddenly, happily, everything was back to normal. I loved the sound of her voice, her laughter, her seriousness about serious matters, her funny attitude to the inessential, the originality of her mind. We spoke together for more than an hour, nothing important, just a conversation.

A day in Charlotte, North Carolina
Halfway through the interview with Barrett C. Dornan, the retired government scientist, my cellphone vibrated, and the

screen showed that I had received a text message. In 2001 text messages were still unusual, certainly within my own circle of contacts. I was unfamiliar with how to send them, but Lil had shown me what to do if one came in. Looking back this seems an inexplicable ignorance about something that has since become so widely adopted, but that is how it was then, at least for me.

I excused myself from Mr Dornan and went out into his garden. I pressed the key to show incoming messages, but the sunlight was too bright for me to read anything. The edge of the garden was fringed with trees, so I walked across the lawn and stood in the shade.

I CHANGED MY FLIGHT. I HAD TO COME TO DC. MARTIN IS HERE TOO. LIL XX

I called her immediately.

'What happened, Lil? Why aren't you going to Los Angeles?'

'Can we speak later?' she said, her voice sounding guarded.

'I want to know why you changed your plans.'

There was a background noise around her I could just about detect.

'Are you in a car?'

'Yes.'

'Are you driving?'

'No – Martin collected me from Dulles Airport. Let me call you back. Or I'll text you.'

'No. Call me when you can. As soon as possible.'

I stood waiting for about five more minutes, trying to understand what had happened. What could possibly have made the plans change? She knew I would be travelling to Los Angeles to see her.

In the end I returned to Mr Dornan in the welcome cool of his air-conditioned house, and tried to resume the interview. He obviously knew something had taken my mind off what he

was talking about. He said he would fix me a drink and went away to get some iced tea. As soon as he was out of the room I took out my phone, and managed to work out how to type and send a text.

WHAT HAPPENED? IS MARTIN THERE? WHY DC? THOUGHT YOU WERE IN LA. PLEASE CALL AS SOON AS YOU CAN. BEN X

I struggled through the rest of the interview, trusting to the fact that once I was at home in my office I could make sense of whatever Dornan was saying for the recording. Lil's unexpected change of plan confounded me. When we were speaking to each other the previous evening everything had been calm and worked out, and we were even making plans about possibly staying an extra day or two in LA. We both knew people there we might visit.

I kept the phone in my shirt pocket so that I would be certain to be aware of any incoming call or message. It remained silent.

When an hour or so later Dornan left me alone in his deeply carpeted and dark-panelled study, I tried calling her again. This time the call went to voicemail, so I left a message.

Five minutes later: TALK THIS EVENING. SORRY, NOT MY FAULT. I LOVE YOU. LIL XXX

At last the interview with Barrett Dornan was completed. I was introduced to his wife Alicia, then accepted her brief tour around their magnificently oversized home, admiring European antiques and paintings, as well as Dornan's showcase of lepidoptera he had collected over the years. When the cab arrived to return me to my hotel I left with what I hoped did not seem too much haste.

I had a vague but insistent feeling about Lil, a despairing sensation that somehow I was losing her. She only ever acted like this when Martin was around, and here it was happening again. How much longer would this man be in her life, and therefore

mine? Why did she always play down Martin's impact on her now the marriage was supposedly over, when it was clear he still had some kind of hold over her?

I decided to wait until she called me.

Finally, after I had eaten dinner in the hotel grill, she did call. I was back in my room, having ripped off my clothes, showered, and sprawled out on my bed wearing only a towel. I tried to keep the sound of relief out of my voice, but the feeling of frustration that had built up during the day kept us circling around each other for a while. Finally I calmed down.

'I'm staying over in Washington tonight,' Lil said. 'I'm in a hotel, the Marriott at Dulles Airport. Martin brought me back here. I'm going to be flying to LA as we planned tomorrow – I will go to the house in Venice, sort out my stuff on my own, and after you arrive we can have our time together in LA, whatever we want to do.'

That was more or less what I wanted to hear, but there were still questions. Why the change of mind? Why had Martin suddenly flown back to Washington, and why had she gone there to meet him?

'There's something in the office he has to be there for tomorrow,' she said. 'He needed those papers signed for the attorney soon, and didn't want to wait. He paid for my flight here from New York, and he arranged for one of his aides to change my flight to Los Angeles tomorrow. I get a seat upgrade.'

'So you've signed the papers, and now it's all right for you to fly on Tuesday?'

'He said it would be OK.'

'Why would he say that?'

'Ben – I've given up trying to understand Martin. Let's just do what you and I want to do. Forget him. Please?'

Gradually she put me back at ease, and we talked on for a

while. The strains of the day were telling on us both, though, and we said goodnight early. We agreed to keep in contact while we were travelling the next day – calls if possible, texts if not. Soon after we hung up, I was in my bed and drifting off to sleep.

Tuesday morning

I was awake early, ate breakfast in the hotel grill, then took the shuttle bus to the terminal. The first leg of my flight, to Detroit, was due to take off at nine a.m. In the cab I tried calling Lil, but she did not answer. I left no message on her voicemail.

As I was walking into the terminal I felt the phone vibrating in my pocket, so I stood to one side and read what she had sent me:

HI. ALL OK HERE, BUT THEY CHANGED THE GATE TO 26. THE LONGEST WALK IN THE AIRPORT! BUT NOW WAITING FOR FLIGHT TO BOARD. SEE YOU TONIGHT. LOVE LIL XXX

My own gate was already on the display – Northwest Airlines 1757, nonstop to Detroit. The sign said they were boarding. I sent a brief text acknowledgement to Lil, and hurried off to catch the flight.

I was relieved to see that there were not many passengers waiting to board. I never liked being on a crowded aircraft. I walked forward with everyone else. The seat I had been allocated at check-in turned out to be next to a window near the back of the cabin, but when I sat down I discovered there was hardly any legroom. I'm tall, although not exceptionally so, and I often find airline seats uncomfortable. The flight to Detroit would take a couple of hours.

When most of the other passengers had sat down I signalled to one of the flight attendants and asked if I could change seats.

'There are spare seats at the front of the cabin,' she said. 'Follow me.'

The front two rows were completely vacant, so I took one of the seats in the front row. I now had ample room to spread out.

Immediately in front of me the door to the cockpit was ajar. I could see the captain and first officer sitting side by side in their white epauletted shirts, headphones on, running through the pre-flight checks, reaching forward to confirm the positions of certain switches, the readings on instruments, and so on. I watched with interest, never before having been so close to the flight deck as this, impressed by the thorough detail with which they went through a technical routine they must have followed a hundred times before.

I glanced at my watch. It was approaching nine a.m., when we were supposed to be pulled back from the gate.

Flight Northwest 1757

There was an announcement from one of the cabin crew, apologizing for the slight holdup in taking off. A passenger had checked in late and was being cleared by security at this moment. In the way of all announcements on aircraft the flight attendant made it sound like a routine delay, which it probably was. No more than a couple of extra minutes to wait, she said. We'll be taking off real soon, and coming round with drinks and snacks as soon as the captain switches off the seat belt sign. Sit back and enjoy your flight.

Where I was sitting I was beside the main door of the cabin, with the ramp outside. I suddenly heard voices and then a youngish man appeared, walking unsteadily towards the air-craft. He had a backpack slung loosely across one shoulder. He was a big guy, tall and broad. His stomach bulged beneath a huge Hawaiian shirt. He was wearing large, floppy shorts. He was deeply tanned, had chains and studs, and headphones were slung around his neck. His hair was a mass of blond curls.

As he held out his boarding pass to the attendant by the door, he said: 'Are we still going to take off on time?' He had a strong Australian accent, briefly bringing back memories of my past life. 'No delay, then?'

'We'll be starting the engines in a moment, sir. If you would take your seat —'

'Didn't you hear what happened? My God, it's incredible! I saw it on the TV just now, at the gate. You won't believe it — a plane went into one of the World Trade Center towers! For real!'

The rising inflexion made it sound like a question, but it was not one. The flight attendant said nothing, but I saw she turned her head sharply towards the open cockpit door. The first officer had heard this and he glanced back at her, then turned towards the captain. One of them pulled the door closed.

Other passengers had heard what the Australian guy said. One of them shouted: 'Yeah — I picked it up on a news feed!'

I turned in my seat and saw that a couple of the others were half-standing in the cramped space in front of their seats, holding up their mobile phones.

'Was it a light plane?' I said directly to the Australian. 'Or something bigger than that?'

Every morning the skies above New York City were crisscrossed by dozens of small aircraft moving about: traffic and weather spotting planes from radio and TV stations, police and commuter helicopters speeding in every direction, weaving between the skyscrapers. I had sometimes tried to imagine the unimaginable, if one of them collided accidentally with a building.

'It was a commercial airliner, I think. A big jet, anyway.'

That stunned me. 'What else do you know?'

'Nothing more, mate. I saw it for a few seconds, then they forced me to come aboard.'

The flight attendant laid a hand lightly under his elbow, urging him away from me, towards his seat further down the cabin. 'We have to pull back from the gate, sir.'

Someone behind me said loudly: 'It was an American Airlines plane. A Boeing 767. They don't know yet if it was an accident.'

Another attendant came to the cabin door, swung it closed and secured it. She spoke briefly on the intercom, checked that the flight deck door was firmly in place, then headed off down the cabin. A few moments later the aircraft was pulled back from the stand, and shortly afterwards the engines started. We taxied down to the main runway, the attendants checking the passengers had their belts on, the seat backs were upright – then they went through the routine of reminding passengers what we should do in case of an emergency, the use of oxygen masks, life jackets, where the exits were situated. Everything normal. Nothing was different from an ordinary flight, the familiar routines were still being followed and the plane was about to take off.

A few minutes later we were climbing out of Charlotte, heading for Detroit.

What happened to the twin towers in New York on the morning of September 11, 2001, and what was to happen a short while later at the Pentagon in Washington, is now so familiar that the events barely need repeating. Everyone who was older than about six years old at the time still remembers vividly what they saw and experienced on television during that terrible morning when three passenger jets on internal flights were hijacked and flown into the World Trade Center and the Pentagon.

What I myself went through that morning was mostly all in the mind. No other passengers were sitting anywhere near me, or immediately behind me. None of the flight attendants were

in sight. I faced the blank wall of the forward bulkhead of the cabin, and the closed door to the flight deck. I felt isolated, appalled, my thoughts full of fear and alarm. When you are flying, or when someone you love is flying, the dreadful news of an air disaster is horrifying. You instantly seek to find out more about it, start haunting the news channels, the TV bulletins, but it's a distant curiosity, a way of trying to cope with the frightful thought that you might know one or more of the victims. In reality, of course, the probability that you do know someone involved in a hijack or a crash is infinitesimally small. But you still worry, you still feel the obsessive need to discover the facts.

I felt utterly alone. The Northwest plane climbed out of Charlotte, bumped briefly through the turbulence of thin cloud cover, then as the control surfaces of the wings were trimmed back, and the engines reduced in power after the take-off, began flying more smoothly. I was struggling to make sense of what I had heard. I knew nothing of the larger events that people around the world were at that moment seeing on their TV screens. All I had heard was the fact that a plane had hit a building in New York.

Everything in me focused on Lil. Lil was flying at that moment. Someone behind me had shouted out that it was an American Airlines plane that crashed – was Lil flying with American that morning? She hadn't mentioned which airline she was booked with. I knew she was on a plane from DC to California – what reason would there be for a detour to New York City?

And many flights went to and from the west coast every day, dozens at this time of morning. Logically, there was little chance she would have been involved.

Even so –

My heart suddenly pumping I grabbed my mobile phone out of my shirt pocket. It was still on because I had forgotten

to turn it off. I jabbed at the quick-dial number for her, but almost as soon as the number was accepted by the phone the 'no signal' sound came through.

I tried a second time – same result. The indicator on the tiny screen was showing the small 'x' that confirmed there was no signal, no network.

In 2001 the use of cellphones on aircraft was a contentious subject, as I was to find out later. The airline companies imposed a general rule that no one should make or receive calls, or send texts, once the plane was in flight. It was said that the planes' instrumentation might be affected. In reality, it was all but impossible to find a usable signal once the aircraft was flying above about ten thousand feet. I did not know of that limitation then, but I do recall glancing out of the window at my side after I tried to contact Lil. No ground was visible through the early heat haze – we must anyway have exceeded that altitude in the first two minutes after take-off.

I shifted position, releasing my seat belt so that I could stand and turn. I looked down the cabin at the passengers closest to me. Many of them were holding their mobiles – none of them was speaking to anyone. They stared back at me as if I might have information for them, so I sat down. The seat belt sign was still on. I buckled up again.

None of the cabin crew were visible in the main part of the cabin. The cockpit door remained closed. After the hijackings on this day, federal and international laws were introduced forcing the cockpit door to be securely locked once the plane had been cleared for take-off, but in September 2001 most crews kept the cockpit door closed but unlocked.

The plane continued to fly, moving steadily through the calm air. There was a feeling of normality, while abnormal thoughts were coursing through me. I imagined that most of the other passengers felt the same way. I was desperate to make

contact with Lil, to be reassured she was safe.

Then I remembered the Airfone – there was a mount for an Airfone receiver on the wall in front of me, but no receiver was there. I checked in the arms of my seat, but there was no capacity for one. For a while many of the main US airlines had Airfone sets, which enabled communication with people on the ground. But because of the sometimes unreliable signal, and the expense to passengers, they had not been widely used. Most of the kits had been removed.

I tried my cellphone again, but there was still no signal.

A flight attendant walked quickly up the aisle and opened the flight deck door. For a few moments I could see into the cockpit – the attendant blocked my view of the captain while she spoke to him, but the first officer was visible to me. He was moving quickly, trying to connect or use some kind of instrument situated too low down for me to see what it was. There was a sense in there of urgent and focused activity, but not panic. The brilliant light of the sky dazzled me.

As the flight attendant closed the door, I said to her: 'Is everything OK? What's going on?'

'Please remain in your seat sir, and keep your belt fastened. The captain will be giving out some information in a moment.'

She hurried away, but I could hear other passengers behind me also trying to get her attention.

About five minutes later the captain's voice came on. He went straight to the point:

'Folks, I know some of you have heard news about an incident in New York City. It seems a couple of flights from Boston have been involved in serious situations. We are still waiting for more details, but nothing we have been told affects this flight. We are continuing on to Detroit as planned. We do need you to stay in your seats with the seatbelts fastened. We will update you with information as we have it. Right now we

expect to be touching down on time in Detroit, in about an hour and a half —'

The planes had come from Boston! Hearing this made me feel lightheaded with relief. Whatever had happened in New York, it would not involve Lil. Her plane had taken off from Washington Dulles. I was horrified at the thought of what the 'serious situation' might have been for the two aircraft it affected, but at least I knew Lil could not have been on either of them.

My cellphone remained unusable but I continued to hold it in my hand.

For a few more minutes the routine of the flight remained, but in the seats behind me many of the passengers were talking loudly among each other. I felt cut off from them and it was difficult to pick out what anyone was saying. I stared through the window at the empty sky around us, trying to imagine or understand what could possibly have taken place in New York.

The note of the plane's engines suddenly altered, the cabin lurched, as if we were slowing down for a descent. Air pressure abruptly built up in my inner ear.

Then the captain again, no longer sounding as if he was dealing with a routine problem:

'Ladies and gentlemen, this is to let you know we have been ordered to cut this flight short. We are about to make a landing in Pittsburgh. We will be on the ground shortly. You must remain seated, and listen for further instructions.'

The aircraft was already banking as we changed direction. The sunlight shafted through the windows at unexpected angles.

Why was an aircraft accident in New York making us land prematurely? I began to feel nervous for the first time about being on the plane. Were we also in danger in some way? Was there something wrong with this aircraft? Why else would we have to make an emergency landing?

55

A few minutes later the captain came on again, for the third and last time. His voice sounded tense and he spoke quickly:

'Pittsburgh airport has now been closed because of another air accident. Detroit is also closed. We are looking around for an alternative destination, which we have been ordered to select as soon as possible. US airspace is now closed to all flights. We are going to try for Columbus, Ohio. Stay in your seats at all times and keep the belt tightened. Listen for more instructions. Cabin crew, take up landing positions.'

Another accident? Near Pittsburgh?

The cabin staff suddenly reappeared, hurrying up and down the aisle making sure the passengers were strapped in, and all loose items were secured. Then they took seats: two of them went to rear-facing pulldown seats across the aisle from where I was sitting. They strapped themselves in, did not meet my eyes and they said nothing.

The aircraft was making several sharp manoeuvres, the engines thrusting noisily before slowing again. The sun's rays kept shifting about the cabin, revealing the number of steep changes the pilots were making to our course and altitude. Through my own window I saw alternate tipping glimpses of the ground, the high sky, the ground again. We were flying low.

The plane steadied at last. When I leaned across to the window I could see that although we were now at a lower altitude than if we had been cruising normally, we were flying level and following what appeared to be a straight course. A kind of nervous calm settled on me. Across the aisle I saw that the two women from the cabin crew were holding hands. They had thrust them down, almost out of sight in the narrow space between their bodies. They stared straight ahead, down the length of the cabin, smiles of professional reassurance on show, but I was close enough to them to see how tightly they were gripping each other's hand.

We flew low and slow for about half an hour. The feeling of stress never eased. I was convinced that something terrible was about to happen to our plane. The other passengers were silent. There were no more announcements from the flight deck and none of the cabin crew moved from their seats. I was trying not to think what might happen to the plane as we crossed closed airspace. What did that mean? If we stayed in the air much longer would we be intercepted by military aircraft? How much fuel was left in the tanks? What if Columbus was closed before we could get there?

I forced a feeling of quasi-normality on myself by trying to make plans. Lil remained my priority. As soon as we were on the ground I should be able to call her. I imagined that her aircraft, like mine, would also be under orders to land somewhere. Once she and I were in contact again we could make our own decisions, travel to join up with each other, book a flight out of the US as quickly as possible. I assumed that only flights within the USA were being banned from flying, that international flights would get away as normal. I began hoping that the airport we had to land at, Columbus or elsewhere, depending on what happened in the next few minutes, would have an international terminal where flights to Britain could be booked.

The aircraft lurched suddenly and the engine note changed – my inner ears popped again. We were now flying close to the ground: I glimpsed roads, farms, clusters of buildings. The plane banked to the left, then more sharply to the right. We seemed to be travelling much faster. There was an increase in noise, again a familiar sensation that regular air travellers are used to as an aircraft heads down towards the runway. I heard the grinding from the wings as flaps were extended, a loud whirring noise and two heavy thuds as the landing gear came down and locked in position.

We were already low enough to see individual trees, the flat roofs of factories, cars and trucks moving on a wide highway. We rushed over them all, heading down to the airport somewhere close ahead. I could see the glittering towers of a city in the near distance. The ground was speeding by below.

We passed over some of the low buildings and odd pieces of machinery often seen at the perimeter of an airport, and I was mentally ready for the bump of the landing wheels, when the engine note increased again. The whole frame of the aircraft shuddered, and tipped alarmingly. We were no more than fifty feet from the ground. The plane rose sharply, banked to the left, and through my window I saw an angled view of stretches of side runways, grass terrifyingly close, many aircraft already on the ground, then to my horror I realized we were actually crossing above the roof of a terminal building. We skimmed it with what looked like less than twenty feet to spare. I glimpsed ventilator fans turning slowly!

The plane levelled out, wings waggling, the engines slowed, the plane shuddered. By some miracle, or more likely after some brilliantly skilful flying from the pilots, we made a swerving and bumpy landing on a second runway. Shouts and cheers arose from the people behind me.

We had had to touch down a long way from the end of the runway, where most normal landings were made. We were already halfway along. The brakes were sharply applied, the engines roared in reverse thrust, and we juddered down the runway, slowing more aggressively than any plane I had ever been on before. When the plane finally came to a halt we were out on the far edge of the airfield.

As the engines died the address system came on.

'Please will all passengers stay seated until the seat belt sign goes out. The tower has ordered us to wait here until a space at a terminal gate is found for us. Thank you.'

The long wait

It quickly grew hotter and more unpleasant in the cabin as the plane waited by the airfield perimeter. The sun was beating down on us. Without the engines running, and with no ancillary power source, the ventilation was off. I made repeated efforts to get a message or a call through to Lil, without success.

The cellphone network was down, or jammed – other passengers were complaining. I stayed in my seat, although I did undo the belt. The plane was going nowhere. The flight crew suddenly opened the cockpit door and strode quickly down the aisle. They did not speak to any of the passengers. They were both strong-looking, capable guys, their eyes shielded by dark glasses. Many of the other passengers were ignoring the instruction about remaining seated and were moving about the cabin. As the two pilots went by they fired questions at them. I wanted to applaud them for their flying skill – they had got us down safely in extraordinary circumstances. But like everyone else I wanted to know what was going on, and they must have had more information than we did. The two men disappeared into the back of the plane, followed by the cabin crew. One of the crew pulled a curtain across.

The Australian guy was sitting away from the other passengers. He had his headphones on and was using a portable game console. The cell network was still down – he looked cool, appearing to be the only one of us not bothered by our predicament.

Rumours were shooting around about what was happening in New York. Someone said there must have been bombs, armed terrorists, perhaps a suicide mission. In fact no one could have known any more than I did. We heard a rear door opening, then slamming closed. Someone at the back of the cabin said

she had seen the crew being driven away – a truck with mobile boarding steps had collected them.

We sweated and complained. Several people used the toilet, which would not flush and so an unpleasant smell drifted around us. I kept looking through the cabin windows, hoping the mobile steps would return to pick us up, or a tractor would come to pull us to the terminal. The cellphone network stayed down. It was becoming an obsession for some of the passengers, who were furious they could not log on to the network.

Finally, a mobile steps truck came for us. After several more minutes of bad temper and complaining from the more volatile passengers, we were allowed to disembark into a shuttle bus. Some of the men shouldered their way ahead of the rest of us.

As we were driven across the tarmac towards the terminal building I was astonished to see the huge number of aircraft standing around. Large and small, cargo and passenger planes, every imaginable US carrier. Many international ones too, most I did not recognize. All terminal gates were in use, so the other jets had been parked loosely in any place that could be found. I remembered an article I had read a few years before, in one of the magazines I contributed to, which pointed out that there were now so many civil aircraft that the industry could only operate successfully as long as most of them were in the air. The realization that every airport in North America must now be crammed with grounded aircraft, exactly like this, dramatized that notion into reality.

As soon as we had moved out of the bus and were walking towards the terminal, the driver reversed away and drove the shuttle back across the airfield at speed.

The terminal
I had no baggage to worry about because I always travel light, but several of the other passengers had to find the baggage claim

(thousands of other people were crammed in the hall) and start what I imagined would be a long and difficult wait for their hold luggage. I was free of that, thankfully. The terminal was in chaos: there were no security or information staff around, so I went across the concourse to where I could see a huge TV screen. A crowd had gathered to stare up at it.

The Aussie guy had already arrived – I saw his now familiar bulk, the backpack on the floor at his feet. I pushed through the crowd and stood beside him.

'Hi,' I said casually.

'Oh, hey man, I saw you on the plane. Wasn't that something?'

We stared up at the TV screen. There was a commentary but because of the extreme level of noise in the terminal it was impossible to hear anything being said. The pictures and captions said it all. There was a sort of running montage of images of the crucial events: the planes slamming into the skyscrapers and exploding inside the buildings, the immense fires that followed, the futile rescue efforts from the ground, the horrific sight of people trapped on the upper floors falling or jumping to their deaths, the abrupt collapse, first of one of the towers, then of the other.

'Jesus, they both went down!' said the Aussie guy. 'That, mate, is just bloody amazing!'

I was appalled by the sight. Even the crowd around us in the terminal was subdued. I thought of the people still inside, the firefighters, the police and ambulances we had seen clustered around the buildings' concourses. It was an unprecedented disaster, terrible even if only one building had been destroyed, but two –

I was silenced by the awfulness of what we were witnessing.

Then the Australian guy said: 'We've just seen the impossible. The towers were built to withstand a big aircraft colliding with them.'

61

'But you saw what happened. Planes full of fuel –'

'That's not enough to knock them down. The twin towers were over-designed, every safety factor doubled or tripled. They can't collapse like that, from the top, straight down.'

'But we've seen it happen,' I said again, uncomprehending. As I spoke, the TV re-ran the footage of one of the towers visibly collapsing and disintegrating, steel columns ejected on each side, a vast crumbling cloud of rubble and destruction, speeding to the ground.

'They're going down, but they're not collapsing. They can't. The towers were built to survive a fully fuelled Boeing 707 crashing into them.'

A huge pall of dust was obscuring the streets and buildings of Lower Manhattan.

'You sound as if you know something about this,' I said.

'I'm a structural engineer,' he said. 'I work with architects. Steel shell buildings don't collapse because they can't.'

'But the fire . . .?'

'Makes no difference. There's no fire hot enough to melt structural steel.'

'What about the fuel in the aircraft?'

'That wouldn't have counted for much after the first few seconds. Aviation fuel burns off too quickly to have any effect at all.'

'But we've seen it happen.' I waved a hand at the TV. 'The planes crashed in, did a lot of damage, exploded, set fire to the buildings.'

'What you're seeing is not a collapse,' he said. 'Those buildings were demolished. That's the only explanation. Someone must have set explosives.'

I was about to protest at the sheer unlikeliness of that, when the scene on the TV suddenly changed.

Another building was on fire, with a huge plume of smoke

spreading into the blue sky. A caption in red letters glared at the bottom of the screen.

'The Pentagon?' I said. 'They hit the Pentagon too?'

'That I did not know,' said the Aussie guy. 'Where the hell else has been attacked?'

We stood in silence in the crowd, occasionally moving forward as other people left. The minutes passed. The TV station kept re-running the scenes of the planes crashing into the towers, the devastation of the collapses that followed. There was no film, though, of the incident at the Pentagon, something we both noticed.

'That place is one of the most heavily monitored in the USA,' said the Aussie. 'But how come there's no CCTV footage? That's ridiculous. Every inch of space outside federal buildings is watched. They must have the tapes. What are they trying to hide?'

I agreed, but we said no more about it. The shock of what we were seeing had the capacity to blank normal thoughts. We concentrated on what we were being shown.

There were more people talking to the cameras, trying to explain what had happened and make the attacks comprehensible in some way. As we slowly edged forward we heard more of what was being said, helped by the captions.

The news stations were interviewing witnesses. Most of them were ordinary people – office workers, tourists, taxi or bus drivers – they had witnessed the crashes from the street, or had been inside the buildings at the time and managed to get out. They had been there, but they didn't always agree with what everyone else said, although they all talked about the shock of seeing the planes crashing.

Several witnesses told reporters emphatically that they heard loud explosions *before* the first plane went in. One even claimed that he heard and felt a massive explosion in the basement of

one of the towers, several minutes before the first plane crashed. This was confirmed by an ambulance driver, who had been on an emergency run to the World Trade Center at eight thirty, more than a quarter-hour before the North Tower was hit. Some witnesses described the aircraft as having no markings. One said it was silvery white, with no windows. A cop said he heard multiple explosions coming from within the towers as they collapsed – this was confirmed by two firefighters, one of whom had been blown off his feet by an explosion in the lobby of the North Tower just as he was rushing to escape. One interview was with a fire chief, white with the dust that caked his hair, face and clothes, shouting answers hoarsely from a street where rescue vehicles, some of them wrecked by fallen debris, stood surrounded by rubble and snaking fire hoses. He warned of more explosions to come.

Politicians were coming forward to express their sympathy, horror or reassurance. A statement was issued by the Vice President, standing in for President Bush, at that time returning from Florida on Air Force One. The mayor of New York City. A senator. Another senator. A buildings expert. A terrorism expert. An explosives expert. A flight expert. A spokesperson from American Airlines, and another from United Airlines, the two companies whose aircraft had been hijacked.

The scene kept switching back and forth, live reports in the studio or from the streets, interspersed with recordings of the earlier attacks. Witnesses in the street, office workers who had managed to escape, relatives and friends of missing people, endless reruns of the terrible footage. All the people we saw were traumatized, some were crying, many were confused, but a few were angry and calling for revenge.

Most of what we saw was about New York. There was still no film of the Pentagon crash in Washington. A huge fire continued to blaze there, but the cameras were not allowed

close enough for any details to be picked out. There had been no major collapse, nor was there any visible plane wreckage around the building.

'Is this what you saw when you were boarding the plane?' I said to the Aussie. On the screen at that moment was what I now knew was an early shot, soon after the beginning: the top storeys of the North Tower ablaze and smoking heavily, the South Tower not yet hit. Both of them still substantially intact, with no hint of the catastrophic collapses to come.

'They were showing it live then,' he said, and after a few more minutes he wandered away.

I was in Columbus, Ohio. I knew no one who lived in the city, nor even anywhere near it. I had nowhere to stay because, as I soon discovered, every hotel within about twenty miles was now full. The air space remained closed, so no planes were leaving. I tried to rent a car but there were none left available. I spent the rest of the day in the airport, trying to locate a hotel room, eating junk food from a stall and when that sold out I bought snacks from a vending machine. Every few minutes I tried to call Lil. The network was down, but around me I noticed that a few of the other people were starting to get through again. Not me – Lil remained unreachable. My phone battery was almost dead.

About an hour after I landed, while I was still watching the TV screen in the terminal, standing in a crowd of several hundred people, I began to piece together the fearful news about American Flight 77. It had taken off from Washington Dulles at 08:20 that morning, heading for Los Angeles. Just before nine o'clock the hijackers attacked the crew and entered the cockpit. One of them took over the controls and turned the plane back towards Washington. At just after nine thirty the aircraft dived at high speed and rammed into the west side of the Pentagon at ground level.

Although her body was never found or identified in the devastation that ensued, then or in the long and agonizing months following, I eventually came to accept the fact that Lil must have been one of the passengers on that plane.

That night, while I was hardly able even to glimpse the consequences of the day, I slept fitfully on the floor of the terminal in Columbus, Ohio.

FIVE

then: 2008–2009

A Russian story

In the spring of 2008 I was telephoned by a man named Bryan Claremont. He described himself as a film and TV producer, and suggested we should meet for lunch in London the next day. He would not say what it was about, except that he wanted to discuss an idea for a film, possibly a feature, possibly a television film. The subject matter had to be confidential until we had met and talked around a few things. Of course, this made me curious and I asked him to tell me at least what sort of film he had in mind, and how I might be involved.

'I saw a programme on Channel 4,' he said. 'It was a couple of weeks back. One of their late night science films, about string theory. You were credited as writer.'

'Associate writer,' I said.

In reality all I had done on that programme was earn a quick couple of hundred pounds by reading through the shooting script to check its accuracy, and pointing out two or three minor errors. A friend who worked for a TV talent agency had put the production team on to me, as a return favour for something else. I did not say that to Claremont, though.

'Yeah, then you know what I mean,' said Bryan Claremont.

'You want to make a film about string theory?' I said.

'No. Something else.'

We agreed on a restaurant close to City Road, and I went there the next day. Claremont was middle-aged, overweight, losing his hair – he spoke loudly and drank a lot of wine, but he was serious and focused on what he wanted. In spite of his warning about confidentiality when we were on the phone I found him easy to talk to. He was accompanied by a young woman he introduced as Jacqueline, his PA. She was silent for most of the time, listening intently to what Claremont and I said and taking written notes. As far as I can remember Jacqueline said not a thing to me throughout the meeting. Her head was bent attentively over her notebook. She drank no alcohol, and for her lunch ate a simple spinach salad. Claremont and I both ordered steaks.

After some general conversation, in which I told him about several of the articles and profiles I had published, and he described the TV programmes on which he had worked over the years, he came to the point.

'I'm interested in a man named Tatarov,' he said. 'Kyril Tatarov, a Russian mathematician, an émigré, living in New York. I believe you know him.'

'Well –' I said, taken by surprise. I did in fact know him, but like Claremont himself I had problems of confidentiality. I described the time in New York when I had interviewed Tatarov at the Courant Institute, which was not something I had to keep to myself. 'I wouldn't claim that I know him well,' I added cautiously.

'But you have met him in person? You did write about him then?'

'Yes.'

'What do you know about the time he disappeared for a month or so?'

So that was what it was. I chewed intently on my steak, as

if working with a piece that was stubbornly tough. I tried to make myself look as if I was remembering.

'You know what I'm talking about?' said Claremont.

'Of course. What's your interest in it?'

Claremont launched into a roundabout story about how he was under contract to an independent production company, working as a supplier of current affairs documentaries to BBC Television, but that his contract was coming to an end. There was going to be some kind of lucrative pay-off and he was planning to invest most of the money in himself and had already set up a small film production company. He had other programme makers interested in joining him and he knew of people who wanted to invest. Everything was coming together, but so far his staff consisted only of himself and Jacqueline.

He handed me his business card – Bryan Julian Claremont, Director, *Theorem Film Initiatives*, at a business accommodation address in London WC2. Telephone, fax, email, website, social media.

'How does Tatarov fit into this?' I said.

'What do you know about 9/11?'

'Probably more than I want to. But that's no different from a lot of other people.' I was beginning to wonder what this was about. 'Why?'

'Tatarov was involved in that. Somehow – I never really found out how, or to what extent. But he refused point blank to discuss it, which made me think he had been more affected by it than he was letting on. Where he works is not so far from Ground Zero. Maybe it was that. Anyway, I went across to New York last month and actually met the guy. He's pretty old now, but his mind is still sharp as a razor blade. He frightened me, in fact. Impressive, but difficult to follow. Your experience too?'

'I'm a science writer. I managed.'

'He wouldn't talk about the time he disappeared, wouldn't

tell me what he knows about 9/11. He said he was in New York on the day, heard the first plane going over just before it hit the North Tower, but watched most of it on TV like everyone else. It was a bit of a wasted trip to be honest. But he gave me some magazine cuttings, and that's where I saw the interview you did with him.'

'That interview was a long time ago,' I said. 'Ten years?'

'Something like that. What about you? Have you any idea what he was doing when he disappeared?'

'No,' I said, dishonestly.

'You don't know where he was, who he was with, or what he was up to?'

'No,' I said again.

'I sense you're holding out on me.'

Remembering that Claremont had warned me that we would be having a confidential meeting, I thought: two can play at that game.

'Depends what you are looking for,' I said.

'So you know more than you're letting on.'

I realized we were sparring, so I let it run for a while. The first bottle of wine had quickly been emptied, and Claremont ordered another. Jacqueline asked for a second bottle of mineral water. Claremont and I continued fishing for each other's knowledge without giving away too much of our own.

I had been with Tatarov for a few hours during the time he disappeared. But he had warned me there were security issues involving the CIA and the FBI, but also probably the National Security Agency and the UK Foreign Office. Amongst other matters they were concerned with his birth nationality, and the fear that the Russian secret service might try to snatch him back. Tatarov himself clearly thought this was something of a joke, but I still had to sign a confidentiality agreement to satisfy the US government.

70

At the time of my first meeting with Claremont, Kyril Tatarov was still alive and well, and as far as I knew was in New York City and working at the Courant Institute.

I had already told some white lies to Bryan Claremont. Tatarov's knowledge of and ideas about 9/11 had become central to his concerns. My lips were sealed because I had promised they would be. Did I know where Tatarov was while he had seemed to disappear from the rest of the world? In the way Claremont meant the question, yes I did know. I was there with him for some of the time. But in a deeper way, that Tatarov himself might understand, I had not the slightest idea of 'where' he was – his capacity for abstract thought and his ability to connect unrelated concepts into a coherent argument were a total mystery to me. Who was he with? Someone like Tatarov was never in company with other people, even though others, including fellow theoretical mathematicians, might actually be present. What was he doing? When I saw him he was talking, sitting in a chair, drinking rather a lot of cloudy and acrid water. Not much worth reporting there. We shared a lunch. He talked a lot, far more than I had expected.

I was wondering what it was about the Tatarov story that had attracted Claremont's interest. What sort of film was he thinking about? Surely not something about 9/11, not now, after so many years? If not that, how did he think he could make a film for a general audience (which is what I assumed he was interested in) about someone who was almost completely intellectual, specialized in a way most people could not fathom, and who was by every normal standard desocialized?

What did Claremont already know? What was interesting to him? Was he himself perhaps a mathematician?

We circled around inconclusively for a few more minutes, then I said: 'What is it you would actually like me to do?

'I need a screenplay and I want it soon. First I will need a

treatment, so that I know what ideas you come up with and how you're thinking. It has to be something I can show to other people, something we can talk about, preferably use to raise more money. You and I would do two deals: the first we can agree now, for you to write the treatment, then after everyone's had a look at it, and if it goes to the next stage, I'll commission a first draft screenplay. Have you ever written a film before? Do you have an agent?'

At last we were speaking a language I was familiar with and we went straight into practical details. Jacqueline wrote everything down.

I try never to agree to a fee before my agent has gone over it with me but for a film there was the question of subsidiaries – the agent would want to know what residuals were likely to come along. Other matters had to be agreed. I wanted to know, for instance, how soon the treatment would be required, so my other work, already in hand, could be finished or postponed. The length would also be important – Claremont said once or twice that he would leave that to me, but I already knew the dangers of sending in work that seemed to the person waiting for it to be too short or too long. We agreed the number of pages, and I made sure Jacqueline wrote it down.

With the business out of the way, Claremont opened up. What he wanted, he said, was a film of mathematical romance. Surprised by the conjunction of opposites, I made him repeat that. A mathematical romance, he said again. Tatarov's temporary escape from the world was to attempt a reunion and reconciliation with the great love of his life, a woman from his past, who was marked by some mysterious problem, which had led to their splitting up. In the present day they are both mature and working on the same theorem. I interjected again that Tatarov's work was an attempt to resolve a conjecture,

not a theorem. Claremont said: 'What's the difference? Who's going to know, who's going to care?'

Claremont was planning the film as a leading role for a famous and garlanded actor called Ted Cannery, or Sir Edward Cannery as he had recently become. Sir Edward had put himself forward for the role of Tatarov. He was to be paired with one of three or four equally eminent female leads, from his own generation. Which one of these great ladies it would eventually be depended on many factors and was not yet decided, but that was none of my business. Filming would take place in winter, in a snowbound luxury golfing resort in the Scottish Highlands. This too had already been settled. There was no need for me to concern myself with practical details.

That was it. The rest would be up to me – what was going to happen and how, what the outcome would be, what the Tatarov figure would discover or resolve or learn or impart was the essence of the story I was to write.

'Does Kyril Tatarov know you are planning to make a film about him?' I said.

'He has been approached.'

'Did he agree?'

'I have someone in New York working on that. We don't see it as a problem.'

'You mean he hasn't responded.'

'Not yet.'

I was thinking about the 'Tatarov figure'. Even as Claremont and I discussed this in the restaurant I had decided that Tatarov must not be named. Most people who eventually went to see the film would recall the incident on which it was based, but only partly, only vaguely. They would not know or remember or care about the details. Because I had met the real man, who was unworldly, odd, abstract, decent, an undoubted genius, essentially a good and important man, I felt he should

be somehow insulated from the efforts to romanticize his few weeks of escape from the endless mental circling around the Pèlerin Conjecture. Kyril therefore soon became renamed in my mind as 'Sergei', and before I left the restaurant he had the surname 'Kalugin'. This in a sense freed me of my knowledge of the real man, and even from those first minutes I was able to sense a fictitious story starting to develop.

It was the first act of fictionalizing, one that would lead to many more.

I did not know how to write a film treatment, although because the money Claremont was offering me was tempting I had not admitted that. In reality I had only the vaguest idea of what a treatment was. After leaving Claremont and Jacqueline I went straight to a cinema bookshop in the West End and bought a book on the subject. It turned out to be not all that instructive. Later, I found some sample treatments on the internet and downloaded the ones that had actually graduated into being made as films, ones I remembered seeing. They were more helpful to me.

A month later I delivered my treatment to Claremont, expecting an immediate response – time was after all of the essence, he had said to me as we parted. A few weeks went by and I was starting to think I would never hear from him again, when a file turned up as an email attachment. It was from Jacqui (the PA at the lunch, now abbreviating her name).

Bryan, Jacqui told me in her email, was extremely enthusiastic about my story. They would be moving ahead to the next stage in the near future. In the meantime, Bryan had had a few extra thoughts of his own. He had made some notes and wondered if I would take a look at them and incorporate them into my draft. She sent them as a PDF. I downloaded, printed. The notes consisted of the draft I had sent in, with numerous handwritten marks.

The first of Bryan's thoughts was there on the first page: 'Sergei' had become 'Ivan'. That apparently random change was of course a clue to what was to come later: the few extra thoughts turned out to be a vast cross-hatch of changes, deletions, restorations, ballooned text, marginal notes in different colours, arrowed moves, and so on.

I was so depressed and demoralized I could not bring myself to look at the treatment again for more than a week. However, in the end I pulled myself together and completed a rewrite. I sent it to Claremont full of foreboding. I had stubbornly renamed 'Ivan' back to 'Sergei', silently ignored the most unworkable of his notes, but I factored in as many other of Bryan's so-called suggestions as I could.

While I was waiting for his response I took a phone call from Jacqui.

'I thought you would like to know,' she started, making an incorrect assumption, 'Bryan loves the way you have set the story on a Scottish island instead of in the Highlands. He was hoping to shoot at Gleneagles, but he thinks this will work nearly as well.'

She paused. I waited for more, suspecting trouble. More changes?

'Is that all?' I said.

'Well the really good news is that we have taken on a new financial backer, which enables us to move to the next stage and Bryan will be giving you the go-ahead to do another draft later this week. Are you still with your same agent?'

'Yes,' I said.

'We'll be in contact. Oh, and there's another note that Bryan has asked me to pass on. Our new backer owns a luxury hotel in the Virgin Islands and thinks we should make the film there. It would simply be a question of changing a few words here and there, wouldn't it?'

I sent in a second draft, then a third. I dug in my heels and kept the Scottish setting in the second draft, but lost the battle of the hotels in the third. The engulfing snowstorm became a tropical hurricane. Then the backer changed his mind, and the promise of finance disappeared. The Scottish setting returned.

It is embarrassing even to remember as much as this of the unoriginal story, but it satisfied Bryan Claremont, and soon after he had read it he commissioned me to write a full screenplay. I silently sent mental apologies to Kyril Tatarov, profoundly hoping he would never see the film, and that if he did he would find it so remote from his own reality that he would not suspect he had any part in it.

When the false replaces the truth

I accepted the commission to write the screenplay because Claremont and I had made a deal, and I needed the money. I had gone over the story in my mind so often that all the details of the plot came naturally to me, and the characters – who were now halfway between how I had originally conceived them and what successive rewrites had made them into – came to life in my mind and more or less wrote their own dialogue. Writing the screenplay was therefore not difficult, and was finished remarkably swiftly, but my conscience continued to prick me.

After another long silence Claremont announced that a second draft of the screenplay was required. He invited me to his new office to go through his notes and decide what must be done. By this time, though, my inspiration had been wrung as dry as my patience. I elected to exercise the option in my contract that would allow third parties to take over as 'joint' writers on the project. I believe Bryan Claremont was as relieved as I was by this decision.

The screenplay of *Sergei and Tanya* was therefore handed over to two well established film writers, who gave the story a

polish or two. They did not work together, the second writer being called in to replace the first after problems with what the film world calls 'creative differences'. Much to my surprise, later in the year the film was actually shot and completed, it gained distributors, it was shown in cinemas, it was reviewed in the press.

I never saw the film myself at a public showing, but Bryan Claremont conscientiously sent me an advance copy of the DVD, and I watched it at home.

Sergei and Tanya was later broadcast on terrestrial television, and from time to time it is still rerun, usually in a late-night slot because of a particular scene involving Sir Edward and the young woman actor who played the journalist Ellie Harsent. The listings magazines and websites normally give the film a two-star rating, and I still hope that Tatarov never saw it.

This long involvement with the film did have one positive result for me. It reminded me of the reality of Tatarov's disappearance, how I became briefly involved in the episode, and what he told me in a guarded, circuitous manner when I went to meet him.

Re-imagining the real incident as an invented one brought home to me the relevance of fiction, of telling a story, when the truth is inconvenient, too complicated to explain or is simply something you wish to hide. Stories can be told.

SIX

then: 2002

Roadside meeting

In the late summer, almost a year after the 9/11 attacks, Martin Oliver Viklund and I agreed to meet in a restaurant on Highway 95 outside the city of Baltimore. It was a franchise of a seafood-and-steak chain, expensive and well regarded by American food writers, but still a chain. I arrived early for the meeting, not by design but because my hotel was in the same area and it happened that way.

The interior of the restaurant was extensive, with several aisles between the tables and booths. There was an impression of solidity and permanence, because the walls had been built from open stonework, and the ceiling was supported by an arrangement of timber buttresses. The restaurant had been designed around an existing mature tree, whose trunk and visible root system dominated the centre of the eating area. The crown of the tree was in the air above the building, visible through some glass apertures. The lighting throughout the restaurant was subdued, each table or booth being illuminated by a small overhead spotlight – the effect, on walking in from the sunlight outside, was a sense of being plunged into night.

I was shown to a large corner table, pre-booked by Viklund's office. It had been arranged for greater privacy than most of the

other tables, with eye-level battens on each side. It was beside one of the few small windows. From the semi-circular couch seat it was not possible to see much of the area outside – what could be seen was expectably part of the immense parking lot. The midday glare was shaded by neutral density screening.

The server came promptly to the booth, and gave me a huge laminated menu board to read. His name badge said he was called Miguel. When he offered to recite the day's specials I said I would prefer to wait for my companion, so he asked me what I should like to drink.

I sipped ice water and waited for Martin Viklund to arrive. I was nervous of meeting him, also curious, and I had mixed feelings about the possibility he would tell me something about Lil's death I did not want to know. I needed to hear it, though – the terrible events of that day the previous September were still fresh in my mind and there were so many unanswered questions. The manner of her death haunted me. In common with many others who had lost loved ones in the 9/11 attacks, I lacked closure.

Lil's body was one of the many that inexplicably had never been found. DNA tracing of many of the victims was proving indefinite, largely because so few remains had been recovered, and because of the poor condition of most of the traces that were. Even after the most devastating of air crashes, human bodies – or grimly detached body parts – are normally recoverable for forensic identification. A man, woman or child, violently killed or burned, torn apart by explosion or impact, leaves many traces that are forensically identifiable. Yet fewer than three hundred intact bodies were recovered from the rubble of the twin towers. Thousands of small pieces of bodies were found, and out of those another sixteen hundred victims were positively identified. But more than one thousand people who were known to have been killed in the World Trade Center, either in

one of the buildings, or on the ground, or in one of the aircraft, left no identifiable trace at all. How could that be possible?

As for the Pentagon disaster, where Lil had died: the authorities were secretive, evasive or in denial. A year after the event they still had not released the information from the flight recorders of the plane that crashed into the building. Why not? Why could we not be told what was being said in the cockpit as the disaster unfolded? Under normal circumstances, what the flight crew might have said in the final moments of a crashing aircraft was often withheld from the public, and understandably. But the plane that hit the Pentagon had been taken over by terrorists, and it was their voices that would be on the tape. The recorded technical data from the doomed aircraft also needed to be known – there were already controversies about radar data, air traffic control issues, and much more.

At the time my meeting with Martin Viklund was arranged the 9/11 Commission had not been chartered, so most people's knowledge of what had happened was vague or vernacular. It was largely based on the media coverage they had seen at the time, or edited replays of it later, or drawn from their own inexact memories of interviews with witnesses and survivors. Wider awareness was imprecise: the media carried endless follow-on news stories and speculation, but in haphazard fashion and only for a few months. Gradually, the attacks of 9/11 became something that was known to everyone but rarely discussed by anyone.

There was an American-led war going on in Afghanistan with inevitable casualties, there were endless rumours about what 'really' happened on September 11, and in general what people knew or thought could not be confirmed because of the closed manner of the authorities. Everything was wrapped up under the slogan: 'war on terror'.

In this environment of official silence a number of conspiracy

theories started going the rounds, in the US and elsewhere. But mostly in America, where the account told by the authorities was soon accepted by the popular media and thereafter gained strength. Because not everything in the account was consistent with what some people believed true, questions started being asked. Airline pilots had pointed out that the planes were flying too fast, too low, making the aircraft almost impossible to control, even by professional crew, and of course outside every known safety parameter. There was no CCTV footage of the alleged hijackers actually boarding the planes, even though all three departure airports had camera surveillance on every boarding gate. Why hadn't the air defence system intercepted the hijacked aircraft?

Still the consensus remained with the official account. It was felt to be disloyal to the victims, disloyal to the country, to raise questions about what everyone thought they had witnessed on TV. It began to seem that doubting was the province of people on the fringe, of groups with anti-establishment agendas, of conspiracy theorists. The official story was patriotic – an American story.

Roadside advice

I had no time for conspiracy theories, but I needed to be told the facts of Lil's death. I knew only that what I knew was not the whole story. This was of course behind my wanting to meet with Viklund, a proposal I had hesitated over for some time, and eventually made only with reluctance. He, or the people working for him, delayed a response for several weeks. This made me suspect he felt much as I did.

He was to me the uncaring husband engaged in divorcing Lil at the time she died, planning to divide money and property, not arguing or fighting about it, but using lawyers as proxies. I was to Viklund – what? The man who had moved in

opportunistically to replace him, who had become his wife's lover? Of course, but was that still an issue? Had it ever been?

I kept staring around the restaurant, waiting for him to arrive. I had almost no mental image of what he looked like – the photographs Lil had shown me were old ones. But that day was already a long time ago, and across the unbridgeable divide created by her death. Much had happened since to erase or edit most of my memories from then.

By this time I had been to Grand Rapids, Michigan, to attend a memorial service for Lil, but especially to meet her family. Elsa and Thomas Trencher were her parents, her twin sister Alison, her older sister Maizy and her brother Jeffery. Martin Viklund had not been at the service, and as far as I could tell he was not expected. No one mentioned him.

After the service – short and sweet, with a calming sequence of fond tributes from Lil's friends and sisters – I went across and introduced myself to Thomas and Elsa. I had no idea how they would greet me, but I need have had no worries. They had heard of me; in fact the longer I spoke to them the more I realized how much Lil had talked about me to them. Martin Viklund was still not mentioned, and Lil's surname written on the memorial cards was given as Trencher.

We all agreed that it was urgent that we should find out for certain the way she had been killed, and that it was a priority for her body to be found and given a decent burial. Our shared grief lay inconsolably in the shallows beneath the calm.

Three months later I was back in the US, waiting to meet Viklund. I glanced through the menu board two or three times, but made no decision about what to eat. The server walked past swiftly, turning the corner beside my table. Smiling, he made an indicative gesture towards the entrance.

I noticed then that two men had entered the building un-obtrusively. They were both wearing dark suits. One of them

did not move from the reception area but stood quietly with his hands folded in front of him. He was looking intently around at all the tables – he looked towards mine, but seemed no more interested in me than anyone else. He turned away, began regarding the other side of the restaurant. The other man was strolling calmly through the dining area, along the aisles, unaggressively and casually, making eye contact with no one. A pod in his ear was wired to something concealed in his jacket.

I peered again through the shaded window, looking outside. I had not until then noticed that three large cars had arrived. They were in the parking lot but not in any of the marked spaces. All three were black, highly polished, the sun glinting from them. They blocked two of the long rows of customers' vehicles which were already parked. Two men and a woman wearing business suits were standing around the cars: the woman had taken up position by the front vehicle, an SUV. One of the men stood beside the last car, another SUV, and the third was positioned beside the rear door of the car in the middle of the group. This looked low and heavy. All three vehicles had drivers waiting inside. The passenger compartment of the central car had silvered windows.

At some signal I could not detect the three people moved at once. They converged quickly on the car in the middle and a passenger climbed out. The four walked towards the restaurant entrance, and briefly moved out of my eye line.

I realized the man who had been in the car was, or must be, Martin Viklund. I did now recognize him from the photos Lil had shown me, but until that moment I would not have been able to describe him from memory. He was of average build, and looked lithe and healthy. He had thickly growing pale hair, cut short, military style. He was wearing sportswear: track suit bottoms, a sweatshirt with a faded NASA logo, bright-white trainers and an orange towel draped around his neck.

As he and the others entered, the maître d' immediately recognized him and with a professional smile signalled him towards my table. He came alone – the others waited beside the door, glanced around the dining area once more, then retreated outside. One of them remained in the reception area. He stood there, he scanned the room.

'Ben!' Viklund slid down on to the bench at the opposite end from mine. 'Great to meet you at last. I have to keep this short, but I guess we have a lot to talk about.'

Miguel appeared, edged a menu board towards Viklund, who waved it away. He asked for two Diet Cokes and some snacks. The server poured ice water, and left. Viklund raised himself up from the seat. As he reached towards me we shook hands. He grasped my shoulder with his other hand.

'You come across from England to do this?' he said. He did not let go of my shoulder.

'No,' I said. 'There are people –'

'There are always people. Look, I need to apologize for how I'm dressed today. Tight schedule this afternoon, but I'm on my way to the gym. Can't eat until later. Do you work out too? You look as if you could use some exercise. Why don't you come along with me after this? We use a great work-out studio down at the Pentagon – not open to the public, but I can arrange a pass for you. What are you – a little older than me? Maybe a year or two – Lilian told me that. You can't be too careful.'

'I get what exercise I need.'

'Yeah. Where are those Cokes? Let's get us a drink too, Ben. You like rye whiskey?'

'I do.'

He released his hand from my shoulder at last, and signalled towards Miguel, already approaching with our Cokes. Viklund ordered one large whiskey and a glass of aerated mineral water for himself.

'You want to talk,' he said. 'We have so much to say. I have to tell you — Lilian was a wonderful woman. No one else like her. I still adore her. You too, I guess. What do you say?'

I was startled by his directness.

'I want to know about Lil, and how she died.'

'Yeah, I guessed it might be that. Well, Ben, what can I tell you about her?'

'Was she on American 77 when it crashed?' I said. 'Her name doesn't appear on the passenger list, the manifest, but she was flying to Los Angeles from Dulles, and —'

'She was never on the passenger list. We don't do passenger lists.'

'What does that mean? The lists published in the press were standard computer print-outs from the airline.'

'The manifests published in the press looked that way, but they were bullshit. We don't know where they found them, or who compiled them. Not us. Lilian wouldn't appear on any list like that. It's standard procedure. Whenever she or I want to fly I get my people at the Department to order up the tickets. It's a Department protocol. Seats are always kept open for Defense officials. We don't get listed on the passenger manifest.'

'But was she on that plane?'

'I guess so. She talked for a while of flying back to New York, but I said it was probably better to take an earlier flight to LA, as planned.'

'Why better?' I said. Viklund shrugged his shoulders, looked away. The man standing by the reception area was impassive. Not watching us. 'You were here on the east coast,' I said into the silence. 'But I thought you were in Los Angeles. That's what Lil told me. That was why she was going. You wanted her there.'

'Lilian told me it was you she was going to meet with. I didn't come into it.'

'We were planning to meet later, after she went to your house in Venice Beach. You wanted her to clear out her property so the place could be sold.'

'She told you that? Not true. The Venice house was sold weeks before. She knew that. I'd already left it.'

'What? Lil said you were there –' Viklund was impassive. I was confounded by his denial of what I had always taken to be absolute facts. I went on: 'Isn't that what the arrangement was? You insisted she had to fly out to California, when she said you could have done everything on your own.'

'By then the house was being lived in by the people who bought it from me. What do you suppose she was thinking?'

'That's what I'm asking you!'

Miguel had brought our drinks while this exchange was going on. I was startled by my own vehemence, but also struggling to maintain my hold on the facts as I knew them, as Lil had described them. I drank some of the whiskey, too much, too quickly. It burned in my throat. I remembered I did not like rye whiskey after all.

Viklund said: 'I had flown back here to DC to meet with her. She knew that, because it was what she wanted. She almost never went to the house in Venice – she said she didn't like it.'

'She told me she hated it.'

Viklund maintained an appearance of calm. He watched me steadily. His blue eyes seemed never to blink.

'You warned her not to fly on Tuesday. That was Tuesday, September 11. Why did you tell her that?'

'I don't believe I did.'

'That's what she told me. She said you were explicitly warning her. Did you – did you know what was going to happen?'

'Did I know what, Ben?'

'The hijacking. Did you have advance knowledge?'

'That's a serious allegation.'

'It's a question, not an allegation.'

'No, I did not have advance knowledge of everything that was going to happen that day.'

'Then why did you warn Lil not to fly?'

'I don't believe I did,' he said again. 'We have a range of regular flights into and out of Dulles and Reagan Airports. The airlines, American and United, always keep vacant seats for us on certain flights.'

'Us?'

'Department officials and staff.'

'Lil didn't work for the Department.' As I said the words it was as if I was hearing them from someone else. I said: 'Or did she?'

'She sometimes worked with me. That day, September 11 – yeah. It was a Tuesday, but we don't normally travel much on Tuesdays. Maybe that's what I said. Why did she think it was a warning? If Lilian was planning to fly to LA on September 11 she would have had to order her own ticket, but the Department would pick up the tab. You want me to look into that for you?'

'I only want to know if she was on American 77 that day, and if so, why her body has never been found. There were sixty-four people on the plane – six crew and fifty-eight passengers, including the hijackers.'

'And another one hundred twenty-five were killed inside the building. A lot of people went missing that day. After the World Trade Center collapsed –'

'I know about that,' I said. 'There weren't as many missing at the Pentagon, but there were some. Lil must be one of them, but because her name was not on the manifest there's a possibility she wasn't on the plane at all. Could it mean that her flight was booked by your staff?'

'It could. Maybe you have something there, Ben. But you

can't rely on the manifest they printed in the press. That was a forgery, not the real one.'

'How do you know that?'

He said nothing. Then: 'You want me to find out if someone in the office booked Lilian's ticket?'

'Yes, I do.'

He slipped a notebook out of his hip pocket, pulled the thin barrel of a ballpoint from the ring-bound spine. He turned a few pages, and wrote something down.

'You have an address here, where my people can find you?' he said. 'Or a cellphone number?'

'I'm in the Best Western, at Baltimore Airport.'

I told him my mobile number and he wrote it down. He glanced at his wristwatch, a large dial with analogue hands as well as a digital display, the sort of watch some runners wear to monitor heartbeat, blood pressure, and so on. He was signalling he wanted our meeting to end, but I wanted to know more.

'Was Lil in Washington before the flight?'

'Yes.'

'So she left from here. And you saw her.'

'Yes.'

'Were you ever in LA?'

'How long is ever? I was there.'

'But you flew back to see her.'

'I got my people to collect her from the airport. She came in from New York.'

'She stayed with you?'

'Always did. I don't suppose you mind. She said you wouldn't.'

'She told me she stayed in a hotel when she saw you.'

'I guess she told you a lot of things, Ben. We were man and wife. Sorry about that. It never changed — good as always. I

expect she told you some story about a divorce?'

I was staring down at the table. 'Yes.'

'There was nothing as definite as that.'

'You were separated.'

He waggled his hand, indicating uncertainty. 'We led separate lives, lived apart, didn't ask questions. She might have meant it that way, and you thought something else. We were like that from the start and went on until the end. I assumed you knew. How could you not?'

I sat in silence, burning inside. How could Lil, out of my life for nearly a year, reach out from behind the hell of 9/11 and still hurt me so? I felt sick at heart to learn of this old betrayal. Could it really be true? I remembered everything she had said about her failing marriage to this man, which I had implicitly believed. How could I not?

The clear, plausible descriptions of the impasse between them, the telling details and anecdotes, the little clues, the off-hand remarks. Martin was always in the past tense. But maybe it was Martin who was lying now, taking a belated revenge on me? Was he testing me to see how I would react or what I might do?

Blindly, suddenly dazzled by the shock of these intimate revelations, on I went.

'Did she or didn't she work for the Department?' I said, knowing now there was more to come.

'In the Pentagon, no. Not there. Her main job was at that publisher in New York City. Senior publicist.'

'I knew about that. Was she doing anything else?'

'If you mean, was she working for the Department, the answer is no. We had separate lives and careers. But she was sometimes useful.'

I waited to see if he was going to elaborate, but he picked up his tall glass of water. The ice cubes clunked as he drained it.

'How was she useful?' I said. 'She told me nothing about this.'

'Did she mention we set her up in a London office? That's an overseas station, run by us.'

'Who do you mean by us?'

'Who do you think I mean?'

'She was working for the publisher, selling UK rights to some of their books. And European translations. I went with her to the London Book Fair.'

'Yeah.'

'I saw her in her London office several times – it was a couple of rooms rented from an agency. The publisher's logo was on the door. They furnished the place, they had a long lease, it was registered in their name.'

'Yeah, yeah.' He clunked the ice cubes again, took one of them into his mouth, crunched it between his even white teeth.

'But you say it wasn't like that –'

'It was a federal overseas station, funded by the US government.'

'So what did she do for your department?'

'Nothing you wouldn't approve of, Ben. Sometimes she did some proofing of reports, papers, stuff like that. Sometimes she wrote material for us. She was useful. She briefed British lobbyists. She tracked down articles we needed to read. She arranged for people to work with us. There are always people.'

It was as if he was describing a stranger to me. Could this be the Lil I had loved and thought I had known? Viklund was describing her as some kind of occasional agent for the federal government. Was that Lil? The committed publisher? The woman in the black wig and shimmering gown, who relaxed by going to vampire conventions? He was lying – he must be lying.

'I can't believe any of this,' I said, feeling angry with myself,

with him, but potentially also now with Lil.

'Suit yourself, Ben. I am telling you only what you said you wanted to know.'

'Then tell me this. Why does the US government act guilty when it does anything abroad?'

'You tell me. I'm not the government.'

'You work for it. You're an insider.'

'No one is inside a government. You are it, or you are not it.'

'Which are you?'

'Not it. I do a job. I have no executive powers.' He was still outwardly relaxed, his arm resting on the back of the couch seat, his fingers a few inches from my shoulder. His demeanour remained friendly, casual, belying what he said next: 'You want to know about guilt? It was you Brits who pioneered guilty conscience about other countries. You and your friends in Europe, all imperialists, led the world in military oppression of developing countries, and when it stopped working, or those countries kicked you out, you couldn't forgive yourselves for having tried. Now you think we're doing the same. No we're not. We're trying to make the world a better place. America does it because it's necessary and there's no one else to do it. There's nothing unusual, nothing wrong in what we do. We are Americans and we're answerable, responsible, but the world is full of groups who envy us, who want to be like us, but they go about it by demonizing us. They fight us to the death for that. If they attack us, we will defend our freedoms. The US is a representational democracy, based on equality and freedom. America is a force for good in the world. We happen to put American interests first, which you Brits don't like, but America stands for the good, and we work for it.'

I said: 'Then why doesn't the good democracy tell us what happened on 9/11?'

'I guess we don't know, or no more than you already know.

There's nothing hidden. What occurred on that day was something no one could have expected. Nothing like it had ever happened before. If the government was at fault it was because we weren't ready. I was inside the Pentagon myself, that morning. If we had been expecting a fully fuelled plane to slam into the building, none of us would have gone to work that day. You think there's a cover-up going on? There is no cover-up, because there's nothing to cover up. We were victims too.'

'The US government knows more about 9/11 than it admits to. Why haven't videos of the crash at the Pentagon been released? Where are the flight data recorders?'

He gestured at me with the palms of his hands wide open. 'I haven't got them. I told you, I was inside the building on the day.'

'If those were released, a lot of unanswered questions would go away.'

'Are you one of those people into conspiracy theories, Ben?'

I made an angry, dismissive gesture.

'I've seen stuff on the internet,' I said. 'None of that convinces me. What we saw on TV that day is the only unbiased information we have – we need to know who was behind it, what was really behind it. People in government, people like you, know more than they have said. My wanting answers is for a personal reason. I'm only interested in Lil, the way she died, what happened to her and why there's no trace of her. I'm certain she was killed but I don't know how, or where she was, or why she was involved. Her death seems incidental to something much larger. To understand why she died I have to know what that larger thing was.'

'Yeah. You do.'

'So is there a reason?'

'I'm interested you say you think the TV coverage was unbiased.'

92

'I said it was the only information we have.'

'Did you happen to see the TV coverage in Syria, Ben? Or what Gaddafi said on Libyan TV? Did you see how Russian TV reported 9/11? You see those Palestinians in the West Bank cheering in the streets? You catch the interview with Saddam Hussein? The Ayatollah?'

'No, but I saw some of them later. The Palestinians were cheering a football result. Everyone remembers that bit of film, but it was not about 9/11. Someone was stirring the news.'

'Was Saddam Hussein biased or unbiased?' said Viklund, undeterred. 'Did you agree with Vladimir Putin?'

'They expressed a point of view.'

'There you go. But if you want an unbiased point of view, there are thousands of American troops in Afghanistan right now. They're out there trying to find out for you, putting their lives at risk. Why don't you wait a while? There's going to be a Senate investigation starting soon, an independent commission set up to give the answers people like you want to hear.'

I had been forced to lean towards him – his voice was soft and even, and sometimes he was difficult to hear in the general noise of the busy restaurant. Now I sat straighter in the seat. Looking up I saw the guy in the suit had come across to our table, and was standing coolly a short distance away.

Martin Viklund said: 'I'm running late. We'll speak again, Ben. Stick around. Eat something – try their year-long aged sirloin, the finest I ever tasted. I've got your number. You'll hear from me.'

He stood up and the tail of the long orange towel brushed against me. Something scented I had been aware of passed my nostrils, momentarily stronger.

I watched as he and the others crossed the parking lot to the cars.

When I saw the price of a steak in this place I knew it was

beyond me. I had no appetite for that much food, anyway. I picked up the tab for the drinks, and left a gratuity for the server. Later, ten miles down the highway I found another roadside restaurant, somewhere that had food I wanted, that I could afford to eat.

Viklund said he would call me. He never did.

SEVEN

now

The inland sea

Returning from London I left the ferry terminal and walked the short distance along the sea front to my house. I looked across at the Cowal hills of Argyll, on the far side of the firth. It was a view I had been soaking up for a few years, but it always seemed new to me, never became commonplace. Sometimes the hills were made to seem distant because of rain or mist or haze – at other times, as on this warm afternoon, they stood out with sharp definition against the sky, the clarity making them appear to be closer, steeper. The colours of the slopes changed almost every day: a blur of green, grey and brown, with patches of pale purple or bright yellow, according to the season. Whenever I returned to Bhòid it was this view that settled me, that made me feel once again connected with reality. The hills of the Cowal were plain, permanent. They lacked the need for interpretation, there was no story that might explain them, no solution to their mystery. They were what they now seemed to be, what they had been for millennia before, and what they would always be.

Sitting on the plane coming back from London, on the train from Glasgow Airport, on the ferry across the firth, I had been thinking lazily about my trip to Paris the following week.

There was going to be some preliminary background work I should have to do that would make the article easier and better to write, but after the visit to London I had little energy for it. I decided to start the work the next day.

Once inside, I brought the house back to life, opening windows, checking the mail that had been delivered that morning, generally tidying up because when I went to London the previous morning I had left everything in a mess. Jeanne and the boys would be home soon.

At the top of the hour I turned on the television to watch the latest news bulletin. I wanted to catch up with whatever new information might have emerged about the wreckage of the plane discovered in the Atlantic.

The main story dealt with politicians and correspondents speculating about an election later in the year, then came a court report of the first hearing of a group of young men accused of operating a terrorist cell in Glasgow. Other stories followed, including a long item about sport. Towards the end of the bulletin, with an enlarged map on the screen of the east coast of the USA, the news reader said that there had been more exploratory dives, and sonar equipment was in use. It had been discovered that the wreckage initially believed to be from a crashed airliner was in fact the wreck of a ship sunk by a German U-boat during the Second World War.

The news programme ended. It was a ship, not a plane? How had that mistake been made? How much like a wrecked aircraft does a sunken ship look, even after years underwater?

There was a beautiful sunset that evening, so I walked across the high ground behind the town, looking at the display of twilight across the still waters of the firth, thinking about my family coming home. I breathed the warm and heather-scented air. After half an hour, in almost complete darkness, I returned

to the house where the landline phone was ringing. It was Jeanne.

'Ben, I know this is going to be difficult,' she said. 'I'll be home tomorrow and I'm going to have to bring Mum with me. The boys are desperate to be back, and I can't manage Mum here on my own. Would you get the spare room ready for her? Only the bed for now, and I'll get everything else done tomorrow, once I'm back.'

Difficult. That was hardly the word that applied. Ever since we moved to live in Scotland there had been the unvoiced awareness that one day Lucinda would no longer be able to manage on her own. Part of our reason for moving north of the border, if only a small part, was that Jeanne could be closer to her mother, but Lucinda's health had deteriorated in recent weeks. Until earlier this year she had been mobile, independent, engaged in her own circle of friends, still working on her long-term project of modernizing her house. But she had suffered a minor stroke, a TIA, and after that there was a sudden marked decline in her health. She had been treated by her GP, was taking medication that allegedly eased the symptoms, and had undergone a series of tests at her local hospital. She was receiving daily visits from social services. She could barely look after herself.

Jeanne had told me several times that the care arrangements for Lucinda were inadequate, and the local authority was proposing she should be moved to a nursing home. Jeanne and Lucinda both rejected that, although for different reasons. Anyway, the boys had to be back on the island for school the following week, and Jeanne herself, who was a successful freelance fabric designer, could not spare more time away. Taking Lucinda into our home was more or less the only option. Jeanne and I had always known that this was likely to happen at some point.

97

'Is there really no alternative?' I said, realizing how plaintive I sounded, even sulkily rebellious. I disliked the sound of my own words. Selfishly, I was daunted by the thought that the way I lived and worked at home was about to change radically. 'You know I need to travel a lot, and that will place an extra –'

'It isn't going to affect you, Ben,' Jeanne said, sharply. 'I can cope. Once she's settled in it won't change anything for you. She's used to the way we live.'

Deservedly rebuked, I knew that this was probably true. Before the present decline in her health Lucinda had been self-sufficient. She had her own car, and every year she took a holiday abroad. She had driven across from Edinburgh to stay with us several times. Our spare room had in effect become Lucinda's room, because other visitors were few and far between. Some of her clothes were kept with us, and a few of her pictures, books and ornaments. A sensitive and observant woman, she always tried to be an inconspicuous visitor, keeping out of our way when Jeanne and I needed to work, spending time with the kids, taking on small tasks around the house. I knew, though, that in recent weeks her freedom of thought and movement had changed noticeably.

'I can't leave her again,' Jeanne said. 'The care visitors only call once a day, and she needs company. It really won't change anything at home. You know that's true.'

As I did. I was regretting my instant and selfish response. I did like Lucinda, felt I owed her a lot, and I was willing to make it work for her. Jeanne and I discussed a few more details over the phone, but the essence of it was that she mainly wanted me to get the room ready and to buy some of the food Lucinda liked.

Before I went to bed I looked at the BBC Scotland news website, and searched for the story about the wreck. The video repeated the report I had heard earlier on the British news from

London, but at the end they went to one of their own reporters, Helena McCardle, who was somewhere on the coast of the state of Delaware.

Speaking direct to camera, she said: 'The cranes were still pulling up parts of the alleged ship when we were suddenly ordered to leave. There was nothing polite about it. A group of about ten Marines came aboard our boat. They were armed. They arrested us, took away the sound and camera equipment, then put us on another boat and we were brought ashore. They closed us down. They gave us back the equipment once we were on land. But we distinctly saw a piece of lightweight metal coming out of the sea, slightly curved. Although it was dirty and crusted from being in the sea for so long it was possible to see traces of paintwork. I and my crew all saw it at the same time. The visible smears were on one side only: a red streak, a blue patch. The rest was indistinct. It looked like airline livery to all of us.'

The report ended. In the studio, the continuity announcer said that Helena McCardle and the rest of the crew had already left the USA and were on a flight back to Glasgow.

Red and blue airline livery. That could have been the American Airlines logo on the tailplane stabilizer. Or the upper part of the fuselage, which was painted in those colours. On the other hand, red and blue were commonly used in the logos of many airlines. I could immediately think of three or four, other than American.

But it would not go away. American! American! The memories and feelings of loss, those long months of endless grief, anger and mystery still reverberated if I dwelt on what happened that day. The nagging sense of absence, of unexplained events, the sudden death of an old lover, the tight-lipped authorities who probably knew, or could discover, the truth.

I remembered the American Airlines spokesperson I had seen

on the news the previous evening. 'None of our aircraft is unaccounted for. That plane cannot be one of ours.'

He called it a plane, not a ship sunk by a German U-boat nearly eighty years ago.

Not lucid

After Jeanne called me to confirm which ferry she and Lucinda and the two boys had boarded I drove the car the short distance to the harbour and parked it as close as I could to the passenger terminal. The ferry appeared in the bay from across the firth fifteen minutes later, slowing and turning, then edging towards the quay. I saw this skilled seamanship every day from our windows – it was a practised, professional manoeuvre, routinely precise and accurate, even in strong winds or rough weather.

After the ship was tied up and the vehicles were going ashore from the car deck, I waited in the passenger terminal for my family to appear. It always took a while for passengers to emerge as they had to walk down the sloping companionway from the saloon deck. A couple of dozen people soon stepped out from the enclosed ramp. They moved out of the terminal, dispersing to their lives. After a short pause I heard footsteps running, clomping hollowly on the metal walkway, and suddenly my son Seth appeared. He saw me at once, ran across the concourse and we hugged.

'Mummy's coming soon,' he said.

'How is Gran? Is she walking OK?'

'Yes. Very slowly. Mummy is holding her. Look – I bought this in a shop.' He held up a small digital device, made of brightly coloured plastic. 'Will you play with me?'

'Later. This evening? We have to take Gran home first and look after her.'

'She's OK. Mummy can look after her. It's got five games and I've already finished one of them.'

Jeanne then appeared, walking slowly, managing two large wheeled suitcases, and weighed down by a backpack and her own holdall hooked over one arm. She was also trying to support Lucinda, who was leaning on her upper arm. Jeanne's hair was windblown or uncombed, falling across her eyes. She looked exhausted. Young Louis was holding his grandmother's free hand, but she seemed barely aware of him. As soon as I saw them I hurried across, took the two cases from Jeanne, kissed her, kissed Lucinda, gave Louis a big hug.

When we had driven the short distance back to the house Jeanne took Lucinda to her room, while I unloaded the luggage from the car and began making drinks and snacks for the boys and a pot of tea for the adults.

Lucinda said almost nothing to me through all this, but smiled many times. She called me 'Ben' once, 'Benjamin' once more, but overall did not have much to say to me. She mumbled most of her words. I saw that her mouth had a sort of irregular sideways quirk, something I had not noticed before, probably a result of the minor stroke.

The next day I spent several hours taking the car ferry across to the mainland and driving to Lucinda's house in Morningside. I packed the car with all the extra things that Lucinda would need, according to the list Jeanne had prepared. I drove back through the central belt of Scotland, then took the ferry across to the island.

That evening I was sitting opposite Lucinda while we were at dinner. She continued to say little, while Jeanne frequently vocalized for her: answering her own questions, maintaining a kind of normal level of conversation. I tried not to stare across the table at Lucinda, wanting to remember her as she had been until recently, not just take note of the changes. But I could not avoid seeing how her hand shook as she raised food to her mouth, nor being aware of the lopsided way her jaw moved as

she chewed. And her long silences – Lucinda of the past had always talked happily through meals.

I was glad to have Jeanne and Seth and Louis home again, enjoyed the games and silly chatter of the boys, semi-rivals to each other, semi-allies against the adults – the innocent conspiracies of childhood.

Later, after the boys went to bed, and Lucinda had retired early, still tired she said after the journey of the day before, Jeanne went to her drawing board to catch up with a design commission she had put aside the previous week. I went downstairs to my study in the basement.

I wanted to look again at the research files I had compiled over the past two decades, begun while I was still obsessed with the way Lil died.

Years ago I had downloaded internet images of the actual plane that on the day was designated American Flight 77. It was a Boeing 757-223, registered as N644AA. Like all the jets flown by the company in 2001 it had an unpainted lower fuselage, polished to a high shine, a long horizontal strip of red, white and blue at window level, and shining silvery blue paint above. The lettering of the company name was a glowing red, with a white surround. The tailplane stabilizer carried the livery in huge letters: 'AA'. One of the letters was red, the other blue, on a white background. All the colours were bright, assertive, proud, prominently patriotic.

I felt a familiar sadness as I looked at the old photographs, knowing what was going to happen to this aircraft, knowing what had happened. The mysteries of 9/11 were still unsolved, years later, now more than two decades later. Few people seemed to care any more.

I leafed through several of the other print-outs I had filed. Almost at once I began to experience the oppressive fatigue-like feeling brought on by the subject: a fascination with grappling

with the problem again, but also a deep reluctance to do so. There were so many unanswered questions that simply to think of one of them brought several others into focus. The dilemma was a real one – Lil had died because this plane had crashed, or because someone had made it crash. American Flight 77 was therefore of personal interest to me, but more objectively it was of general interest in any case.

Of the four aircraft destroyed on 9/11 there were extra mysteries about the fate of AA 77. After it took off from Dulles International Airport at 8:20 a.m. it was tracked as a normal flight until about 8:50 a.m., when air traffic controllers lost radio and radar contact. The transponder had either stopped working or had been turned off. At this time, controllers on the ground were unaware of the other hijacks going on – following standard practice they assumed that American 77 had crashed, and declared an emergency. A search for wreckage on the ground was instigated, but it was called off almost immediately as news of the other hijackings came in. The controllers then assumed correctly that American 77 had also been hijacked.

About half an hour later an unidentified aircraft appeared suddenly in Washington air space. The area of sky around the White House and Capitol Hill is a closed, protected zone into which civil aircraft are never allowed to fly. For that reason ground controllers assumed at first that the intruder must be a military plane, an impression that was reinforced by the high velocity and low altitude at which it was flying. It was diving and turning at great speed, such that several controllers thought the radar trace had to be from a jet fighter aircraft. Several eye-witnesses on the ground, close to the Pentagon, saw an aircraft flying low at very high speed in the last few seconds before the impact, and some described it emphatically as a military plane. One of them even said it looked like a cruise missile. Many of

them described the aircraft as painted white or off-white, with none of the familiar AA markings.

If not American 77, what was it?

But these were not the only witness accounts. There were many people in the area at the time – traffic along the adjacent freeway was halted by gridlock, and drivers and passengers in the vehicles had an uninterrupted view of the Pentagon. Some of them said that it was beyond doubt an American Airlines plane – they saw the livery, glimpsed the windows.

Then there was the question of the direction in which the aircraft had flown. Some witnesses said the aircraft appeared from one direction, while others emphatically disagreed, and pointed towards buildings and local landmarks they swore the plane had flown above.

Both eyewitness versions of the incident rang with authentic feeling, while being in conflict with each other.

Intriguingly, several other witnesses, including independent journalists, reported seeing a white-painted Boeing 747 circling above the White House at the same time as the Pentagon crash, and this was later confirmed on film – it was a type of electronic surveillance plane used by the US Air Force. Its presence there, on that day of all days, and at that time, has never been officially admitted, nor has it ever been revealed what it was doing there.

Whatever type of airborne object was the cause of the crash, something certainly did collide violently with the Pentagon that morning. In March 2002 the FBI released what they claimed was the only CCTV film of the crash. It was four frames in length, showed an indistinct object scudding across the Pentagon lawn at high speed then exploding with massive force. The blurry recording only added to the confusion, and clarified nothing.

There were other mysteries too: the immense speed and intricate manoeuvring of the technologically complex aircraft in its final minutes, allegedly flown by an amateur pilot, an almost

total lack of visible wreckage after the crash, the inexplicably small size of the hole made in the Pentagon wall, and the secretive nature of the Pentagon hierarchy that barred investigators from discovering what had happened inside the building after the crash. Finally, there was the lack of credible evidence about the physical condition of the flight data recorders, not to mention the misleading evidence eventually gleaned from one of them.

As usual, looking at this material made me feel depressed. When collecting it I had always avoided the opinions of politicians or theorists or radicals, or any evidence that appeared to be part of some kind of agenda. I made a point of listening only to whatever live witness interviews could still be traced, or the evidence of impartial experts, taking a special interest in the statements of engineers, pilots and scientists.

Even on that basis of verifiable fact I was left with the knowledge that there was little truth in what had become the official account, but also that so much else was inexplicable and often illogical.

More than two decades had passed since the day of the attacks, and still nothing made sense.

I put away the two folders I had opened.

I wanted to see Jeanne before we went to bed, but before I closed my study I saw that it was nearly time for another television news broadcast. I watched it through – the wreckage found on the Atlantic seabed was not mentioned. By the time I went upstairs Jeanne was already asleep. I climbed into bed beside her but lay awake for a long time, unable to sleep.

In the morning I listened to the radio, I read three web newspapers, I watched the twenty-four-hour news on BBC Scotland's rolling coverage. Almost nothing to be found, except in a passing reference there was a reminder that some flights to and from the USA might be delayed by the need to detour to a

slightly longer route. Much the same on the internet feeds from Fox News, CNN, MSNBC. The only mentions I could find on the internet were a day or two old. No information on aircraft wreckage at all – but there were a few references to a ship that might have been sunk during the Second World War.

I was just about to abandon the search when I came across a blog put up by someone in Canada. It included a video recording of one of the newscasts, and what gained my immediate attention was that it was from Helena McCardle again, a familiar figure on Scottish television news, who routinely reported American events.

The previous evening I had seen her describing the way she and her crew were roughly ejected from the search area. Somehow, the Canadian blogger had come across the actual footage that they were shooting at the time, just before they were arrested. The faint logo in the top-left of the picture showed the familiar schematic diagram of Scotland's shape, and the words: BBC SCOTLAND. The filming was from one of the several boats hired by different media outfits.

The clip started with McCardle talking to camera, describing the pressure that was being put on them and other journalists to leave the area. The camera suddenly swung to one side, pointing unsteadily towards a heavy lifting barge, maybe two hundred metres away across the sea. Then the camera zoomed in powerfully on the crane to reveal a new piece of metal dripping and swinging as it was raised from the sea. It was impossible to make out details, but as the sheet twisted in the daylight, there was a glimpse of bright paintwork beneath the accumulations of time. A red streak, a blue patch, exactly as McCardle had described on the late news the night before, a news slot which had apparently been recorded after this one.

The video ended suddenly: there was a violent intrusion, the camera shook and the picture went black. Voices shouted in

protest. The picture returned for a second or two: a glimpse of an aggressive, manhandling figure in a military uniform, helmet and visor. Then blackness again. Then silence.

I remembered that we were told McCardle and her crew had since flown out of the USA.

I backed up the video, saved it to my archive.

American? American?

Lucid

The boys returned to school the following week, and daily life settled into the familiar routine built around getting them up in the morning, packing them off to school on time, collecting them in the afternoon, preparing their supper, putting them to bed. Midweek, I made my visit to Paris. As I went through Glasgow Airport I could not help but notice the long queues of travellers waiting to go through passport control to flights to the USA, England, the Middle East. I slipped through the Schengen portal, a well-staffed procedure that was quick, courteous and non-intrusive. In Paris, I prepared a review of an exhibition at the Palais de Tokyo: artwork that had been created as by-products of industrial, medical or scientific processes. I stayed overnight, flew back to Glasgow in the morning and was working at my desk after lunch.

The following week it was Jeanne's turn to be away – she went to London to spend some time at the design studio. She had to be away from home at least one night, possibly two. The familiar daily routine shifted into one of its two subsets, the first subset being the one where Jeanne did everything while I was away, the second being this one, where I took over.

Lucinda had become part of our lives, and in fact everything was starting to work out satisfactorily. Her movements were slow, her speech was slurred, she sometimes seemed to be incapable of understanding what we said to her. However, she

was able to look after herself in the house so long as we were aware of her, ready to move in quickly if anything went wrong. She took on small household tasks, tidying up after the boys, vacuum cleaning the carpets, washing dirty dishes. She fed herself with simple snacks: sandwiches, a boiled egg, pasta, a salad. She enjoyed a glass of wine or three in the evenings. She did not need our help getting into or out of bed, and she used the bathroom alone.

One day, about a month after Lucinda arrived, Jeanne had to make another trip to England, this time to Birmingham, where one of the studio's clients had a print works. She was to be gone for three days and two nights. On the first day Lucinda spent most of the morning sitting in the garden, enjoying the sunshine. She slept in the afternoon. I watched a film on TV in the evening, and halfway through Lucinda wandered in, muttered something inaudible, and a few moments later I heard her going to her room.

She slept late the next morning. When she appeared I sensed at once that some kind of change had taken place. I was immediately tense, wary of a new development, a problem I should have to deal with, but Lucinda made herself some coffee and sat at the kitchen table across from me. Nothing was said.

Then, as I was about to pick up my own cup of coffee and head downstairs to my office, Lucinda suddenly leaned forward across the table. She looked at me urgently. She made a sound, a sort of tight humming noise.

'What is it, Lucinda? Do you need something? Can I help?'

She repeated the sound, then shook her head – not a negative reply but an expression of frustration. Her mouth looked straighter than before, almost back to normal, and the semi-vacant, haunted look in her eyes was gone.

'Mmm –' she said. Again she shook her head. 'Mm – memories. I have memories.'

'Do you want to tell me about them?'

She raised herself up, pressing her hands down on the table top. 'Benjamin – will you listen?'

'Of course.'

'Listen, Benjamin.'

'I will.'

We repeated these words a few times, in the way that recent exchanges with her had often to be said more than once. But now she looked determined, struggling to overcome the difficulty.

'I have memories,' she said in a rush, as if the inhibition had finally fallen away. 'All the time, there are memories. Do you have memories, Benjamin? Before, before this happened, the attack, the illness, memories were there, a part of me. Normal, the same as everyone.'

She swallowed, trying to settle her breathing, but for a long time she said nothing more. I waited, thinking the burst of lucidity had ended as quickly as it began.

Then she was back, her voice gaining strength: 'I remember everything now, everything, but they are not memories, not the same. Some of them are lies, stories. When I was a girl –'

She came to a halt again. I leaned across the table, held up her coffee cup, offering it to her. She took it from me, sipped it, then put down the cup with a steady hand. She regarded me with a knowing, adult look. She pressed her fingertips lightly against her forehead, an old gesture of hers which I used to see in arguments, or discussions, when she was assembling her thoughts.

'Are you going to tell me about the lies?' I said.

'No no no. I want to remember again. I have always been proud of my strong memory. Memory is truth. Memory is our only reality. Can you hear what I am saying, Ben?'

'Of course.'

She spoke in a hurry once more, but she was articulate, she did not slur, and her words were well formed.

'It's so clear now. Let me tell you something. When I was a girl, not a wee bairn, a girl. I was a teenager. About fifteen – that's definite. I know this is a fact. I was fifteen. There was a building in my village and it burned down. I can see it now, remember it – an old house, a big house, on its own, up on a low hill. It was empty, it had always been empty ever since I knew about it. There was an accident, or maybe someone set fire to it deliberately. As the heat intensified the windows blew out and the smoke poured up, thick smoke rising through the windows. Then the flames. I saw the flames creeping up the wall somehow. I watched it for a while, until suddenly the roof fell in and there were sparks everywhere and for the first time I was frightened. I thought people would say that it was my fault, so I ran away.'

'But it couldn't possibly be your fault,' I said. 'There's nothing to feel guilty about. Not then, not now.'

She was shaking her head determinedly.

'Ben, you don't understand. This is what I *remember* – the smoke smell, the crackling noise, the roar when the roof fell in. The heat. I know what clothes I was wearing that day. Everything. The sky was blue, no clouds. There was no wind so the smoke went straight up. And I remember the feeling of guilt.'

I said: 'You know, Lucinda, Jeanne and I have been worried that you might be starting to lose your memory. But this is obviously –'

She banged her fist down on the table, so angrily that the cup and saucer in front of her rattled.

'No! You think I'm getting old, demented. Not true. I suffered an ischemic attack, and I know what that is. What I'm trying to tell you is that this memory is of something that never

110

happened. There was no old house, no fire. I didn't see it, I wasn't there, I *couldn't* have seen it. This is the point. There had been a house there once, on that hill. I have a vague memory of it from when I was little. A scary old house. But it was demolished. Whoever owned the place sold the land to a builder and a small estate of modern bungalows went up. They're still there, five hundred yards from the house where I grew up. I could take you to see them. By the time I was fifteen, when I have this clear memory of seeing the old house on fire, everything had changed. It could not have happened.'

'Then are you joining two memories together?'

'No – that's not it. I remember the old house I used to see when I was a small child. I remember the bungalows that were built to replace it. Those are the reality. The fire can't have happened when I remember it, and if it did – I wasn't there to see it.'

I pressed her for a few more details, but she was adamant. The memory of the fire was valid and felt real, but it must have been false.

After this Lucinda seemed to sag a little, and said she thought she might like to take a bath and then maybe a short nap. I was mentally jubilant that she had started making a tangible recovery and wanted to hear more of what she had to say, but I helped her climb the stairs and left her to it.

I wondered if I should call Jeanne and tell her about the change in Lucinda, but she had told me she would be in meetings all day. I wanted to hear more from Lucinda, to be sure that the improvement was not a short-lived remission, and that a genuine recovery was taking place.

She came down for lunch. Her movements were slow and awkward, but mentally she said she felt good. She made herself a bowl of soup, fanning it with her hand. Once again we sat opposite each other at the table.

'The memory of the house fire is not the only one,' she said. 'There are others. Events from the past that I seem to remember, but know at the same time that they are false.'

'What about real memories?'

'Yes, there are those too.'

'You seem much better today,' I said.

'The stroke shook me up, scrambled my brain for a bit, but I think I'm getting over it. You must see the difference?'

'Yes, of course.'

'Listen, Ben – I'm full of memories I've made up, untrue ones. Jeanne is my only child – so how can I remember her having a brother? His name was Robert and he was a year older than Jeanne. I'm convinced of this, but I know it's impossible because he simply never existed. Never born, never there. And my husband, Dougal – he died a few years ago. He never learned to swim, yet I have a memory of him, clear as seeing a film in a cinema, swimming across a river. The river is a real one, not far from my house, but he would never have done that. He could not have done that. He was terrified of water. Then there are other recollections, just as clear and convincing, but because I have no way of testing them I can't decide if they're real.'

While she was upstairs resting an idea had come to me. One of the incidental advantages of the work I do is that over the years I have built up a wide-ranging library of non-fiction books. Before Lucinda came down for lunch I had been into my study and found a couple of titles. They were on the table between us.

I said: 'Lucinda, a few years ago an American psychologist and mathematician called Freyd identified a condition he called false memory syndrome. He discovered that false memories were often experienced by people recovering from traumatic shock. The shock could be emotional, physical or mental – any or all of them. It was the shock that somehow allowed the mind

112

to create false memories. People recovering from a serious road accident are typical. Soldiers returning from war also sometimes develop false memories. One psychologist said that she had discovered that victims of stroke were particularly vulnerable.'

Lucinda was staring straight at me. I knew she was looking, acting, talking like her old self. Somehow the temporary damage caused by the TIA had started healing itself. I felt again an impulse to call Jeanne straight away. It was a cause of celebration, a return to normality.

'So you think I'm losing my mind,' Lucinda said.

'No – the opposite. False memories are a part of the process of recovery from the shock.'

'But they're still distracting me.'

'I think they will pass.'

She said: 'How do you know so much about this?'

'You know what I do for a living. Everyone I meet for an interview, or go to for information, obviously knows more about their subject than I do. If there's time before I meet them I try to find out what I can, simply to keep up. So I accumulate books and cuttings and a thousand web pages. False memory syndrome is a psychological theory – it's controversial, but it's current. You can borrow these books, if you like.'

The hydropathic hotel

Two weeks later Lucinda was still living with us, but the situation had returned to being difficult. She had become a constant but unacknowledged source of aggravation between Jeanne and me. The remission in her post-stroke condition turned out to be temporary – within hours of Jeanne returning from her trip to Birmingham, all Lucinda's recovered articulacy, self-awareness and wish to communicate that I had briefly witnessed was gone again. I tried to describe it to Jeanne.

'She's done this before,' Jeanne said. 'The last time I went to

Edinburgh she seemed almost normal, but then without warning she started mumbling, drifted mentally, needed me to help her dress, and all that.'

'I thought it was a real recovery,' I said. 'She seemed virtually normal.'

But she was not, or for some reason was choosing not to be. Her condition made her the central figure in our household – everything had to be worked around her needs, her difficulties. Seth and Louis suffered most, I think, because they were caught between all three adults, each of us making a superficial effort to act normally around the others. Jeanne and I were suppressing anger and frustration about the problem of Lucinda. Lucinda was doing what she did, a quiet, disconcerting presence, clearly struggling inside. It was a state of affairs that could not continue, but I at least had no idea how to disrupt the cycle of irritation and silent vexation that built up.

Lucinda had returned to her state of inarticulacy, to needing assistance in moving about the house, to waiting for us to cook for her, to leaving a mess of her clothes that needed washing, to spilling liquids carelessly on our floors.

One morning, irritated because of her behaviour when she first came down, I confronted her. She had moved to sit in the garden at the rear of our house. It was a day of light but cool wind and thin cloud cover, an end of summer feeling. Rain was forecast for the afternoon. I went out to speak to her.

I said: 'Lucinda, would you like me to take you inside?'

She raised her head to look back at me, but with the move half-completed she let herself droop again.

'Why are you doing this?' I said. 'I know this is not the true you.'

She emitted her almost inaudible humming noise, saliva shining around her pursed lips.

At present, Jeanne was making more trips south to see the

people who gave her work – I could not blame her for wanting to be away from the house for a couple of days every week, even though it placed more of a burden on me. My own work was going through a quiet period, so in practical terms there was no problem.

'Hydro,' Lucinda said suddenly.

'What was that?' I said.

'Hydro. Can we – hydro?'

'Do you mean the old hotel, with the mineral spring?'

'Hydro.'

'It's not there any more,' I said. 'The building was demolished ages ago.'

She started fidgeting on the garden seat, looking agitated. 'Benjamin!'

'What is it?'

'Listen. Will you listen?'

'Yes. I'm listening.'

A long silence, while she pressed the palms of her hands down against her lap. I could hear her controlling her breathing. Her eyes were closed. Then she said: 'We went to the hydro. You and I. I would like to go there again.'

'I can take you to where it was. But the building is not there any more.'

'Can we go now? Is there time?'

'The boys won't be out of school for several hours. We have most of the day.'

'Hydro.'

'I'll have to get the car out.'

She said nothing more. I went to the garage and moved the car into the street outside, so that she would not have to walk too far. When I returned I discovered that Lucinda had gone up to her room, put on her jacket and was now waiting for me in the hall.

'I want to know what's going on,' I said.

'And I want to see the hydro.'

'All right – but why are you acting like this?'

'I'm not acting. Sometimes I feel better.'

'Whenever Jeanne is around you have a relapse. But if Jeanne is away for more than a day you do this –'

'Jeanne, yes.'

'Why, Lucinda?'

'She's my only girl. I love her.'

'And I love her too.'

I waited for her to say more but she added nothing. I left her in the hall while I went to pick up my camera. I ushered her gently out of the house, helped her down the stone steps to the road, then held the car door as she took the front passenger seat. I clipped her in with the safety belt. When I climbed into the driver's side she was sitting erect, her eyes closed, breathing steadily. It occurred to me that it was almost as if she was focusing herself, like a camera, or a computer or some other digital device sorting data again after a period of downtime.

As I started the engine, she said: 'Benjamin – this reminds me of the first time. Long ago. Do you remember that?'

'The first time of what?'

'On the island. When we came to the island.'

'That wasn't so long ago,' I said, now realizing what she meant. 'Fifteen years, perhaps?'

'More than that, but yes. For me – you know, time telescopes as you grow older. You can remember events, or things you did, but putting them into the right order is more difficult. That was the first time I'd been here, to the island, and wasn't it the same for you?'

The whole trip had felt a little weird from the start. I had to get to Scotland, but it was one of those periods when I was hard up for cash. Jeanne and I had been together only a short time,

yet she suggested I could stay at her mother's house near Edinburgh as a base, saving hotel expenses. I barely knew Lucinda at the time, but once I was there she had offered to drive me across to the island.

'I had been in Scotland when I was a child,' I said. 'But never this far west. I had no idea how beautiful Bhòid is. It's largely why Jeanne and I came to live here.'

I drove slowly along the coast road. We passed the ferry terminal with its lines of trucks and cars waiting to return to the mainland, past the parade of small independent shops, the visitor centre, the winter gardens. All now so familiar to me. Less familiar was the feeling of disjuncture Lucinda caused me, when she seemed able to dig deep into her physical condition and pull herself out and away from it, back to a strong semblance of normality. She made me nervous – I felt it was possible she would revert without warning, at any moment.

'So you do remember?' she said.

'Of course I do.'

'And you came here to Scotland without Jeanne.'

'That's right.'

'Why was that?'

'It was for an interview I had been commissioned to write. I often travel away for work like that. Even though Jeanne and I had known each other for several weeks we weren't yet living together and there was no reason for her to be with me. She always has plenty of work of her own.'

'So why this island, why Bhòid?'

'The person I was interviewing was here.'

By this time we had passed out of the main part of the town and were following the coast. Houses lined the road, but behind them the land rose steeply, quickly becoming hilly farmland with stretches of forest. To our right was the great tranquil expanse of the firth, spreading out towards the steep slopes of the

117

green Argyll mountains. The day had become windier, but for the moment we were still in sunlight – the forecast rainfall was soon to arrive, the mountains wreathed in dark cloud. The sea shimmered with light. The view gave the promise of a seascape going on forever, an endless sea, opening out to the ocean a long way to the south, an infinitude of unseen islands.

I remembered it had been like this on the first day, more than a decade and a half earlier, when Lucinda and I drove out to the hydro.

The rain finally arrived as we reached the village of Port Bannatyne, where the main yachting marina on the island was located. Dark grey and brownstone houses, some of them with shops at street level, lined the inland side of the road, a few steps away from the edge of the sea. They were backed by the steep, wooded hills behind the village. I turned left into Quay Street, the lane that ran up from the old pier – until the port was extended in Baile Bhòid this jetty in Port Bannatyne had been a regular landing place for the island ferries. At the top of Quay Street was the former main entrance to the hydropathic hotel, marked by two large gateposts. I parked and turned off the engine.

'That's where it was,' I said, indicating the sloping meadow beyond the gateposts, all that was left of the hotel. 'Would you like me to walk up there with you?'

Lucinda was staring ahead. Houses enclosed us on both sides of the narrow street. Greenery rose ahead of us. On a windowsill of the house beside where I had parked the car a large ginger cat was sitting upright and alert, sheltered from the drifting rain by a balcony above. The field of uncut grass and wild flowers rose up towards a plantation of trees. In the days of the hydro what was now a pasture had been a banked and sculpted garden, with a winding drive up from the gatehouse, an ornamental lake, statues, fountains.

The rear of the building had been high against the edge of the woodland, where a narrow garden of forking paths was laid, encouraging the guests, the voluntary patients, to exercise by wandering in the shade, or to find the small glades where seats for relaxing had been set out. Now there was just a line of trees.

The demolition work had left no visible scars in the earth, or maybe the passage of time and the reclamation of nature meant that any damage done by the tractors and wrecking balls was obscured by new growth.

'I can't believe it's gone,' Lucinda said. 'It was such a vast building.'

'Some of it was already falling down, even then. All of it, apart from one wing, had been condemned by the local authority. No one was allowed near. The only part of the building still usable was the wing where Tatarov was working.'

'Tatarov?'

'You must have heard me mention him. When we came here last time I would have talked about him as he was the only reason for being here.'

'Yes –'

But Lucinda was drifting. I could sense it. Her hands, which she had clasped together in her lap, were now apart, resting limply at her sides. She continued to hold her head up so that she was looking towards the site of the old hydro, but her eyelids were drooping.

'Shall I take you back to the house, Lucinda? You look tired.'

'What happened to the girl you were with?'

'Girl? Who do you mean?'

'You know. You must remember. She came with us to see the hydro that day. A young woman – quite pretty, I thought, with auburn hair. You and she were in love. She sat in the back of the car behind us.'

'Do you mean Jeanne? Your daughter?'

'Of course not! Jeanne wasn't with you. The one I'm think-ing of was an American. Her name was Liz – maybe Elizabeth? I parked the car about here, in this little lane, and she ran up the hill. The old building loomed over us. She was taking pho-tographs, so excited to be here in Scotland.'

'I don't know anyone called Elizabeth,' I said.

'You called her Liz. Yes, she was called Liz.'

'Lucinda, do you mean Lil?'

'Lil! That's right – but she wanted me to call her Lily or Lilian. You must remember her!'

I was watching the expression on Lucinda's face. There was no guile there, no challenge, nor any hint of a return to her health difficulties. For those few seconds I felt I was glimpsing her as she had been, the old her, the way she looked when I first met her as Jeanne's middle-aged mother, the way she looked on the day we came here to the hydro. I could sense her intelli-gence was there, just beneath the shallow impact of the stroke.

'Lucinda, you never met Lil.'

'She was here with us. I remember her well. Wasn't she a girlfriend, someone you knew at the same time as you were dating Jeanne? I couldn't understand that, why she came to the island with you that time. I didn't like to ask, but I kept won-dering if Jeanne knew you were here with another woman. I was embarrassed by that, but once I started to know Lil I really liked her. What happened to her? Did she return to the USA?'

'Lil died in an accident,' I said. 'You couldn't have met her.'

'Benjamin – that's terrible news! She was so lovely! What happened to her? What sort of accident was it?'

'There's no way you could have met Lil,' I said again. 'She died a long time before I met you, before I met Jeanne. We were here in – when was it? 2006, I think. Lil was killed in 2001, nearly five years earlier.'

'What sort of accident was it?' Lucinda said quietly.

'It was a plane crash. And not an accident, in fact. She was murdered, because the plane she was on was hijacked.'

'But I met her when she was here!'

'Lucinda – that's not possible.'

'But it is! This isn't one of those false memories you were trying to convince me about. I told you I know the difference between ordinary memories and . . . the others. Are you trying to upset me?'

'No – but you're mistaken, Lucinda. I'm so sorry.'

'Memories are the only reality I can trust. You're making this up.'

'I'm not, and I wouldn't. Lil was special to me – I was in love with her long before I met Jeanne, but she died in the crash, and that meant it was the end of everything.'

Confusion was rising in me, even so, a match for Lucinda's damaged state, a terrible fear that because I couldn't prove what I was saying, or even show evidence for it, I was the one who was misremembering. I had to test her, confront her, to prove her wrong.

I said: 'Look, after we came here and you parked the car, and this young woman, Lil, started taking photographs – where was I?'

'You stayed in the car with me. Then you opened the door, went around to the back, took out your travel bag, and you and I walked up the hill behind Lilian. There were gates here then. And a path, and some steps.'

'So we all went to the hydro together?'

'No. You said goodbye, and walked up through the gardens on your own.'

'OK – and what did you do after that?'

'I returned to the car. I drove around on the island for a while, then I went back to the town. I waited for the next ferry and drove back to my house.'

'I thought you waited for me. You were here, you stayed here on the island, and collected me after I had finished the interview. I remember waiting for you down there, by the old pier.'

'No. I went home.'

'And Lil – was she with you? Did you take her back with you to your house?'

Now Lucinda looked puzzled. 'No – I don't think so.'

'So was she with me?'

'No, I'm certain of that. I remember you walking up the steps on your own.'

'So where was Lil? Not with you, not with me.' I was angry with Lucinda. I had to get all this out. There was no logic in what she was saying, and I had to prove it. 'It's a false memory. Can't you see that?'

I glimpsed a start of tears in Lucinda's eyes, and she turned away from me. I felt guilty for confronting her like this. I should have been more tolerant. But she had shocked me. How could she have ever known about Lil?

Lucinda and I sat unhappily in the car together, staring up the hill through the rain-streaked windscreen of the car, past the rows of houses, through the space where the gates had once been, looking for the ghost of the demolished hydro building, the ornamental gardens, but seeing only the alert cat sheltering beside the car, the windswept trees, the wild flowers, the dark-clouded sky, the place of a remembered past. Memory was a reality, but so too was this.

EIGHT

then: 1996, 2005

Two interviews (1: New York City, 1996)
I was twenty-nine years old, trying to make a living as a free-lance journalist and I had been offered what felt at the time would be a career-defining commission. In the short term at least it was better paid than any other work I had been given to date. Money was invariably an influence on the work I took on. I flew to New York with a brief to interview and write a profile of Kyril Tatarov.

At this time Tatarov was working in the Courant Institute of Mathematical Science in New York City, close to Washington Square. The CIMS is an independent division of New York University and is one of the most prestigious mathematical schools in the world. Kyril Tatarov had enrolled as a graduate student in 1952, finished his doctoral thesis and remained at the Institute as a faculty member. He was engaged in research and development. For some years he was instrumental in pioneering work on the development of computer software for mathematical modelling, but he was later involved in purely theoretical research.

At the time I met him he was in his mid sixties, already one of the most important theoretical topologists and geometrists in

the world. At the start of our conversation he said how much he feared growing old.

'I'm sixty-three, next month sixty-four,' he said, which I wrote quickly in my notebook. I had not been sure of his age before I met him. 'This means that as a mathematician the best I can hope to be is competent. Once you pass about forty it's useless expecting to have original ideas any more. Those come from young minds only.'

'But you are still doing your best work,' I said, and Tatarov nodded gently.

'Good of you to say that, and I hope you think it too.'

I was interested in what he might have to say about Russia. He had been born in the Soviet Union. He and his family emigrated to the USA when Kyril was seven years old. He was now a naturalized US citizen, and had lived most of his life in the USA. He told me he had almost forgotten any Russian he might have known from childhood, because once they arrived in America his parents insisted that he and his sisters only speak English. I wondered if he had any interest in present mathematical theory in Russia, or if he would ever return to Russia now that the Soviet Union had ceased to be.

'Mathematics was the enemy of the Soviet creed,' he said immediately. 'Russia, the Soviet Union, it's the same thing for mathematicians. No different today. Math creates arguments, but in Russia the régime disallows argument. Russia expects conformity. Math is about patterns and patterning, but only the Supreme Soviet could create or allow patterns. Mathematics is based on logic, but state socialism only functioned properly by forcing people to live and work in a reality that was illogical, unpredictable, unreliable, full of disappointment. Mathematics is for the few, for an admitted elite, for specialist minds – it is incomprehensible to government servants. They think math is in code, that it is subversive, and in the narrow terms in which

they operate they are probably right. They will never know why. But above everything else, mathematics requires learning, training and the use of knowledge, so non-mathematicians do not understand it, never will understand it. The Party did not like being unable to understand. They instinctively punished people they did not understand. At the heart of mathematics is the search for truth, perfection, a sort of beauty, but the Soviet régime believed it held the monopoly on such matters. Of course, Russia now is the same, except that instead of the Party they have capitalist oligarchs with vast wealth and what they mistakenly believe is power.'

'So you will not go back?' I said.

'I have been back twice. Brief visits.'

'Your wife is American, I believe.'

'My wife is dead. She died three years ago.'

'I'm sorry — I had no idea.'

'Neither did they.' He gestured to include everyone else in the building. 'They did not even know I was married until six months after she passed away. My work is here in New York. My life is the work I do.'

I moved the questions to a more general area.

'Could you describe to me what you mean by beauty in mathematics?'

'You are of course not a mathematician, but then I am not a writer. Beauty is for me the essence of mathematics. Ugly math is wrong math. It is the work of mathematicians to seek the beauty that lies somewhere inside a conjecture. The beauty resides within patterns. A painter makes patterns with shapes and colours, a dancer moves in patterns, a poet makes patterns with words and rhythms. For mathematicians it is the theorem that reveals the pattern of an idea, just as Michelangelo's hammer and chisel released the shapes he knew were concealed inside the blocks of marble.'

I next asked Tatarov to explain the difference between a conjecture and a theorem. I had the non-specialist reader of the magazine in mind, but Tatarov regarded me with amazement and, I think, contempt.

I began to blush, felt perspiration springing on my neck and brow, as he said: 'A conjecture is the question, a theorem is the answer. Of course you know this. Everyone knows this.'

As what I thought might be a safe way of escaping from the faux pas, I enquired in general terms if he would like to describe what he was working on at that time. I had no idea that his reply would be the key statement, the revelation of what Tatarov saw as the truth.

He said: 'I am attempting to solve the Pèlerin Conjecture, or, if you prefer to describe it that way, derive the theorem. Jean-Louis Pèlerin was French, one of the greatest mathematicians of the twentieth century. His conjecture concerns what is known as a topological knot theory – it has remained unproven for nearly one hundred years. I am applying to it a radical means of developing the theorem, a pattern that exists, or possibly exists, or might exist, by means of a sociological theorem. Are you writing this down, Mr Matson?'

'I am,' I said, not wishing to admit that my shorthand skills were being stretched to their limit.

'The sociological theorem can be expressed in non-mathematical terms as the Thomas Theorem. You will have heard of that, of course.' (I had not. I continued to write my notes at frantic speed.) 'Thomas, in fact there were two of them, both named Thomas – they said if a situation may be considered real then it will have real consequences. The situation may be defined. It is the situation that causes the action, the reaction, the fact. This interpretation, this definition, is not objective. It is subjective. Actions and reactions are affected by *subjective perceptions* of situations.

126

'The Thomases were sociologists, working with human behaviour and human society, but to me they were forming a beautiful conjecture that could be expressed as math.

'It is most interesting to me that Pèlerin's Conjecture, involving the problem of movement and shape in infinitesimal fourth dimension variables, might possibly be resolved by an equivalent to the Thomas Theorem, by the reality of its consequences. This is the work that is absorbing me. I have several brilliant young men and women who are studying this with me. We hope to publish a first draft theorem within the next five years, possibly longer.'

I sat in silence for a minute or two, writing in my notebook, a pretence to try to convey that my mind was engaging. I was nervous of him – I took a breath.

'Professor Tatarov, would you kindly express the Thomas Theorem in terms my readership will understand?'

'Of course. The Thomases said: *If people define situations as real, they are real in their consequences. In other words, the interpretation of a situation causes the action.*'

He watched me closely as I wrote this down in longhand.

When I had finished, Tatarov said to me: 'You have no more questions.'

I did not.

'You understand what I have said?'

'Perfectly. Thank you, Professor Tatarov.'

Two interviews (2: St Kilda, Victoria, 2005)

In 2005 a congress was held in Sydney, a gathering of academics to discuss the current state of quantum mechanics and field theory. Most of the leading mathematicians and particle physicists in that particular area of study would be present. One of the newspapers to which I occasionally contributed offered to send me to Australia to report on it for them. I had loved

Australia during my spell of youthful excesses, so I was thrilled by the prospect of another trip there. I leapt at the opportunity. (I wondered if I should see Kyril Tatarov, but in the event I did not. I later discovered that he had been invited, but he declined.)

With about six weeks for preparation I did what preliminary research I could, seeking information about the backgrounds of the most important men and women who would be there to present papers. I read as much of their recently published work as possible, but predictably I struggled to understand the abstruseness of both quantum physics and field theory.

While this period of research was going on I made a positive effort to track down someone in Australia I had briefly met and wished I had known better and for longer. I knew that finding the man I wanted would be a long shot, but in the event I was lucky.

This was in the days before the widespread use of social media, so I advertised on blogs and message boards based in Australia. I described myself as a professional writer conducting serious historical research. I said I wanted to re-establish contact with an Australian structural engineer who happened to be on an internal flight within the USA, September 11, 2001 – Northwest Airlines Flight 1757, Charlotte, North Carolina, to Detroit, Michigan, diverted mid-flight to Columbus, Ohio.

My search was successful – a response came the following day, when I received a tentatively worded email from the man himself. His name turned out to be Charles Thewlis. He lived and worked in St Kilda, Victoria.

We exchanged a few emails, preparing the ground for a meeting. He remained guarded throughout, insisting that our messages be transmitted under a particular security and

anonymity protocol. With that set up between us he communicated more openly.

He said that he would be willing to meet and discuss the events of 9/11, on condition that I did not quote him directly or name or identify him in any way. He also said that although he had certainly been a passenger on the plane to Detroit he did not recall speaking to me or anyone else, on the aircraft or in the terminal building at Columbus Airport. I accepted that, but it did not take long to establish that he was the guy I had briefly met that day. I assured him that my sole interest in 9/11 was to understand what really happened on the plane that was said to have struck the Pentagon.

In a later email he told me that other professionals – engineers, architects, builders, and so on – had spoken out about the unreliability of the official version of events, but they had invariably been warned off by vaguely identified government agencies and officials. The standard response to enquiries was to say that the hijackings had been thoroughly investigated, the results had been passed on to the 9/11 Commission, whose report had been published in 2004, and that the matter was now closed.

Thewlis told me, and at the time I took it partly as a warning, that he knew of many people – engineers like himself, but also eyewitnesses, families of victims, scientists, airline pilots, researchers – who had been silenced in some way after trying to publicize their doubts about what might really have happened. He spoke of people being warned about losing their jobs or given early retirement, or paid undisclosed sums as hush money. It was all hearsay, but he had heard about it from so many different sources that he had to believe some of it was true. He said he was willing to meet me and speak openly, but it would be in confidence and he would not put anything in writing. He added that because of work and family commitments

he would not be able to meet anywhere but close to where he lived and worked.

A few weeks later, when the congress in Sydney was over, I flew down to Melbourne, my head still spinning with the concepts of the quantum universe to which I had been exposed for four days: Hilbert spaces, condensed matter physics, perturbation theory, non-entangled quantum states, and much more, way beyond even those basic premises. I felt dazed by it all, overwhelmed by abstracts, confused by infinity and the infinitesimal, concepts which until then I had thought I comprehended.

I checked into a hotel close to the airport. The next day I took a tram to St Kilda.

I met Thewlis in a coffee bar at lunchtime. It was crowded with office workers, with much coming and going, and the racket of coffee-making pressure machines. Thewlis had arrived early and taken a relatively secluded table at the rear of the room. I recognized him straight away, although in the interim his image had changed. He looked slimmer, fitter, he had cut his hair and he was wearing a grey business suit and spectacles. He immediately restated what he had already told me by email, about having no memory of meeting me that day – but, he explained and I readily agreed, there had been a lot to take in that morning.

As soon as we had been served with snacks and coffee we got down to business. Time for him was short.

I said: 'Just about everyone on the planet has seen the video images of those two World Trade Center towers collapsing –'

'In fact, three of them collapsed,' he said, his accent making it sound like a question. 'The third one, WTC 7, is the most important, even though no one was directly killed by it. Building 7 was a huge skyscraper, one of the highest in New York City, and it was destroyed in plain sight. Few people realize how

revealing that destruction was. It's the strongest evidence we have of what happened in New York that day. Did you know there is no mention of WTC 7 anywhere in the 9/11 Commission Report, even in passing?'

'I didn't know that,' I said. 'But the point I was making is that everyone saw the towers collapse. They had just been struck by jet airliners fully loaded with fuel, which exploded on impact. The buildings caught fire, and collapsed. I need you to explain to me what you said on the day, that those buildings did not collapse, that they could not collapse.'

'They fell, but they did not collapse. All three towers had immensely strong skeletons of structural steel. They had massive central cores, the girder members being nearly eleven centimetres thick at the base, but there were also many exterior columns. On the twin towers, the outer walls, the vertical frame that could be seen from ground level, were basically a phenomenally strong exoskeleton. There were many unseen extra storeys below ground level, car parking, cleaning and services area, generators. The building was embedded deep in Manhattan bedrock. Each of the twin towers weighed about half a million tonnes, and was capable of withstanding hurricane force winds. The highest known recorded wind pressure is about five thousand tonnes. The buildings were designed like sails, so that lateral pressure created by high wind, or for that matter a violent impact from a speeding jet aircraft, would be redistributed to other supports as the building flexed. Many of the survivors who were actually inside the buildings when the planes hit reported the movement and sound of the structure recovering from the impact. There had been a bomb attack on WTC 1, the North Tower, in 1993, and after that the specification was amended and the buildings strengthened. They were then capable of surviving a hit by a fully loaded, fully fuelled Boeing 707 or Douglas DC8 – the design redundancies

131

would accept the shifted load. The jets that struck the two towers on 9/11 were more modern than the specified aircraft, but similar in size and weight. In short, after the aircraft crashed into the buildings, neither tower was at any risk of collapse.'

'Yet they came down. There were huge explosions, and fire.'

'The explosions of the aircraft were mostly contained within the buildings. Again, the inherent strength of the design easily withstood the blast. There would have been an unbelievable amount of superficial damage but the structure took the strain. That was what was intended.'

'And the fires?'

'They weren't hot enough to damage the steel structure. Steel only starts to sag or distort at about 1,500 degrees Celsius. Aviation fuel never burns at more than about 1,000 degrees, and only then if there is a strong current of air. As everyone knows, the weather in New York on 9/11 was calm and almost windless. Anyway, most of the fuel that was spilled in the crashes burned off in the explosive fireballs that were visible for the first few seconds. The conflagration that followed was relatively normal, the sort of fire associated with office buildings: paper, carpets, curtains, wooden fixtures, plastics, office machinery. These burn at no more than about 250 degrees, which would hardly singe the steel structure. The black smoke that everyone saw proves it was a low temperature fire, a burning office building.'

'Yet the buildings still collapsed,' I said.

'Did they? Those buildings were felled, demolished. Most of the people in the same line of work as me drew the same conclusions. Someone had planted shaped explosives, and the buildings went straight down, into their own footprint, at free-fall speed. If the collapse was caused by the aircraft damage, as they claim, it would have affected only the

floors above the impact zone, and a few below. The law of conservation of energy is absolute. Most of the floors of the buildings were below the impact, yet they too collapsed. When I finally reached Detroit I went to my associates' office. Everyone there was unanimous – we had witnessed controlled demolitions.'

'Why was WTC 7 the most important? That's what you said.'

'It's what Americans call a smoking gun? Evidence so strong that on its own it is proof enough. Building 7 was not hit by any aircraft. It was damaged by wreckage from the North Tower, and it caught fire. But the damage was mostly on one side of the building, which was immensely strong: it had twenty-four steel columns at its core and a further fifty-eight columns around the perimeter. The videos reveal there were around ten fires inside the building, but they were all normal-size office fires, and nowhere near hot enough to weaken the structure.

'Somehow, people knew in advance the building was about to fall: police and fire officers warned that a collapse was about to happen. The leaseholder of the building said on the record that he authorized the "pulling" of the building – "pull" being the demolition industry's word for what they do. Demolition charges take weeks to set up correctly, so the explosives must already have been in place, ready for use. When the building went down it too fell at free-fall speed, vertically into its own footprint. There is no question of what destroyed it.'

I had come across these theories before – controlled demolition was often mentioned in online videos about the 9/11 attacks. Many of these videos seemed unreliable to me, obsessed with conspiracies.

There were strong arguments against the demolition theory based on simple logic: for instance, if people set up

the charges how did they know that aircraft were going to hit two of the buildings weeks ahead? The collapse of both the North and South Towers appeared to begin on the floors where the planes had struck – so how did they arrange for the demolition to begin there? Did the hijackers tell them in advance which levels they were planning to impact? If it was a plot by Islamic extremists, surely someone in the buildings might have noticed these people drilling and banging around the steel girders for several weeks on end? Building 7 was full of highly sensitive government offices – how did the terrorists get past the security checks while carrying their immense spools of wire into the building, their drills, their crates of explosives?

It was incredible, fantastic, impossible to believe. But here I was in a busy and reassuringly normal lunchtime coffee bar, listening to Charles Thewlis, a civilized and clearly professional man who spoke calmly, deliberately, and with every sign of expertise.

He reached into his briefcase and brought out several sheets of paper and photographs.

'Take these with you,' he said. 'They are details of other steel buildings which suffered catastrophic fires. They all burned more destructively, and for much longer, than either of the twin towers.'

I glanced at them then, but have of course examined them more closely since that day.

The first concerned a fire in a thirty-eight-storey tower in Philadelphia, in 1991. It burned for eighteen hours – nearly twenty times longer than the South Tower, and ten times longer than the North Tower. It did not collapse.

The Parque Central Complex in Caracas, Venezuela, was a fifty-nine-storey building which caught fire in 2004. Seventeen levels near the top of the building blazed out of control for two

days before the fire burned itself out. Although it was seriously damaged, the building did not collapse. It was repaired and returned to use.

The following year a thirty-two-storey office block in Madrid, called the Windsor Tower, was engulfed by fire after an electrical fault. It burned from top to bottom for twenty-four hours. Although a few of the upper levels fell through on to the floors immediately beneath, the main structure remained intact.

Thewlis said: 'World Trade Center Buildings 1 and 2, the twin towers, suffered partial fires for about one hour near the tops of the buildings, yet the entire buildings fell. The floors below the level of the aircraft crashes, which were totally undamaged by the impact of the planes, the explosions and fire which followed, also fell. Practically everything inside was pulverized as the buildings fell. This included the thousands of computers, photocopiers, chairs and desks, and other large pieces of equipment, all of which in a few seconds turned from complete, undamaged, working objects into a fine, choking powder. Building 7 was the same, but no aircraft collision was involved. Those three towers in the World Trade Center are the only steel buildings ever to fall.'

'And you maintain they were deliberately demolished?'

'Without a shadow of a doubt. Quite apart from the video evidence, in which anyone can plainly see what happened as the buildings fell, there are many reports of explosions just before they collapsed. Few of these explosions can actually be heard on the soundtracks of the videos, because by the time they occurred media workers had been moved to a safe distance and were filming through long lenses. However, more than one hundred of the firefighters and police officers at the scene independently reported hearing loud explosions inside the buildings just before they started to fall. The few

explosions that can actually be heard on the recordings were either ignored by the 9/11 Commission, or they were disputed. The investigators from the National Institute of Standards and Technology went further. They specifically denied any such explosions had occurred, and claimed that not a single report of explosions had been made. The police and fire reports are a matter of documentary fact, yet NIST denied them.

'Apart from the first responders on the scene, who we can safely accept were experienced in major fires and other accidents, several victims were killed by explosions in the lower floors, and some survivors reported being close to them. One young man, killed inside the ground floor foyer of one of the buildings, and whose body was eventually recovered, had the front of his face and chest burned and smashed by an explosion, yet the other side of his body was unharmed, untouched. One of the surviving workers in an office high in the North Tower described how after the plane crashed, and the fires began, he and several others hurried down the emergency stairs from the eighty-second floor to the fourth floor. They were attempting to enter the lobby when a big explosion sent them flying. The survivors from that managed to crawl outside and still had time to get far enough away from the building to escape being hurt by the collapse.

'As happened to Building 7, both of the twin towers fell vertically into their own footprints. Any building that collapses after a structural failure always follows the line of least physical distance. That means it will usually tip over and fall to one side. These towers went straight down, through themselves. That's the line of maximum physical resistance. This can only mean that the central core, the massive steel uprights, had been compromised – they had been cut through or broken. The demolition was deliberate, and it was controlled.'

'Surely there must have been security measures inside the buildings?' I said. 'If demolition workers were going through the building setting charges, why didn't people who worked in the building notice them?'

'I don't know,' said Thewlis.

'Who set the charges?'

'I don't know that, either.'

'When were they set?'

'I don't know.'

'Who arranged or authorized the demolition?'

'I don't know.'

'How did the people who set the charges know in advance that hijacked aircraft were going to smash into the buildings?'

'I don't know,' he said. 'It beats me.'

'Do you have any theories at all?'

'I'm an engineer. I don't do theories. All I know is that what we saw on television, and what people who were in New York actually experienced, was not the same as the official explanation of events. The US government looked into it and they made their findings known.' He added: 'And now the subject is closed.'

'What happened at the Pentagon?' I said, which of course was the one event at the forefront of my own interest.

'That's another story,' Charles Thewlis said. 'And it's something else I do not know. I can't help you.'

Bullshit

I switched off my recorder. I listened briefly on the earphones for a sample of the recording – there was an endless background clatter of voices, movements, coffee machine noises, music. But I could hear Thewlis's words and that was enough. I had listened to and transcribed worse interview recordings in the past.

When he saw my recorder was off Thewlis drained his cup of coffee and picked up his briefcase. He was about to leave.

I said: 'I'm really grateful for your time.'

'You're welcome. You're clear on our agreement about confidentiality?' I nodded my acceptance. 'As you know, there's plenty of material online about the attack on the Pentagon. There are also some books coming out – mostly from small or indie publishers, but they're not too difficult to find.'

'I've already turned up some of the books, as well as the online stuff. Why do you say you don't know about the Pentagon?'

'I can form an expert opinion about what happened to the World Trade Center because I know what I'm talking about. The Pentagon attack was different. Part of the building collapsed there too, but given that the building had been hit by something travelling at high speed, which exploded on impact, the structural collapse was in my terms completely explicable. The Pentagon was built using conventional methods. It does not have a steel skeleton. I can't add anything to that.'

'Another unprecedented event,' I said.

'Not exactly. There was a similar crash back in 1992. A Boeing 747 cargo jet operated by El Al crashed into a block of apartments near Amsterdam. That provides an interesting comparison with the Pentagon. Not because it was similar, but because there were differences.'

'Tell me more?'

'There was a fault with the aircraft. One of the engines detached soon after take-off, damaged the wing and collided with the engine next to it. That also fell off. The plane was barely flyable, and as the flight crew struggled to regain control it crashed into the building. There was a huge explosion followed by fire. Most of the fatalities were inside the building, but the rescuers found all the bodies and every one

of them was identifiable. The wreckage of the plane was of course present at the scene of the crash and it could be pieced together later by crash experts to determine what caused the accident. The flight data recorder and the cockpit voice recorder were both found, both had survived the crash as they had been designed to do, and both contained readable data. It was a terrible human tragedy, but there was no mystery about it.

'Everything about the impact at the Pentagon was the exact opposite – a mystery about the black boxes, many unrecovered bodies, and as far as anyone could tell from the visible crash site there was hardly any aircraft wreckage.'

I had already seen some of the photographs on the internet. FBI agents were walking on the lawn next to the crash site, picking up with their hands small pieces of what looked like parts of a plane. No sign of wings, fuselage, tailplane – not even the wheels or engines, which are the strongest parts of any aircraft. But I understood the flight data recorder had in fact been found.

'What's the mystery about the black boxes?' I said.

'I'm not clear on that – the problem is discussed in some of the books and videos. It's a complicated story, and I don't have any specialist information about it. I told you I don't know, and I'm not backing off from this. I'm an engineer, not a crash investigator.' He was already on his feet, ready to leave, and he extended his hand to shake mine. 'I have to get to a meeting. Mr Matson, I'm sorry but I'm genuinely strapped for time today. If you email me, remember always to use the protocol I sent you.'

'Thank you,' I said.

'Are you heading back to the UK now?'

'Tomorrow,' I said.

'If what happened at the Pentagon proves anything it is that

the entire official account of 9/11 is bullshit. It's no great shakes to find this out. Everything the authorities have said, claimed, argued, released, everything from beginning to end, is lying, deceptive, dishonest bullshit. You won't mind me saying that, I know. Don't quote me, though,'

'I knew someone on that plane.'

'American 77?'

'Yes.'

'I was wondering about that, why you are interested. Was it a relative?'

'The woman I was in love with.'

'That's really terrible. I can see why you would want to know more. But never forget the single reality: everything the authorities say about 9/11 is bullshit.'

Later

The twenty-four hours of my return flight between Melbourne and London gave me plenty of time to think about what Charles Thewlis had told me. In the months that followed the brief meeting with him I took a renewed and more active interest in the alleged facts of 9/11 – books could be easily bought online, as well as the hundreds of videos which were available to watch.

I started to notice that most of the books were from small or independent publishers, or had been self-published by the author. Very few books came from established, mainstream publishers. The majority of the internet videos were also obviously the work of amateurs, or enthusiasts, or conspiracy theorists, all with some kind of personal agenda: footage was copied and repeated from one video to the next, many of the images were blurry, the narrative was sometimes quirky, the captions and text pages often mis-spelled.

The personal agenda of these people was possibly like my

own, based on personal loss or lack of closure. They gave everything an immediacy, but the dubious quality also minimized the videos' usefulness as research material. Apart from natural journalistic interest in the subject in the hectic period following the attacks, mainstream or professional broadcasters and news channels had little new to add after the first few months.

The subject of 9/11 seemed increasingly to be a vernacular concern, one that for some reason the professional media shied away from.

One of the first problems of researching the subject was soon clear: there was too much to take in. Almost every aspect of the events of that awful day came under suspicion: the climate of secrecy and official silence at its lowest level aroused curiosity, and in the worst cases it provoked paranoia about global economics and political alliances and subterfuge between nations and corporations and people in high places.

This introduced the second problem: of being able to discern the unarguable facts from the labyrinth of rumour, allegation, conspiracy theory and sheer amateurism of argument.

Some of what Thewlis said turned out to be true, or at least highly probable. There were certainly people who had been close to the events, sometimes perilously close – first responders, police officers, firefighters, paramedics. Some of them had initially spoken out to journalists or TV crews, about what they had seen or heard that conflicted with the official version, but then either went silent or became unreachable, or refused to say more. An objective researcher could not help but wonder why.

The media initially let loose a storm of reporting and investigation in the weeks and months that followed the attacks. Questions were asked, anomalies were examined, politicians were challenged, the alleged facts of the hijackings were aired

and questioned and in some cases exposed as untrue. But events moved on, and 9/11 gradually became something that was no longer of immediate interest.

Once the 'war on terror' was given a name, and the real war in Afghanistan began, then troops and aircrew from America and other western countries were putting their lives at risk. In many cases they paid the ultimate price, and returned in body bags.

The nature of the problem changed fundamentally. It became local, more personal, more urgent.

It was a family tragedy when your son or daughter was killed in action. The town they came from grieved for their loss. The country they came from had increasingly to deal with the dilemma of pursuing the war further, or withdrawing.

It became steadily less relevant to understand or remember the root cause of the conflict. The actual events of 9/11 seemed less important.

It was not only in the USA that this process was taking place. A newspaper journalist in Germany, for example, sensed there was something wrong with the events as explained by the US government, and started a weekly column for his newspaper. Here he exposed intriguing omissions, contradictions and official deceptions as they came to light. This went on for about six months, until one day his editor told him, gently but with unmistakable intent, that readers were becoming weary of hearing about 9/11. The column disappeared.

There were official reasons given for closing the case. At the end of 2002, after much pressure from victims, survivors, the press and Congress, the US finally agreed to set up the 9/11 Commission. Martin Viklund had told me this was coming.

The report was published in 2004. Although it gave a good appearance of impartiality and thoroughness, there were many serious shortcomings that were never fully addressed. The

investigation was under-funded and placed under time constraints. There were serious conflicts of interest. Much of the evidence taken by the Commission had been obtained by what the CIA called 'enhanced interrogation techniques', a euphemism for torture – for that reason it was unreliable in every way. Evidence was taken without oath from senior officials, notably the President and Vice President, who agreed only to a short interview, with no electronic recording, and the notes to be taken by hand by one person only, and which would never be made public. That evidence too would be unreliable, if publicly known. There were serious omissions in the published report – as Charles Thewlis had pointed out to me there was no explanation of why and how Building 7 collapsed, although a revised version of the report, published in 2011, allowed that this event had indeed happened. Still no explanation, though.

With the existence of the report, even though it was incomplete, inaccurate and unreliable, the authorities had a means of sheltering from further investigation. Serious attempts by researchers to find explanations of events, or corrections of inaccurate information, were routinely stonewalled: a standard response from government spokespersons went along the lines of: *we are declining your request at this time – the issues surrounding the events of 9/11/2001 are documented in the 9/11 Commission Report.*

When senior politicians, such as Dick Cheney and Tony Blair, were lobbied to re-open the investigations and publicly settle all the outstanding issues, the response was similarly standardized. The security services, they claimed, had become so involved with dealing with the after-effects and consequences that it was unrealistic to remove these operatives from such vital work and re-investigate matters which had already been thoroughly examined.

In other words: the consequences of the 9/11 attacks had become deemed to be more important than the original events. The unreliable quality of our knowledge of the original events was no longer relevant. The need to interpret the consequences had become greater than the need to understand the cause.

It was a clear variant of the Thomas Theorem, which Kyril Tatarov had described to me during our interview in 1996. *If people define situations as real, they are real in their consequences. In other words, the interpretation of a situation causes the action.*

But those consequences were so severe, so long-lasting, so extensive – the Middle East in turmoil, hundreds of thousands of deaths, literally millions of people made homeless, the use of chemical and biological weapons – that a truthful explanation of those original events was still essential.

More fires

Charles Thewlis and I met in St Kilda in 2005. As part of my continuing researches I was careful to note any subsequent fires that occurred in steel-framed high-rise buildings. There have been several.

At the end of December 2015 the sixty-three-storey Address Downtown Hotel in Dubai caught fire as a result of an electrical fault. A huge blaze spread rapidly up one side of the building (allowing safe evacuation of almost everyone inside), but later strong winds spread the inferno to the rest of the hotel. By midnight of the same day, most of the fire had been controlled. The damage was severe and extensive, but there was no collapse.

Eight months later, also in Dubai, a seventy-nine-storey residential block called, perhaps inappropriately, the Dubai Torch caught fire for the second time in two years. The flames spread rapidly throughout the building, and much debris fell catastrophically into the streets below. The tower did not collapse.

In June 2017, the twenty-four-storey Grenfell Tower in

London caught fire after a faulty domestic appliance exploded. The fire spread rapidly throughout the entire building, killing more than seventy people, and injuring many more. The fire raged destructively for nearly twenty-four hours before being brought under control. Although the building was completely uninhabitable after the fire it did not collapse.

After our meeting in St Kilda that day Charles Thewlis and I had no further contact with each other.

NINE

then: 2001–2006

The ugly untruth

It began with Lil, it went on because of her, in a sense it will never be concluded without her.

I learned from Kyril Tatarov his concept of beauty in maths, that wrong maths was ugly maths. John Keats wrote, two hundred years before 9/11:

> 'Beauty is truth, truth beauty,' – that is all
> ye know on earth, and all ye need to know.

The attacks on New York and Washington left scars, not only on the fabric of buildings and cities, but on thousands of lives. Beyond those, invisibly, stealthily, disgracefully, the lies and omissions of certain unknown people left a scar on democracy, on the history and standing of the world's greatest free country, on all of Western society, on the world as a whole.

After my meeting with Charles Thewlis I knew I should have to confront this ugliness, and if not solve or resolve it, then at least I wanted to gain an understanding of it.

Conspiracy theories

Most people accepted the official account, as I had done at the beginning. Perhaps that acceptance came from the relief of

learning that there was an explanation, any kind of explanation. It was also because of a complex subconscious belief, a kind of shared instinct, that in an open and sophisticated democracy the politicians and military leaders were expected to be truthful. To question or challenge that assumption would be to question the very foundations of our democracy.

There could be no conspiracy in the way the internet theorists meant it. People who have power in a democracy, presidents and prime ministers and deputies and generals, do not form conspiracies. They run the country.

What they do is prescribed and proscribed by law, by culture, practice and precedent, by the checks and balances of the judiciary, the press, the parliament or congress, the forum of public opinion. Not everyone votes for them, but most people accept the result. The people in power do wrong sometimes and they can make serious errors, but they also build hospitals and schools and fund scientific research, they maintain law and order, they collect taxes and they spend money, and every few years they have to face re-election.

To enquire why such people did wrong, why they arranged for the deaths of thousands of people, or why they had allowed those deaths to happen because of some secret and shameful policy, was not a question most ordinary people were willing to ask. It would be a question too far.

But I had found out enough about the science, the logic, the sheer impossibility of the official explanation of 9/11, to convince me that even if it was already too late to halt or reverse the consequences, at least the victims and their families deserved a full and honest explanation, an owning up.

The truth could hardly be worse than the prevailing myth.

I had practical objections too, to the notion of a conspiracy. If 9/11 was the result of a conspiracy it would have required vast organization, meticulous timing, cooperation between

many different agencies working directly or indirectly for the government, with links to other agencies abroad, the power to manipulate the media, the ability to manage in advance the reaction of ordinary people all over the world. Too many secret decisions would have to be made, too many people would have to be trusted to keep their mouths shut. Only one whistleblower would be enough to wreck the plan.

There was a precedent of sorts, though. Between 1942 and 1945 the US government set up a highly secret project to develop, test and eventually deploy atomic bombs against the Japanese. The Manhattan Project grew rapidly from a core of highly specialized scientists and academics into an organization of about 130,000 people, all sworn to secrecy. The secret held. That was during a war, though

Were another 130,000 people in on the 9/11 conspiracy? Was every single one of them still content to maintain the fiction of their story? Was the prospect of a new war, a war on terror, enough to keep them quiet?

Then there is the fact of the live television coverage, which is the way most people discovered what was happening. Because of the suddenness of the event only a handful of people would have seen American Flight 11, the first plane, strike the North Tower at the moment it happened. Those were the people in or around the building, or in the streets below. By the time live television cameras were on the scene, the upper storeys of the North Tower were engulfed in fire. Film of the American 11 impact was soon handed in and shown on every TV channel; it turned out to be the only footage most people ever saw of the North Tower crash.

Soon, though, the TV coverage became a mix of live feeds from cameras on the spot, reporters hastily sent to the street, studio or phoned interviews with experts, re-runs of what had happened earlier and videotapes from other cameras that

happened to have a different viewpoint. The rush of shocking images was complemented by the television presenters' voices. Almost from the start reporters and commentators were adding to the confusion: speculating, repeating themselves, asking questions, talking over interviews, interrupting interviews, cutting away to new developments.

When the Pentagon attack occurred, the confusion of different locations, different scenes, different incidents, was doubled and tripled. By the time I myself reached the airport terminal building in Columbus, Ohio, and was able to catch the TV feed, it certainly took several minutes of concentrated attention to work out exactly what was going on.

This freewheeling rush of images, recordings, re-runs and endlessly speaking voices, difficult and appalling though it was to make sense of, speaks emphatically against any idea of state intervention, of news manipulation, of presenting an official interpretation, of any attempt to make what was being shown fit in with some preconceived conspiracy.

However, something started to take shape.

The need for answers, the enquiries into what was known, the suspicions of who the culprits might be, the shock of the hijacks, the opinions of experts, the interviews with high officials, gradually created a story that emerged almost surreptitiously.

The story was shaped to fit into what few facts were known: planes had been hijacked (air traffic controllers confirmed that, and desperate phone calls were made from passengers and crew), those planes had actually crashed into the towers (we saw it happen), the buildings had collapsed (we saw it happen). Again, this speaks against any idea of a planned conspiratorial explanation. How could any of that have been pre-arranged?

The final reason I could not accept the conspiracy theory was for me the hardest to shake off. It was fear.

For me to believe that some US governmental agency had been

complicit in the deaths of all those innocent people required me to overturn a lifetime of assumptions about the world I had grown up in.

I assumed that in an enlightened civilized society, with a free press and an independent judiciary, where personal freedoms were inalienable rights, where the sciences and the arts were highly developed and culturally integrated into our lives, where there was a high level of education – in a modern Western democracy, in other words – then there was no danger from the people we elect into positions of power.

To question that assumption was to create a sense of what psychologists call cognitive dissonance. This means: when cognition starts to fail, when we suddenly see the world differently, we lose our feelings of security.

We assume that a government is essentially on our side, even if we did not vote for the party who takes power or the president who wins the election. We continue to assume this even when we do not agree with everything they do. If we let that go we feel fearful and anxious, and our defences kick in.

The only defence I personally had against that kind of anxiety was denial. I could not handle anything else. I had lost Lil, which was bad enough. To add to that personal loss the realization that she might have died because the US government was responsible made it much worse.

Denial lasted for a long time. I suffered my grieving alone, I meekly accepted as true what the authorities had said about 9/11. I wanted to go back to my life, to move on. It was a dark time. Eventually, though, I started to overcome that feeling of fear. I began to feel it would be better to find out the truth for myself, not to blame anyone, not to accuse anyone, but I needed to know.

I was mainly concerned to find out the reality of the crash at the Pentagon, because Lil had died in it. I soon realized that of

everything that happened, that was the incident most shrouded in secrecy.

But before even that, before I went to meet Charles Thewlis in St Kilda, I had made a discovery about the Atlantic island of Bermuda.

Bermuda

Most of the people who died in the 9/11 attacks were civilians. Almost without exception every passenger on the four crashed aircraft was going about his or her normal daily life. The people who died in or around the twin towers were people who had jobs there, or who were visiting, sightseeing. The flight and cabin crews in the aircraft were civilians, although most of the pilots and co-pilots were ex-military. Inside the Pentagon, the majority of deaths were those of civilian workers.

The exceptions were the fifty-five military personnel killed inside the Pentagon and the nineteen alleged hijackers. Firefighters, police officers, paramedics and other emergency responders had civilian lives, but at the time they died they were on duty, working as professionals.

In total, just under three thousand people died that morning.

The attacks were almost immediately characterized as an attack on America. They took place within the USA, the buildings were American, the aircraft were American built and operated, most of the corporations and businesses in the twin towers were American and the majority of the victims were US citizens. It was an inherently American story.

It was, though, a tragedy of global reach.

The citizens of more than ninety countries were killed. Just over two thousand six hundred Americans died and they were of course the most numerous. But other countries suffered significant human losses, including India, the United Kingdom, Russia, South Korea, China, the Dominican Republic, Canada,

several European and African countries – about twelve per cent of the deaths that day were of non-Americans.

Many more civilians died subsequently. Hundreds of rescuers, survivors and witnesses suffered fatal lung disease from breathing the toxic dust the buildings were reduced to. Fatalities directly traceable to the events of 9/11 have continued for more than two decades.

Of all the immediate deaths in the World Trade Center the country with the highest per capita death rate was the tiny island of Bermuda. Three young Bermudans, who worked in offices in the South Tower, perished when the aircraft struck. When the news was received in Bermuda, it was said that every person on the island felt directly affected, directly bereaved. The island went into national mourning.

Whatever motives there were that lay behind the attacks I could not see how the murder of these three young victims could justify any cause, political, military or religious. The same would of course be true if there had been only one such victim, or five thousand, but the realization of what these deaths meant to such a small country hit me hard.

My wish to establish the facts began there.

American 77

I discovered there are several ways of identifying an aircraft. The flight number is the simplest, the one that passengers learn and use when they fly. It's printed on the booking confirmation and the boarding pass, displayed on the departures board in the terminal and when the flight is called it's located to a particular gate number. However, it's a temporary identity. There are many aircraft in the airline fleet and any one of them, of similar type, can be used with the flight number, on that day, from that gate, in that terminal, at that airport.

Passengers trust this information because they must. The

system is familiar and universal. No one who travels by air questions it.

The aircraft itself is identified by a tail number. This is always painted permanently and prominently on the fuselage of the plane, usually towards the rear.

Individual parts of an aircraft are also identified by serial numbers. These are stamped indelibly on each part, and catalogued by the airline. On a day-to-day basis the serial number ensures that repairs and replacements are quickly and accurately enabled. After a disaster the serial numbers can be used by rescuers and investigators to identify the plane and help establish the cause of the accident.

On the morning of September 11, 2001, American Airways Boeing 757-223, tail number N644AA, was boarded as Flight AA77 from Gate 26D at Washington Dulles Airport. This I could easily verify from public records. Few passengers remember such details. The flight of American 77 is of historical significance, though. The details are therefore important, and it's reasonable to assume they are factually correct.

I even had a personal, informal verification. Lil had texted me from the gate just before she boarded the aircraft, complaining that the gate had been changed, and that the flight was now departing from Gate 26 – the longest walk in the airport. (I found a map of the terminal, and she was right – Gate 26D is one of the remotest gates in the airport, at the far end of the long boarding area.)

I am therefore certain that this was where Lil boarded her plane that morning.

But her name never appeared on any published passenger manifest.

I sensed my first hint of doubt. When I met Martin Viklund he explained that he and his staff, and presumably in this case his wife, never had to book seats on United or American

internal flights, that seats were routinely reserved for them. This was why Lil's name was not on the published passenger list. He said.

Was that really what happened? Was it conceivably true that government officials had pre-booked seats whenever they flew? I had never heard of that before, and subsequently found it impossible to check. Did they fly anonymously, and were not listed on the airport and airline computers? Was it true at that time, on 9/11, and is it still true now? I had only Viklund's word, but it had a certain ring of plausibility when he told me, while leaving doubts afterwards.

The absence of Lil's name on the manifest reduced the certainty that she was on that aircraft.

I remembered that during our last phone conversation, when I was still in Charlotte, North Carolina, she had said, 'I get a seat upgrade.' That sounded to me like a seat that had been booked conventionally. Another inconsistency.

And one more, in some ways for me the worst: in that same conversation she told me she was spending the night at the Marriott hotel in the airport complex. But Martin Viklund told me the unwelcome news that she spent the night with him.

Someone was lying to me but I did not know who it was. It was a microcosm of the larger story: it was a superficially credible account until you looked at the details, when nothing could be trusted because of small, betraying inconsistencies.

In spite of all this I still felt sure Lil must have been on the plane that started its flight from Gate 26D, at Washington Dulles, on that day, in the morning. She had told me so.

FDR and CVR

There is an urgent and thorough search for the aircraft's 'black boxes' after every plane crash. As well as fire and rescue responders, all investigators, from the country where the crash

takes place, from the airline that operated the plane, from the aircraft manufacturers and from the statutory bodies who oversee civil aviation, are involved with the search. The electronic recorders are the best and most reliable guide to discovering what went wrong and why the aircraft crashed.

The two instruments are known as the FDR (flight data recorder, which records practical information about many aspects of the flight: speed, height, direction, fuel use, much more), and the CVR (cockpit voice recorder, which records not only the words of the captain and the first officer on the flight deck, but conversations with air traffic control and other sources).

The recorders are practically indestructible, designed to withstand massive G forces, explosions, heavy impact, extreme heat and prolonged submersion. Despite their common name they are coloured bright orange to help searchers find them, they automatically emit an identifying signal, and are normally mounted near the tailplane – in many crashes the tail area is the least damaged.

Since they first went into use, these recorders have in almost every case been successfully discovered and retrieved from the wreckage, and from them invaluable evidence has been extracted. The only known incidents where the black boxes were not found involved planes which crashed in deep ocean, or on inaccessible mountain peaks.

'In almost every case' – but not in the cases of the four aircraft crashes on September 11, 2001. There is no objectively reliable recorder evidence available from any of those planes. This is not only unprecedented, it is inexplicable.

Eight recorders should have survived, two from each plane. All four of the aircraft crashed on land, in the technologically sophisticated territory of the USA. Where the aircraft were involved in destructive explosions and building wreckage (at the World Trade Center, and the Pentagon) huge numbers of

responders with advanced rescue equipment were quickly on the scene. Although all four crashes were extremely violent, the recorders should have been well inside the survivability parameters designed into them.

Of the two aircraft that hit the World Trade Center, no recorders were ever admitted to be found. Two rescue workers reportedly did discover three of the instruments in the rubble, and they promptly handed them over to the FBI. Nothing more has been heard of them.

From United Airlines Flight 93, the aircraft that crashed in the countryside near Shanksville, Pennsylvania, the recorders were apparently found and handed in. No data from these recorders was ever made public. A transcript of an alleged voice recording from the cockpit was produced to a court in 2006. Much of it was in Arabic, which added to its plausibility, but it was a transcript and not the original recording, and was given no proof of origin, which added no plausibility at all.

From American 77, the aircraft that most concerned me, the recorders created an extra mystery, another twist to the story. They threw into further doubt everything I previously believed about what happened to Lil.

Both the flight data recorder and the cockpit voice recorder were recovered − according to reports on American television and in responsible newspapers the recorders were found in the debris of the Pentagon, close to where the aircraft had smashed into the Pentagon wall. The discovery was made at night, at just before four o'clock in the morning of September 14, nearly three days after the actual incident. Both devices were promptly handed over to the FBI. The FBI reported to the press that the cockpit voice recorder was damaged on the outside and the data recorder was charred, but that the Bureau was confident the data could be recovered from both.

For the next five years nothing more was heard about the

American 77 recorders. Although the data from most crashes is normally made public, sometimes it is held back. In particular, the words actually recorded on the cockpit voice recorder might be distressing to the families of the crew, and if nothing was said by the doomed crew that might reveal the cause of the accident there is no advantage to making it public.

However, taken with the non-release of the data from the other flights, and the knowledge that the Pentagon recorders were reported to be in recoverable condition, the silence was agonizing for the families and friends of the victims on the plane. I know – I was one of them.

As the weeks and months and years went by, what began as a need for closure was aggravated by a growing anger.

The data was needed, because the evidence of eyewitnesses was so inconsistent. Was it an American Airways Boeing 757, as should be expected and many people positively confirmed? Or was it the smaller type of aircraft, reported by a substantial number of other witnesses – a Boeing 737? And why did several witnesses say it had no airline livery and was painted white all over, was too small, flying too fast and low for a jetliner, and looked more like a cruise missile? Local air traffic controllers were unanimous: they said that when the aircraft first appeared on their radar they assumed it was a fighter aircraft, because of its high speed and extreme manoeuvres.

Why did the only CCTV images available show blurrily what appeared to be a small craft flying at zero altitude and immense speed across the lawn of the Pentagon?

Professional pilots had come forward to say that no large civil aircraft could possibly fly as fast as that, as low as that, without becoming uncontrollable, possibly suffering structural failure. All passenger jets have strict speed limits related to whatever altitude they are flying at: they are designed for high speed only at great heights, where the air is thin. They have

to fly slowly when near the ground, or risk breaking up. They are hard to keep level when at zero altitude, because of the turbulence from ground effect, a problem greatly worsened by increased speed.

In 2006 a man called Moussaoui was brought to trial in the USA. He was accused of being part of the hijack plot. He confessed to that, claimed he was a member of al-Qaeda, and during the trial repeatedly boasted that if he had not been arrested he would have been involved in even more damaging attacks against the USA. Part of the evidence that was produced during his trial was a photograph of the cockpit voice recorder from American 77.

This picture showed that far from receiving only superficial damage, as convincingly described by the FBI when first handed over after it was located in the Pentagon wreckage, the recorder had been all but destroyed in the crash. It was claimed that the actual recording, on tape, had fused into a block of unreadable plastic. (This was the first known occasion when a cockpit voice recorder had not survived a crash.)

Following this, researchers began making intensive requests under the Freedom of Information Act, and after a delay the National Transportation Safety Board finally released the data from the flight data recorder. It was intact, recoverable, it had somehow survived the same impact that allegedly destroyed the almost identical unit beside it.

The data from the FDR was released in the form of a detailed Excel spreadsheet. From this, it was possible to reconstruct the whole flight of American 77 from the moment it pulled back from the terminal gate until the moment it slammed into the Pentagon wall.

Well, not exactly. The data ran out exactly six seconds before the moment when the plane slammed into the wall. Six seconds before the crash the aircraft was still intact,

still travelling at immense speed, but, according to the data, flying too high to hit the wall. From that position, six seconds before the end, the aircraft could only have flown *above* the Pentagon. It would have been frighteningly low, a mere three hundred feet, but it would have missed its target. It certainly would not have been able to skim low over the lawn at an impossibly high speed, as the 9/11 Commission claimed, as radar records revealed, and as the blurred CCTV image appeared to show.

It was the first of several mysteries, all of them controversial.

The function of the flight data recorder is to explain what caused the crash, not to create new problems.

The fact of the missing last six seconds of American 77's flight was not the only new anomaly to emerge. The data is date stamped, as it must be – similar to the way a computer re-stamps the date of a file when it is altered or saved. The internal date stamp recorded in the flight data recorder said: *Date modified, 9/13/2001. 11:45 pm.*

In other words, the last time the data was recorded or saved ('modified') was more than two and a half days *after* the collision with the Pentagon wall, and about four hours *before* it was allegedly discovered in the rubble, 'close to where the aircraft struck the building'.

Who modified it?

How could this data be taken as accurate? It was patently unreliable. Was the recorder incorrectly set? Or had someone secretly discovered it in the wreckage, taken it away and interfered with the data, then placed the recorder back into the rubble, ready for it to be 'located' a few hours later? Or was it a fraud, taken from some other plane, then planted in the rubble? Or was the whole thing a half-bungled fake?

The internal data does identify the plane as a Boeing 757, American Airlines, Flight 77, and the tail number is correct. But

was this entered, altered, typed in, 'modified', before it was left out for the searchers to find?

Much of the data values normally available from the flight data recorder are missing or blank. There is no note of engine performance, flap use, cabin pressure, and almost everything else.

But some information is revealed. Most intriguingly, the data shows that at no point during the flight was the door to the cockpit opened, violently or otherwise. How then did the alleged hijackers break in and take control of the flight deck, as described by passengers making terrified calls to the ground? Was the captain still at the controls as the plane circled above Arlington, before it plunged down towards the Pentagon?

The 9/11 Commission report states that the controls of American 77 had been taken by one of the hijackers, named Hani Hanjour. This man, along with others of the alleged hijackers, had taken flying lessons in the United States in the months before the attack. If that was correct, then Hanjour sitting at the controls of American 77 introduces a whole new problem of credibility.

American flight instructors who had given flying lessons to Hanjour came forward after the attack. They said that he was incompetent as a pilot. He had no aptitude for flying, nor had shown much interest in learning. One instructor said that Hanjour was the worst student flier he had ever worked with, incapable of maintaining straightforward level flight in even an entry-level single-engined light aircraft.

Yet this man, allegedly, had forced his way into the flight deck (somehow without opening the closed cockpit door). Disbelief added to impossibility: armed only with a small knife he had ejected a physically strong and professionally motivated captain from his seat, the first officer too, and had taken over the controls of a huge and sophisticated jetliner he had never

flown before. The plane was heavy with fuel, passengers and cargo. Hanjour had allegedly flown it for several hundred miles at high altitude, then taken it into a high-speed diving turn, nearly three hundred and sixty degrees at low level, before skimming it at 460 knots (529 mph, 851 km/h) across a lawn and into the side of a building.

Professional pilots, familiar with the Boeing 757, said such a manoeuvre would not be difficult for a useless pilot like Hanjour – it would be impossible.

It would be impossible, in fact, for anyone. If flown at high speeds in dense, sea level air, the slightest error or touch on the controls of a heavy commercial jet would tilt or dive it into the ground. Several long-experienced commercial pilots even tried to reproduce the alleged last few seconds of American 77's flight on simulators, but invariably failed.

But this is the aircraft that took off at 8:20 a.m., flew for the rest of the flight with its cockpit door firmly closed, allegedly hijacked somehow half an hour after take-off, and at nine minutes past nine was six seconds away from the Pentagon, three hundred feet above. It was the aircraft whose flight data recorder was forged. Or it was an aircraft with no FDR at all.

The only large jets that fly in American airspace without a flight data recorder are military aircraft.

Some of these have had their wings and control surfaces modified to allow stable flight when flying at high speeds at low altitude.

TEN

then: 2007

D. L. Glenister

I was in my office at home. It was late in the evening – I had my curtains closed, the extra heating was on. It was the middle of January 2007, and a cold rain was being blown hard against the windows. It brought a feeling of the wild to the London street where we had our apartment. I was working in a pool of light from my desk lamp, with several notes and papers from my 9/11 files spread out before me. I was watching a video on YouTube, one which raised the intriguing matter of the seismic record of New York City on the day of the attacks. This of course revealed seismic peaks during the two moments when the planes crashed into the twin towers, followed a while later by the collapse of each one. Much more interesting, though, was the discovery that the seismic record showed large concussions *before* the planes struck the towers, and a series of concussions (explosions?) *after* the towers were hit, but *before* the towers fell.

Jeanne walked into my room suddenly, switched on the overhead light and sat down in the easy chair I used when watching TV in my office.

'Ben, we need to talk,' she said.

'OK – what about?'

I put the video on pause, but when I glanced across at Jeanne and saw the determined look on her face, and the tension in her body language, I hit exit, then powered down the computer.

While it was still going through the closing-down routine, she said: 'This has got to stop.'

'What?'

'You're doing it again. You're spending your whole life researching the stuff about 9/11. Where's it getting you?'

'I'm researching for a series of articles, possibly a book,' I said.

'No – you've been saying that long enough. You're just obsessed with it and it's eating up your life.'

'No it's not. It's a hobby, something I do when I'm not working on anything else in particular.'

'It's an obsession. Why won't you admit that?' She waved a hand dismissively at the bookshelf behind where she was sitting. 'Look at all this material you've collected. Aren't there enough 9/11 conspiracy theory books already? How many more do you need to read, and what possible use could another book about it be?'

'I don't believe in conspiracy theories,' I said. 'And each one of those books is about different areas of the 9/11 attacks. It's a huge, complex subject.'

'It's so huge it's going to destroy you.'

'I don't think so. I'm starting to understand it at last. You remember last year, when I went up to Scotland and interviewed the Russian mathematician? Kyril Tatarov? He gave me a whole new insight into the problem, and I've been trying to work that out, understand what he meant, ever since.'

'As far as I can tell, most of the time you watch homemade videos by conspiracy nuts who think Tony Blair and George Bush arranged the whole thing.'

'That's partly true,' I said. 'There are hundreds of videos like

that. But don't you think that by now I can tell the difference? I watch that sort of thing so I can eliminate it. Anyway, every now and then one of those nuts comes up with something that I hadn't known before, and occasionally it even turns out to be true.'

 'And what's the point of that, Ben? How much evidence do you need to prove whatever it is you want to prove?'

'I'm not trying to prove anything. I just want to know what happened.'

'No, there's more to it than that. Why are you so interested?'

'It's the biggest event of our time. Everything dangerous or aggressive that's happened in the world since 2001 has its root cause in 9/11.'

'But why does it need *you* to work it out? Leave it to others. What makes it special to you? It's that woman you were involved with, isn't it?'

'Lil? Do you mean Lil?'

'Of course. What was it about her?'

'In the way you probably mean it, nothing special – except she was killed by whoever arranged the 9/11 attacks. She didn't deserve that. Look, Jeanne, you know everything I've ever told you about Lil. You know what she meant to me, back then. She was in my life long before you and I met. I was in love with her, we thought had a future, we were planning a life together. I can't pretend otherwise. She was as real and important to me then as you are now. But she was killed. She's in my past. You know how it was. Yes, you're right – I wouldn't be interested in 9/11 if Lil hadn't been a victim. Well, I would have been interested, but no more than anyone else. I became obsessed, that's the word you used, but only obsessed with the need to find out what happened to her, why she and thousands of others died that day. I thought it would be simple, as simple as the official story tries to make it –'

'There you are again. I'm sick of hearing about the official story.'

'Me too – but that's all we have. If I could make myself believe that story then the whole mystery of Lil's death would be solved. But the story is full of lies, full of half-truths. Evidence they won't release, false data they have released. It's self-evidently not true, and they won't admit the truth. I've moved on – this isn't about Lil any more.'

Jeanne was looking away from me now, staring down at the worn old carpet that was already laid in the room when we moved into the apartment. I had always intended to replace it, but had never got around to doing so.

'You're still obsessed with 9/11,' she said after a few moments. 'But it's going to hurt you. Let it go, Ben. You've become static, locked in this. I don't want that. I want to get out of this flat, find somewhere better for us to live, move out of London if we have to.'

'OK – maybe when the weather improves, we can go and look around for a house somewhere. In a couple of months?'

She shrugged, looking irritated with me.

Then she said: 'Did I ever tell you how my father died?'

'You said once he had a heart attack. You've never told me much more than that.'

'Mum doesn't like me talking about him. Did I say how it happened? I don't suppose Mum said anything about this.'

'She said Dougal, your father, died when he was in Washington, but she didn't give any details. It's the only time she ever mentioned him to me. It was last year, when we were travelling together to Bute, when she drove me to the interview with Tatarov.'

'She doesn't normally like discussing Dad. How did the subject come up? She rarely even talks to me about him.'

'She asked me about Lil, and I mentioned Lil's husband had worked in the Department of Defense.'

'That probably explains it. You didn't talk about 9/11 with her, did you?'

'Not really. She clammed up, and I realized it was not a good subject with her.'

Jeanne stood up from the chair, but then leant her backside against the overstuffed arm.

Half-standing there, she said: 'Dad was fit, active, well. Not overweight. The doctors said a heart attack can hit anyone, but I don't believe that. Because of his job he had regular check-ups – twice a year. He always came out of those reassured. He ate healthily, he had never smoked in his life, he sometimes liked wine with a meal, but he was not at all a heavy drinker. He used the gym two or three times a week, and always swam. He'd been a junior swimming champion at county level, when he was at school. He kept that up all his life. Then one day, while he was on a trip to the USA, he dropped dead. He travelled a lot in his work, and after the funeral our GP said that maybe that was what caused it, the stress of flying so often. I don't think so. Dad always said he enjoyed flying, because it gave him a chance to read and sleep.'

'Lucinda told me he was a lawyer.'

'Dad was a mercantile lawyer for a big insurance syndicate. He wasn't the sort of lawyer who goes into court. He worked for underwriters, assessing losses, negotiating disputes about who was responsible, or if more than one party was involved, what proportions they shared. He was involved with international matters, usually about infrastructure: harbours, bridges, land disputes, dams, shipping, freight haulage, airlines, so he had to be abroad much of the time. He spent at least six months every year in Africa or the Far East or the USA. It didn't matter to me because he always came home between trips,

166

gave me a lot of his time. He was a writer too.'

'I saw his books in Lucinda's house. D. L. Glenister?'

'That's him. He wrote two books. They're standard works on international mercantile law. Very dry texts, the sort of thing no one sits down to read but if you work in international law you have to refer to them. D. L. Glenister is an authority. The books are still in print, still current. Mum's pension is supplemented by them. I'm convinced that it was that part of his life that killed him.'

'Writers get killed?'

'Not usually – but lawyers often make unpopular decisions. Dad died when he was on one of his business trips, staying in a hotel in Washington. He was trying to negotiate compensation for people who had lost relatives when the Pentagon was attacked. He phoned Mum the night he died – everything was normal, routine. He told her he had been called in the next day to a meeting with a senior official in the Defense Department, which was unusual. He normally only ever met lawyers and applicants. But he saw nothing suspicious about it – he took statements from all parties. He never made it to the meeting. The next morning a member of the hotel staff found his body in his room. His death certificate was drawn up almost immediately, the same day Mum was told he had died. It was from a doctor who worked for the US government. Then they shipped his body home. In a sealed casket. They never said why they did that.'

'Are you saying someone killed him?'

'No, I'm saying he died of a heart attack. That's what the death certificate said. But something induced the attack.'

'What do you think happened?'

'More than a year before he died he told me that he had discovered something really interesting. He said that during one of his earlier trips to the US he had worked on an insurance

167

claim from the families of some of the victims of 9/11. Dad was liaising with the Justice Department in Washington DC. It was a class action, a group action, complicated by the fact some of the victims were US citizens, and some were from European countries. It was typical of the sort of work Dad routinely did. This was about six months after 9/11. It gave him access to files and correspondence, as it would be bound to, and he spent a week going through the matter in the usual way, preparing the case strictly according to the law, taking written statements from the families, and much else. But somewhere in that work he came across some other documents – he said it was obvious he was not intended to see them. I don't know what they were, but in the course of the week he discovered information about 9/11 he found intriguing. When he came home he could hardly stop talking about it.'

'What did he say?' Suddenly I was listening intently. 'You've never mentioned this before.'

'Well – to put it bluntly, he became a conspiracy theorist. He was certain that what he called a cartel of vested interests – Russian oligarchs, arms manufacturers, shipping lines, the CIA, members of the Saudi royal family, all sorts of connections – had conspired to create the events of 9/11.'

'Did he have proof?'

'No, but he had theories. The thing is, he started doing the same as you: he was endlessly looking online, buying books and DVDs about 9/11, downloading documents, putting the theory together, travelling abroad to meet people he thought might have extra information.'

'He did this at the same time as his legal work?'

'No – he had been with the syndicate long enough to take a sabbatical, and he spent most of that time investigating 9/11. He told us he was writing a book – in fact, he did write a book.'

'A book? Do you have a copy, did you read it?'

'No – listen. He finished the book, sent the manuscript to a publisher he knew, in the same group that had brought out his law books, and was given a deal for it. A new book by D. L. Glenister. They were excited about it, said his earlier books gave this one a special authority. They said they would make it a lead title in the following spring list, paid him an advance – I don't know how much, but I think it must have been a large one because he told me how pleased he was. He was less pleased after he delivered the manuscript, when they said that part of the deal meant they would take over all his notes and research material – they said this was in case they had to defend themselves from legal action. Dad objected, said he could handle it himself, but the publisher insisted it was a condition of printing the book. So Dad reluctantly handed everything over, and waited for the book to appear.'

'So his notes have been lost?' I said.

'He always kept copies of everything. But if he kept copies of those notes I've never found them. Mum's house is still full of his stuff. I tried looking for them once, but there are several packing cases in the basement crammed with his old papers. When Mum found out what I was looking for she became upset, pleaded with me not to go on.'

'Would she let me search for them?'

'Ben! You've already spent too long on this.'

'OK. Tell me the rest.'

I realized that one day it might become possible to look properly for them.

'A few months went by,' Jeanne said. 'His sabbatical ended and he returned to work. The book was not published on the date agreed, and when Dad queried what was going on, he was told by someone claiming to be an editor that they had no record of receiving any manuscript submission from him. When he protested and spoke to the guy he knew in management, he

was told the publisher's holding company had made a policy decision not to publish the book. The contract was terminated.

'That was the week before he went on what turned out to be his last trip to America. He was summoned unexpectedly by some important official in the Defense Department. Then an alleged heart attack in the middle of the night. Don't you think there's a chain of events? What do you suppose I think actually happened to him?'

'Did your father tell Lucinda the name of the official who wanted to see him?'

'I don't know. It's possible – but she never told me.'

I felt a tautness in my chest, an uncanny certainty. The official might have been Viklund.

But not him? Surely not Viklund!

Jeanne's voice had remained steady throughout all this, but now I looked at her more closely I could see her eyes were full of tears. She moved across to me and we held each other for a while. I felt the wetness against my cheek, running down to my neck.

I said: 'I'm really sorry, Jeanne.'

'I don't want anything like that to happen to you too. The 9/11 conspiracy world can be dangerous.'

'I'll be careful.'

'Dad was careful. That was his profession: careful with details, picking out the relevant facts, assessing what various people had to say about the facts, coming to a considered, deeply careful decision. And listen – Mum doesn't like you talking about 9/11. She gets upset when she finds out you're researching the same material. I do too.'

'I'm really sorry, Jeanne,' I said again, and put my arms around her once more. 'All I'm doing is finding out.'

But afterwards I tried to remember the time I was travelling with Lucinda, and how unknowingly I had opened up to her

about Lil and 9/11, revealing how deeply involved I was. She had told me none of the details about her husband's death. I had said nothing about who Lil's husband had been.

Jeanne was right, though – enough was enough. The sheer complexity of the 9/11 story, all the conflicting evidence, the unexplained mysteries, was a kind of obsessive lure, an unending saga of detail. Maybe I should let the whole thing go, at least for a while?

Later that evening I put away my files and did not look at them again for several weeks.

ELEVEN

now

Orange and blue

I noticed the woman one afternoon as I was starting one of my regular sea-front exercise walks. She was crossing the road outside the entrance to the ferry port. I could hardly avoid seeing her — by the conservative, workaday standards of the island her appearance was unusual. During the summer weeks there were many oddly or colourfully dressed visitors in Baile Bhòid, especially around the Port Bannatyne yachting marina to the north of the town, but autumn had already arrived and many of the sailing boats moored in the marina over the summer had been winched ashore. Visitors to the island were relatively few by this time.

The woman's hair had been dyed bright orange and gelled into spikes, and as we passed each other in opposite directions I noticed she was wearing vivid blue eye shadow. We glanced briefly at each other as we walked by. I was surprised to see a brief flicker of recognition in the way she looked at me, but I did not know her and after walking on I thought nothing more about her.

I was using the walk that day to think again about the problem of Lucinda, and what we should do about her. She had recently declared herself entirely recovered. Her health and

memory were back – she said she was feeling fit and able and would like to return home. Her episodes of mute incomprehension seemed to be over, at least for now. Jeanne and I were broadly in favour of her going back to her house, but there were other matters to think about.

There was no knowing how long this recovery was likely to last, or how we would be able to cope if a sudden relapse made her as dependent on us as recently. Or, as was likely, more dependent. Would her local authority provide care workers to call on her, or would they say we should have to fund that ourselves? Maybe she should talk to a GP? The surgery was close to where she lived and although Lucinda had registered with our local clinic she said she had known her GP in Morningside for many years. If she went back perhaps there was a neighbour we could trust to keep an eye on her?

Then there was the opposite possibility, that she might be able to live exactly as she said, which was to return to her life as an independent adult, self caring, self sufficient. She was only in her early seventies, the same age as many of the friends who lived close to her in Morningside, who apparently still drove their cars, took holidays abroad, went to theatre and concert performances, and so on. It was tempting to accept that might be possible, but Jeanne felt it was risky. I tended to agree.

Nothing had been decided yet – even Lucinda seemed content for the time being to stay on in our spare room.

I walked as far as another of the former piers, which was where paddle steamers had moored during the busy summer holidays decades ago, then turned around, crossed the road and began walking back towards the town. Traffic swept by intermittently. A fine spray from the sheen of rainwater on the road drifted behind the cars, but a wind had started blustering in from the firth so the spray never touched me. The hotels and guest houses along the sea front were still open for the end of

the holiday season, but most of them had signs outside saying rooms were available. I knew that within a couple more weeks, when the first of the autumn gales arrived, most of these places would close for the winter.

I always liked the shortening days, the fresher air, I liked the dark skies, the white-capped waves in the deeper stretches of the firth and the lowering, clouded bulk of the fringe of mountains. The island would be reduced to its core population. Then life on Bhòid returned to the sense of isolation, existing on the edge of the elements, an island state.

When I walked back as far as the parade of shops along the sea front, the woman with orange hair was waiting for me on the traffic island opposite the large tourist store. She raised a hand in recognition, then crossed towards me. There was no traffic anywhere – the town was for the moment silent.

'You're Ben Matson, aren't you?'

'Yes,' I said, somewhat startled by her direct approach.

'I recognized you. I've been looking for you.' She laughed aloud, a defensive signal. 'You will think I'm rude.'

She surprised me, but I did not think her rude. I still had no idea who she was.

'Do I know you?' I said. 'Have we met before?'

'Yes – but you obviously don't remember. I'm Jaye. Jaye Hume.'

Then it clicked – the night at the flat in London. Weeks had passed since then. 'Oh, yes.'

That had been a shadowy meeting. I had barely seen her in the half-light from the television, nothing by which to recognize her now. That evening I was depressed and lonely, watching TV, wishing I had gone to a hotel. I had a vague memory of the way she looked when she came into the room, at first standing slightly behind me, a tall woman with only a towel around her, who moved forward to crouch on the floor in front of the

screen. I remembered her hair because it was uncombed and it had partly blocked my view of the screen. Had it been coloured orange then? I hadn't noticed, hadn't seen. As she sat by the television, the towel, wrapped negligently around her body, started coming loose. The encounter had been borderline embarrassing, unsought, an accident of meeting. But even so, a brief moment of chemistry: an offer of intimacy, half made by her?, half refused by me? Perhaps she had meant nothing by it, perhaps I had refused her clumsily. It had come to nothing. I had been distracted by the television news report – the crashed aircraft in the deep ocean off the state of Delaware.

I was nervous of her, standing there with me now in the centre of my town. I glanced around with a sudden feeling of needless guilt, an associative memory of the brief attraction that had passed between us, as if someone I knew might see us and realize about our first meeting. Cars and trucks were driving away as they disembarked from the ferry that had recently docked. Many of them went past us as we stood there.

'Could we go somewhere and talk? A bar perhaps, or one of these cafés?'

I said: 'It's not really convenient just now. My kids will be home from school –'

'Then later this evening?'

'Could we make it tomorrow?'

She looked up and down the sea-front road. Then she shrugged. 'OK.'

I was thinking of Jeanne, out of the house at present, picking up the boys from school. They would be back shortly – I thought of the noisy chaos that usually rattled around the house for half an hour after the boys came in. It was a time when it was difficult to work, so I usually messed in, talked to Seth and Louis if they wanted to tell me something, made a cup of tea or coffee for Jeanne and me, gave the boys something to eat

after school. That was my life now, something commonplace, the gentle pleasures of having a family. What, anyway, would Jeanne think if I turned up at home with this colourful woman in tow, someone I clearly already knew?

Lucinda would be there too, her immediate future still being thought out, probably anxious to talk about it again, hoping to resolve everything this evening. She was anxious to go home. If that was to happen there would be a week of going to and from Edinburgh, transporting her and her stuff, then starting up her house again, sorting out the utility suppliers, settling her back in. Jeanne would probably have to stay there with her for a few nights, which meant I should be at home for the boys. It was not going to be an immediate or quick transition.

I was preoccupied with all this, the minor travails of family life.

'I do need to talk with you,' said the woman with the bright orange hair.

'I'm on my way home.'

'Could we talk there?'

'Can't you just say what it is now?' I said. 'Is it important?'

Two more cars went by in a rush, their tyres noisy on the damp road surface, making me raise my voice with the last words.

'Tomorrow will be all right,' she said.

'Do you have somewhere to stay tonight?'

'I've booked in at the B&B along there. The one with the palm trees outside. I'll wait across the road from the building in the morning.'

She was indicating the row of large houses in the same road as where I lived. Further along. I knew the place she meant.

'It's just that I have a family problem to sort out at the moment – I need to talk to my partner about it this evening.'

'You don't have to explain. I assumed you'd have other

things going on. I was not expecting to find you straight away so I planned to be here for a couple of days at least. I'll see you tomorrow.'

She said no more but walked away in the direction of the B&B. After a few paces she raised an arm in farewell without looking back. I did not follow because for some reason I did not want her to know exactly where I lived, or for her to come knocking at the door. I knew I was acting as if guilty of something. I reversed direction, walked across to the newsagent's shop and for five minutes I browsed the magazines. There was no sign of her when I emerged, so I walked briskly to the house and let myself in.

That evening over dinner we all agreed that Lucinda should return home in the next few days, and that Jeanne would stay with her for the first nights. Lucinda said she would visit her GP, accept any treatment that was prescribed and then would keep us regularly informed about the state of her well-being. While the move went on the boys would stay with me – I had no work trips planned for the next couple of weeks at least. We could work it out.

The unifying subject

In the morning I went out to find Jaye. She was sitting in one of the old Victorian seaside shelters opposite the B&B, leaning forward with her elbows resting on her knees, smoking a hand-rolled cigarette. As I walked towards her the steep hills of Argyll were looming beyond her, bright with the morning sun. One of the ferries was crossing the bay, heading for the mainland. When Jaye spotted me approaching she took a last drag, then flicked the cigarette towards the water's edge. She stood up. Her hair of course was still orange, but today she had not put on the electric blue shadow around her eyes.

I led her along the sea front, past our house, then into the

centre of Baile Bhòid. She told me about the room she had been given at the B&B, the view across the firth, the calming sight of the ferries' businesslike arrivals and departures. She said she loved to see the boats, the sense of being cut off from the mainland. She told me she had been to the island before, but not for several years.

I took her to Jamie's, the best of the coffee bars on the front, the one that stayed open all year round.

I apologized for my offhand behaviour the day before. She said she was not bothered by that. We ordered lattes, and waited while they were brought to the table.

'I remembered what you told me,' I said. 'You're in the production office of one of the video companies in the group.'

'Yes, but since then they've cut back. There's only one company now, and anyway my job doesn't exist any more.'

'What are you doing instead?'

'For now I'm freelancing, but they say I can probably go back to the job in a few weeks. They've given me some work, projects I was working on before.'

'Will you go back?'

'If they'll have me. If I want to be there.'

'You don't sound sure.'

'I need to get across to the USA for a while. At least for a weekend, perhaps longer. I could afford a couple of weeks. The company have a shoot coming up in New York, which gave me the idea of doing my trip at the same time, if they paid my fare. In the end they didn't select me for the team. When I tried to talk my way into it they suggested the leave of absence. I got the message.'

'So you'd have to pay your own way.'

'That's right.'

'Then why are you here on Bhòid?'

'I wanted to see you. I couldn't find an address for you,

178

but I knew you were on the island. I tried asking about you at the bookshop, but they said they didn't know where you were.'

'I think they do.'

'Well, they wouldn't tell me.'

'Why did you ask at the bookshop?'

'You told me you were a writer.'

'I'm a journalist. Not quite the same thing, but they do know me at the shop. What is it you want to talk to me about?'

'The old hydro hotel, in Port Bannatyne. I know you've been there.' For a moment I thought she meant the short visit I had made recently with Lucinda, but of course she would not know about that. 'Do you have any way of getting me in to have a look around?'

'There's a problem with that,' I said. 'The whole site has been cleared.'

'Already?'

'Ten years ago. Longer ago than that, probably.'

'I had no idea. The original house was in danger of collapsing, and they pulled that down while we were on the island, but I thought most of the hydro was going to be saved. It was beautiful and historic.'

'Apparently not. They knocked the whole place down. You seem to know a lot about it.'

'Of course. I have an interest in it. The same as yours.'

'And what is that?'

'Indirectly, the Russian mathematician. Sergei Kalugin – I can never remember his real name.'

'You mean Kyril Tatarov?' I said. 'How do you know him?'

Now she regarded me with a direct stare, the first time her gaze had steadied on me.

'Because of the film – you and I worked on it together, with

Bryan Claremont. You wrote the screenplay, and I was Bryan's production assistant. We shot some of the film on location, inside Kalugin's study, in the hydro.'

Suddenly, belatedly, I made the connection. 'You were – Jacqueline?'

'I still am, but everyone calls me Jaye.'

'You signed yourself Jacqui.'

'Jacqui Hume. That's what some of the people at work call me.'

During those interminable weeks of drafts and redrafts of the wretched *Sergei and Tanya* screenplay I had met Jacqueline in person only two or three times. Then I had barely noticed her, a slight figure at a desk in another room, beyond Bryan Claremont's. Most of our working contact was at a distance, by email, text messages or telephone. Now, sitting closely opposite her, I could see the resemblance of Jaye to my memories of Jacqueline, blurred by the passage of a decade and a half, the distraction now of her spiky hair, the unexpectness created by a different context.

I smiled across at her to show I now recalled who she was, but I did not say how much, back then, I had grown to dread her telephone calls, to detest the sound of her voice. Her name on an incoming email had made my nerves jangle in anticipation of complaint, trouble, interference with what I had written. I was in a constant state of creative frustration because of the irrelevance of many of the script notes she passed on from Claremont and his financial backers. For most of the time she was my main contact with the producers, and inevitably I focused much of my irritation on her.

When I finally released myself from Claremont and his contract, I quickly put behind me everything about the film. I had barely thought about Jacqueline, Jaye, since.

A silence between us started extending. To break it I said:

'That film. I watched part of it on DVD. Then it was on television, but I never watched it through.'

'Some of it was pretty good,' Jaye said. 'I liked the scenes in the hydro, the ones we shot on location. The scene in the faucet room is great, where the guy is wrapped with a towel soaked in freezing cold spa water.'

'I don't remember seeing that. Is it one of the scenes I wrote?'

'I think it was put in later.'

I was trying to work out when this must have taken place. Tatarov was certainly still alive at the time the film was made, but he had left Scotland and returned to New York a week or two after I interviewed him. That must have been in 2006, because I had started seeing Jeanne not long before then. I worked on the script in 2008, and the film came out towards the end of the following year. I was under the impression the hydro had been demolished as soon as Tatarov and the other people left. Yet they could not have started filming for at least two years afterwards.

I said that to Jaye.

'We did have to shoot some of the interiors in a studio,' she said. 'But we began in the hydro itself. The building was still standing unoccupied after Tatarov and the Americans left, but, by the time we were ready to shoot, workmen were already pulling the oldest part of the place down. The eastern end was derelict and unsafe. You must have seen how huge the main building was — it was long and narrow, running along the slope of the hill, with at least four wings. And the grounds, of course. The area where the Americans had been was in the wing at the west end, and that was still intact when we were there. Bryan made a deal with the owners that we could film inside the building for two weeks, but the demolition team made so much noise and vibration, dust drifting everywhere, that after a few days we had to pull out.'

'Were they using explosives for the demolition?' I said.

'No – just tractors and wrecking balls.'

Jeanne and I moved to Bhòid in 2017, and Louis had been born not long after. Seth was then about two years old. I never went near the hydro, at that time or afterwards – we must have driven past the site dozens of times, but the hydro was not easy to see from the road because of the village houses and the trees. Most of the surviving photos from the days when the hydro was open had been taken either from the end of the pier, itself long gone, replaced by the quay in Baile Bhòid, or from a boat sailing in the firth. From that sort of viewpoint the Victorian mansion stood proudly along its hillside, seeming to loom over the village, but when you were actually there at sea level it was more or less hidden. Many trees had grown to maturity.

'What happened to Bryan and you?' I said. 'Are you still working with him?'

'No – that job was over when the film was completed. You probably haven't heard, but he died a couple of years later. He didn't produce any more films. He used the credit on *Sergei and Tanya* to make several TV commercials, but then he fell ill. I only found out several weeks after he died.'

Feeling surprised and slightly stunned, I sat thoughtfully for a few moments. I remembered Bryan Claremont well in person, although I had not liked the way he worked, endlessly changing his mind, demanding rewrites on what felt like someone else's whim. Nor Jacqui, Jaye, for that matter. That period was in the past. Little of it mattered now. Some of the work I had done over the years was merely a transit to something else – that was how the *Sergei and Tanya* screenplay was to me.

'What about you? Are you still out there shooting films?'

'I never was – I'm a backroom worker. Or I was until they laid me off. I almost never went on shoots, if that's what you

mean. Most of the people who work in the film industry aren't around when the camera is turning.'

'I think I realized that, when I was writing the script.'

'It was a shit idea for a film, wasn't it?'

'I never said it in so many words to Bryan, but yes. He managed to get it made, though, and people went to see it. It even received a few good reviews. I learnt a lot from the experience.'

'Bryan was fascinated by Tatarov.'

'I assumed he must be. I found much of what Tatarov said puzzling.'

'Do you remember the first time we met?' Jaye said. 'When Bryan was talking to you about his idea for the story?'

'Of course. What Bryan didn't know, and I couldn't tell him, was that I had actually been to the hydro to meet with Tatarov. It was during the time the media thought he was missing. I didn't even know at the time that there was press speculation about him. But when I met Tatarov he made me promise to keep everything he said confidential. So the one thing Bryan wanted to talk about was the one thing I couldn't.'

Jaye said: 'I was taking notes when you were talking with Bryan. Afterwards, I was with him when he read through them, and he said then that you must have been holding out on him. He said he was certain you had been with Tatarov.'

'What was he actually looking for?'

'He wanted to make a film about 9/11. It was a big subject for him. He was planning to make it next, after he finished *Sergei*. He was certain that Tatarov knew something profound and important about 9/11, and he saw *Sergei* as a way of laying out the groundwork. He wanted you on board for that reason.'

'So what was going to be his angle?'

'He believed Tatarov had worked out there was a kind of explanation for the attacks through the medium of television. Everyone was watching, all over the world.'

'I was too,' I said. That long day, standing in the airport terminal in Columbus.

'Do you remember where you were?' she said. 'The day it happened?'

'Yes, of course. I was on an aircraft –'

She said without listening to me: 'I can never forget what happened to me. I was seventeen, still in school. The head teacher came into our classroom and led us to the assembly hall. All the other senior students were there. Juniors were not allowed in. The staff had set up a television and were showing the live programme from the BBC. The first thing I saw was the fire in one of the skyscrapers, the North Tower, black smoke pouring out. Then they showed the second plane going in and smashing into the South Tower.'

'So you saw it live.'

'Well, the programme was live, but they were running recordings as well as live feeds from America. It was difficult to work out how it had started. They kept re-running the same footage. It was confusing, and that made me more interested. Why weren't they showing the story straight?

'That year I had begun a course in media ethics, the syntax of film and TV. I loved the subject – nothing else I learned at school was so interesting. So although I found the 9/11 stuff horrific like everyone else, I was fascinated by the unstated language of the broadcast, with what seemed to me were hidden meanings. I was reading the work of a man called W. Hugh Baddeley, a classic theorist of film and television documentary making. He was concerned by the way a straightforward factual event could be filmed as it happened, then manipulated by film makers to have other meanings, by their choice of camera angles, by montage, by using distraction, juxtaposing images, by use of cutaways and commentary, by suspending images so that the viewer never quite saw everything. The American TV coverage of 9/11

184

was an almost classic example of that. It seemed designed to obscure what was going on, rather than make it clear. There was almost no information, nothing straight, factual. It was all guesses and speculation and questions. By over-revealing the wrong details, by interrupting interviews, by constantly moving to another scene, they were in effect hiding the events in plain sight. They were abandoning every rule of visual documentary journalism, making it impossible for them to convey reliable information, or for the viewers to receive it. The effect was that the audience had to make assumptions about what they were being shown.

'Then the BBC coverage made it even worse. They started re-running the re-runs, sometimes blocking out the American commentary and putting in their own. They had their own experts, explaining and speculating. Bryan told me that it was the same everywhere.'

'To be fair, nothing like it had ever happened before,' I said. 'It couldn't have been planned. They were just trying to cover a major news story, thrust at them without warning. It was confusion.'

'The US government knew it was going to happen. There were warnings.'

'They denied that. They said they had no advance information at all. It was a surprise attack.'

'They were given detailed warnings.'

'Yes, but even if there was a general threat of hijackings, there had never been suicide attacks using aircraft.'

'Bryan said there were explicit warnings, in detail, in advance. The US government was warned that there would be suicide missions in American commercial aircraft in the USA. The warnings were passed on to the US by other countries. Britain, Russia, Italy, France, Germany, Israel, Egypt, and more. At the end of August, Mossad, the Israeli intelligence service, told

the US that nineteen trained terrorists were in the USA, with four of them having flying lessons. Mossad even provided a list of their names.'

'I do find that hard to believe.'

'Some people believed it. Officials cancelled their own flights that week. People from the White House, people who worked in the Pentagon. They damned well knew something was about to happen. Journalists are well informed, have contacts at every level. The media weren't completely unprepared.'

'Surely people cancelling flights must have been a coincidence?'

But then, I remembered – Martin Viklund had altered and cancelled flights that week. All that confusion with Lil, the lies, the changes of flights, the change of story. Where she was, which plane she would be on.

I said: 'So if that was true, why was the media complicit?'

'I'm not certain of that, but it was the media coverage that interested Tatarov. Everyone knows what happened because they saw it on TV. Tatarov was working on what he called a social theorem.'

I remembered then that he had told me about that. In his own way, stating not explaining.

My own viewing of the TV coverage had been in the worst circumstances: I was already upset, worried, tired. Disoriented by the flight on the plane from Charlotte, concerned about Lil. The place was crowded. The TV picture was unsteady, and there was so much noise I could barely hear anything.

But on that day I nevertheless came away from the television coverage with an understanding. A story had emerged somehow, almost as if I had made it up myself: al-Qaeda terrorists had hijacked the planes, caused a shocking number of deaths, terrible damage. It was a story I found coherent. It had awful

consequences, but it was a story with a rationale that made a kind of sense.

Jaye went on: 'I watched television with everyone else until school finished. I hurried home because I wanted to see the rest, but my mum was there, already watching, and she was crying. As soon as I came in she rushed to me, put her arms around me. "Your dad had to go back to New York last night," she said. "I can't get hold of him. I'm terrified something has happened to him. All the lines are down." The television showed the cloud of dust and debris that had fallen over New York.'

'Were you able to contact him?' I said. 'Was he all right?'

'No – the worst had happened. Much later we found out that he was in the North Tower on business. He was a software consultant. There was a particular program his firm had written for the client – that morning he was in the client's office on the 94th floor, where the plane went in.'

I felt something lurch inside me. 'Oh, Jaye, what can I say? You too.'

'Ben, I know something similar happened to you. I heard you talking to Bryan about it. Someone you knew was on one of the planes.'

'Her name was Lil, my girlfriend at the time. She was not on American 11, the plane that went into the North Tower. She was on the one they say hit the Pentagon.'

Jaye said: 'They never found my father's body. Not a trace of it, nothing they can even take a DNA sample from.'

'It's the same for me. Lil's body has never been found.'

Jaye's hand came across the tabletop and gripped mine.

'It's shit, isn't it?' she said. 'These people are lying to us. Why can't they simply tell the truth? If they didn't conspire, they fucked up. It's almost as bad to fuck something up, but not quite. Why won't they admit it?'

'Bryan told me he had someone involved too.'

'That was his son, Cliff. He was twenty-one, had gone on vacation in New York. The day before, September 10, he had taken the tourist elevator to the viewing platform at the top of the North Tower. Cliff met some people there, and changed his plans. He left New York City that evening without telling anyone, so his father assumed he was still in New York the next day. When he couldn't get hold of Cliff, Bryan told me he went through the worst hell he could imagine. But Cliff called him later – he had gone upstate and was staying with the people he had made friends with. So that was all right.

'It was because of Cliff that I met Bryan, which led to my job with him. I went to a 9/11 victims' counselling session in London. More than one hundred people who had family members killed turned up. Bryan was there, and so were several other people who had had similar traumatic false alarms. Until that evening I hadn't realized just how many ordinary people had been affected. These were people who lived in Britain, most of them in the London area. I thought how many thousands more of us there must be, all over the world, still in shock, still suffering.'

I wished I had known about such a meeting – it might have helped me too.

I said: 'You're planning to visit New York? Will this be the first time, since 2001?'

'It's my third trip,' Jaye said. 'I go to the area in Lower Manhattan where the towers were. I sometimes see some of the same people. I always go on the anniversary. The people look the same, unable to grieve, staring around, looking at the memorials, always seeming drained of emotion, emptied out. There's the skyscraper built as a replacement, of course. It's irrelevant to me, as it is for everyone who lost someone. Afterwards I go to talk to the laboratory where they are still trying to identify DNA traces. I feel informed but depressed. I come home and

try to live a normal life. This time I'm making the trip for my mother. She died last winter.'

To the hydro

I went home, caught up with emails and other routine work, had lunch, then went out to the car. I picked up Jaye in the town, and drove her the two or three miles along the island coast to Port Bannatyne.

As we were driving, I told her again what we were going to find at the old site, but she said she still wanted to see it. I parked the car close to where I had stopped with Lucinda, then we walked up to the access road. Almost as soon as we were out of the car the extra elevation gave us superb views across the village roofs towards the Kyles of Bhòid, the narrow inlet that runs between the northern part of the island and the Cowal peninsula. We both stood to admire the astonishing Scottish scenery, the mountains, the wide and turbulent sky.

We climbed over a broken gate to get into the grounds of the former hotel, avoiding the muddy puddle around the remains of the post, then walked erratically up the hillside, which was overgrown with rhododendrons, gorse and tufted grass. There was no trace at all of the former buildings. We headed for the tree line, surveyed the view down the hillside, across the pale water, the big and empty hills, the looming clouds.

'Bryan told me he came here to meet Tatarov,' Jaye said.

'Here? He met Tatarov on the island?'

'Didn't you know?'

I remembered back to the first meeting with Bryan Claremont – we were for some reason fencing about what we knew of Tatarov. I felt loyal to the old mathematician's request for confidentiality, also the warning he had given me. But there was additionally the 9/11 dimension, which at that stage did

not seem relevant to Claremont. Things were never quite what they seemed.

'I didn't know Bryan was so interested in the 9/11 attacks,' I said. 'He never said.'

'Did you tell him about your involvement?'

'No.'

'According to what Bryan told me, from the outset what he and Tatarov talked about was dominated by Tatarov's worries. He wouldn't meet Bryan in the hydro itself, but in one of the bars down there in the village.' The wind was stiffening, blustering up the slope, and some of Jaye's words were being lost. She went on: 'He told Bryan that only when he arrived at the hydro had he realized that it was an undercover outfit. He thought they were CIA and that he had walked into a trap. He feared he was going to be sent back to Russia, or employed in espionage somehow. One of the women had taken him aside on the first day and shown him a printed extract from the USA PATRIOT Act. She wanted him to sign his name on the page, which he did, but he wrote in Cyrillic and used his patronymic, Alexeyevich. He thought they wouldn't realize what he had done, that it would give him something to deny later, but they were on to that. You must have seen him not long afterwards. Did you get any sense from him of what was going on?'

'I came here to the hydro to prepare an interview for a mathematics magazine published for schools,' I said. 'Nothing was said about Bryan Claremont – anyway Bryan's name wouldn't have meant anything to me then. The whole experience was bizarre. The hydro had been taken over by the American people Tatarov was with, but once I was in the building I didn't pay attention to the others. I couldn't gain any idea of what they were doing. I wasn't here for long – two or three hours, perhaps. I recorded enough with Tatarov to be able to write the essay I had been commissioned to produce. Then I left.'

We had both started moving away from the trees, down the overgrown hill towards the village. It was just a piece of open ground, nothing resonating there of its past. We stumbled over roots, strode across the traces of old pathways where the ground was level for a short distance, circled around the prickly gorse.

I helped Jaye over the broken gate, then she held out her hand to steady me. The puddle we had been able to step over on the way up was more difficult to avoid from this direction. We walked down towards the car, as the rain started up again.

Four victims of 9/11

I took Jaye to the house because I wanted Jeanne to meet her. I had after all spent a large part of the day with her. The children were still at school, and Jeanne or I would have to go to meet them, but there was still time for introductions and a drink.

We sat in our living room, the kids' toys pushed back against the wall and out of the way. The large bay window looked out across the shallows of the firth and the entrance to the harbour, but the rain was streaming down the window panes, making the view indistinct. Lucinda brought in tea for me and herself, coffee for Jaye and Jeanne. One of the ferries was tied up at the quay, a thin, almost indiscernible wisp of dark smoke rising from the twin stacks. The rain was drifting now, a fine, drenching mist. The hills across the bay were hidden. No other boats were in sight.

I told Jeanne and Lucinda that I had met Jaye several years ago, that she worked in the production office with Bryan Claremont, that she had wanted to visit the hydro again. We talked about that, the disappearance of the old place, what they had managed to film when on location there.

'You know, I've never actually seen the film,' Jeanne said. 'Do we still have a copy?'

'I think the DVD is on the shelf behind you,' I said. 'We

could watch it this evening, if you like. I've only ever watched it once.'

'I thought you hated it.'

'He still does,' Jaye said.

'No – hate's not right,' I said. 'I didn't like working with Claremont on the screenplay. Jaye wasn't much of a help, but we've made our peace over that. It was a long time ago. It wasn't a good experience.'

'I wasn't there to help you,' Jaye said.

'I know, I know. You and Bryan finished the film, and there were a few good reviews.'

'What do you think of the film, Jaye?'

'I don't think it's a failure. I know Ben thinks that – but it's not as good as it could have been.'

'The script was terrible,' I said. 'I blame no one but myself for that.'

'We never got it right, that's all.'

Jaye turned away to glance through the window. Lucinda was sitting in the large armchair in the bay. Even though the sky was darkening with the imminence of heavier rain her features were made indistinct by the daylight from the window behind her, but I could see she was staring intently at Jaye. Her face was fixed, her eyes unwavering.

She said not a word while we chatted innocuously about working with Bryan Claremont and his band of ever-changing financial backers. I said nothing about Tatarov. I had nothing to say about the hydro. 9/11 was a closed subject around Lucinda. I felt they were all difficult subjects, for varying reasons. I glanced at my watch, noting that the boys would have to be collected from school in about thirty minutes' time. The daily deadline, the likeable chore.

Then Jaye mentioned her upcoming visit to the USA, saying that her father had died in the World Trade Center. I saw Jeanne

look towards Lucinda, but her mother said nothing. Jaye explained what she was doing now, working for herself, finishing off some of the industrial videos she had been producing for the company before they let her go. She pointed out what she saw as a paradox, that they were paying her more now as a freelance than they had paid her while she was on the payroll.

Lucinda continued to stare at her.

If Jaye was at all aware of this long regard she did not appear to react to it. She too glanced at her watch a couple of times, because I had mentioned to her before we went in that we had to collect the boys. The weather outside in the firth was deepening. The wind was up.

Lucinda said to Jaye abruptly: 'Do you have to be somewhere else? You seem anxious to leave.'

'No – I'm sorry. It's just that I don't want to overstay.'

'How did your father die, Jaye?'

'I wish I hadn't mentioned that. It was years ago.'

'Ben's obsessed with the World Trade Center. Is that because of you?'

'No. I –'

Jeanne stood up, making a pretence of collecting the cups we had been using. 'Mum. That's enough.'

'No – I want to know. You were the one on the plane that crashed. That's right, isn't it?'

'I'll collect the kids from school,' Jeanne said. She looked towards the window. Outside, the rain was starting to fall heavily. 'I'll take the car. Lucinda, why don't you come with me? And Jaye, you can meet the children when I bring them back.'

'Jaye?' Lucinda said, leaning forward suddenly in her chair. 'Why do you call yourself that?'

'Well, my real name, the one my parents gave me –'

'It's Lil, isn't it? Or Liz? I can never remember exactly. Benjamin, which is it? Is this Lilian? We went to the hydro, you

know. I saw you there.' Her hands were gripping themselves into tight little fists. 'I know Benjamin says it wasn't you, but I know what I see. You've mussed your hair and you've put on weight, but your name was Lil then.'

Jaye looked uncomprehending, as well she might. Jeanne, heading for the door, stopped in her tracks. She looked across the room at Lucinda, then at me. I stared back at her. Everything in that moment seemed about to change, or to change back. Our plans for Lucinda were suddenly in abeyance. Nothing was clear any more about what should we do about her, what we could do.

The rain swept loudly against the window, like gravel being thrown from above. Outside, the ferry switched on its upper deck lights, signalling it was about to cast off from the berth. The brilliant yellow beams glinted on the rainy windows. Our window frame was briefly shadowed on the wall, blurred by the weather.

Another shadow, incomprehensible, insoluble, too huge to accept as real, filled all four of our lives, dominating the harmless room where the boys often played. We were all in the dark, in the shadow of 9/11, victims, or remnants of victims, losers of our lovers, relatives, inadvertent characters in the story that insidiously weaved through and around our lives, untrue, unreliable, irrational, and as yet unfinished.

TWELVE
then: 2001–2006

The silence

I was forced to remain in the USA during the hectic, emotional, frightening days that followed the events of 9/11. For the first twenty-four hours I tried calling Lil's mobile phone at regular intervals, a depressing repetition, but soon realized it was hopeless and I did not continue with it after the first day. Three long, uncomfortable and frustrating days of delay dragged by in Columbus, Ohio, but finally I was able to book an internal flight to Newark, and from there I returned to New York.

I went directly to Lil's apartment building but her door was closed and locked. The hall staff said they had not seen her since before the World Trade Center was attacked. Her mail and newspapers were building up in her hallway mail box.

New York City was slowly returning to something like normal, although a huge tract of Lower Manhattan was closed to all except rescue and recovery teams. Trucks were moving through the zone of the collapsed buildings, carrying away the thousands of tonnes of rubble, dust, and bent and broken steel. Every night, on every TV news channel, there were pictures of the recovery activities. Huge cranes and tractors had been brought in to pull away the remains of the buildings. Several reports revealed the almost unbelievable news that the rubble

was still on fire, that there were vast pools of molten steel down below. Water was being pumped in, with little apparent effect. Smoke and steam swirled around the site, and all the workers were in heavy protective gear. I saw a film of one of the immense steel beams being lifted out of the tangle of wreckage, and as it swung in the air it was obvious that several yards of one end of it were glowing cherry-red. Others were twisted and bent grotesquely — several were riddled with large holes, like cheese.

I had found a hotel room in midtown. Using it as a base I did what I could to establish every fact about Lil: who might have received calls or texts from her before she went to Washington, who had seen her, what if any messages had she left. No one appeared to know any more than I did. I enquired about Martin Viklund — few of her New York friends had met him, and the two who had seen him occasionally said they barely knew him, and had no idea where he might be. They all knew he worked for the Defense Department. I visited the publisher Lil worked for and discovered much the same, with the unexpected additional fact that the corporation had no idea she was married, and had her registered as a single woman, name of Viklund. I contacted Lil's family in Michigan and spoke on the phone to her sister Alison, who was Lil's twin. Distraught at the news of Lil's likely fate, she said the whole family was devastated, but that she would be flying to New York the following week to sort out Lil's belongings. The family knew little more than I did, and had also been trying to contact Martin Viklund. His absence from Lil's life, according to the family, now and in the past, was a matter of focused bitterness. A staff member at his office in the Pentagon had merely noted Alison's call, and said the message would be passed to Mr Viklund directly.

Everyone in New York I spoke to about Lil, her colleagues at the office, the staff at her gym, the people who ran the

neighbourhood independent movie house, even the two people who worked in the coffee kiosk where Lil called every morning when she went to the office, seemed shell-shocked in general by the attacks on the twin towers, but stunned by the realization that Lil had been one of the victims. Most of them were uncertain on which plane she might have been.

While I was still in New York the newspapers published the passenger manifests from all four lost aircraft, and it was from these that I discovered that her name did not appear. It was another mystery to add to all the others. Dozens of bodies were still undiscovered, and so far few of the ones they had found could be positively identified.

I tried several times to contact Martin Viklund through the Defense Department. No success.

It was during this time that stories started emerging about people who had made desperate cellphone calls to their families or loved ones. Most of these calls were made by people who had been inside the twin towers as the planes went in. Some of them were from people who had somehow managed to escape. On the day, mobile communications became increasingly difficult and erratic, because the cell networks around New York were routed through the mast mounted on the top of the North Tower. Coverage continued for a while, but after the tower collapsed it was more or less impossible to make a call.

The entire cellphone network across a large part of the USA was soon jammed by people trying to contact their families, seeking or giving reassurance, or reporting fears or known tragedy.

The calls were mostly logged by the network providers, and in due course it became possible to identify which calls might have been made by people before they fell victim. Some calls had been recorded, for a variety of reasons, and a handful of them were reported in the press, presumably after the families

had given permission. They contained tragic similarities, a terrible sameness of panic, fear, forced calm, outbursts of love and empty reassurance. I could barely bring myself to read them.

Nagging at me was an unanswerable question: why had Lil not tried to call me?

But calls were made

I could not afford to stay indefinitely in the US, and after four days I flew back to London. I was haunted by what had happened in Washington and New York, and my helpless closeness to it. I was bereft of Lil's love and companionship, I was missing her, blaming myself for not being with her when it mattered, wishing I had not been impatient with her in the hours before she boarded American 77, thinking back obsessively over stupid things I might have said to her, or insensitivity about her feelings on some small matter. These are the memories that maddeningly return to you when you are unable to say goodbye. Above all I was yearning to hear from her somehow, or best of all discover that she had, against all logic, survived.

None of these jagged feelings could be resolved. I was in a vacuum of helpless emotions – sad, angry, confused, puzzled, determined to solve the mystery, above all convinced that she was the victim of a terrorist plot against the West in general and the USA in particular.

Far away, in Asia, American vengeance on Afghanistan was being carried out. The so-called war on terror had been declared by President Bush within a week of 9/11. Military action against the Taliban in Afghanistan began in the first week of October.

This mobilization occurred with astonishing, unprecedented speed. Within less than four weeks of 9/11 a major retaliatory attack was launched against a landlocked, mountainous country on the far side of the world. How did that happen so quickly?

Professional observers, journalists and defence analysts in the UK and Europe noted that a complex military operation on this scale would normally require several weeks or even months to plan and organize.

It was as if the action, described as a reaction to unprovoked antagonism, had in fact been in an advanced stage of planning before 9/11.

I wanted none of that. I simply cared about Lil.

The puzzle of why she had not contacted me continued. An increasing number of calls from passengers trapped in the doomed aircraft were becoming known.

I thought hard about Lil, and what she might have done when she realized the seriousness of the situation she was in. She was an early adopter of cellphones and had been using them regularly for five years. She normally carried at least two: one for business, the other for personal calls. There was the possibility there was a third, because once I received a call from her from a number I did not recognize. I never asked her about it. At the time, mobile phones were neither lightweight nor compact. I assumed that on the day of the attacks she would have been carrying both phones, but at the very least she would have had her personal one with her.

This was the one I assumed she used for the brief text messages she sent me before she boarded the plane. At the time I had not noticed which handset she used, because receiving calls or texts from her was routine and normal. When I thought to check the number, though, I discovered she had been using the business line.

Lil would normally make about a dozen calls a day, usually a brief exchange, a contact arrangement, a meeting, a question that needed an answer. When I was with her in New York she called me at least five times a day – when I was in the UK and she was in New York the calls were less frequent but lasted longer.

At that time, the sending of text messages was not nearly as popular or universal as it later became – most texts had to be paid for, and there was a limitation on how many you could send. Lil said she usually preferred to speak.

She often used her mobile when flying, or tried to. I was uncomfortable with that, knowing that the airlines explicitly forbade their use during a flight. The one time I challenged her about it Lil shrugged it off. She said cabin crew sometimes told her to switch off, but she was certain there was no risk to the aircraft's electronics.

She thought this because Martin, her husband, had told her always to use her business phone, which he had provided. This, he said, connected to a secure network, one that was used by the government and was safe to use when flying. She told me this might or might not be true, but to her it was irrelevant. She found it almost impossible to connect with a network, any network, once the aircraft had taken off and was climbing. Neither of her handsets worked at normal flying altitudes. She did call me from some of her journeys, but always while the aircraft was on the ground, or taxiing.

One thing I was certain of: she would have tried to make contact with me.

But on the day I received no calls from her. At first this was nothing to worry about – we were intending to meet later that day in Los Angeles and we were both taking long flights. After my plane landed in Columbus, I made repeated failed attempts to get through to her.

Rational evidence quickly emerged that several other calls had in fact been made from the doomed aircraft, at least intermittently. Some of the passengers had managed to get through to their families.

Only a few such calls were logged from the plane Lil was said to have boarded but there were more from the other hijacked

aircraft. Notably on United 93. This was the aircraft that crashed in Shanksville – passengers and crew made nearly forty calls before the flight catastrophically ended. Some of these were recorded by the network providers, or the airline dispatcher who took the call, but I did not listen to them when some were played on television broadcasts. They were more depressing and disturbing than anything I had ever heard before. I hated the thought that the voices belonged to real people who knew they were about to die, and who did in fact actually die a short time later.

But because those calls had come through I wondered anew if Lil had tried to talk with me.

It then emerged that six mobile phone calls had been made successfully from American 77, while still in flight. Four of these could not be identified: both the caller and the recipient were unknown, but there were two other conversations which were fully logged. The first was from one of the flight attendants to her parents – the other call, a few minutes later, was widely reported in the media. It was eventually to have a huge influence on the way the hijack was understood.

This was a call made by a passenger well known on American television as a political pundit. She called her husband as the hijack violence started. Her husband was himself a fairly prominent public figure: he was a senior attorney in the Department of Justice, working for the administration. After the attacks he gave several televised interviews. He said his wife had described how the entire crew, including the pilots, had been herded by the hijackers to the back of the passenger cabin. (I only found out later that according to the flight data recorder this was the plane on which the cockpit door had never been opened during the flight.) The hijackers, the woman told her husband, were armed with what he described to the media as 'cardboard cutters', then later as 'box cutters'.

The frightening details aside, I was interested to learn that all six of these calls were made from cellphones, a fact verified by the FBI. Was it possible that one of the four unidentified calls had been made by Lil?

Two of the calls from other hijacked aircraft that morning were positively identified as from cellphones, by the family members who received them. They gave evidence to the FBI investigators, stating emphatically that when they received the calls they recognized the familiar name and number displayed on the screen.

The FBI circulated the news.

Calls from nowhere

Whether or not Lil had tried to call me was a personal matter, a disappointment, something that added to the miserable compulsion that I had somehow let her down. I did not want to dwell too long on the other calls that had been made. My loss seemed a small problem, a tiny part of the larger tragedy.

As the weeks and months went by, though, I began to hear and read informed comment about the technical limitations on phone calls from a plane flying at cruising altitude. By this time, recorded radar traces from ground stations and Air Traffic Control had been logged for the four aircraft. The route of each one was exactly known, as well as the speed and altitude at which it had been flying.

The passenger calls had by this time become part of the vernacular history of 9/11. The information about box cutters used as weapons on American 77, known only from the interviews given by the victim's husband, had an impact on passengers flying everywhere in the world. Based purely on hearsay – this loosely described event, unsupported by any evidence – all passengers were afterwards banned by airport security from carrying sharp-edged instruments, no matter how small.

There was a growing argument about the limitations of mobile phones. It was said by engineers that it was impossible for any of the calls to have been made. The planes were flying too high and too fast to allow anything more than a few seconds of contact, and then the signal would have been of poor quality and likely to break up.

The science was clear. Once a plane attained an altitude of more than about eight thousand feet it was above the range of the cellular network. The masts which relayed calls and other communications were not designed to send or receive signals vertically. They were horizontally aligned towards each other. Once the plane was above about ten thousand feet it was shown that a connection was almost impossible.

Because most commercial jetliners, including the ones hijacked on 9/11, cruised at heights of between thirty-five and forty thousand feet, they were emphatically out of range.

In 2003, two years after the attacks, the FBI, apparently having taken note of the scientific argument, released a revised assessment of the phone calls alleged to have come from the aircraft. All but a couple of the calls, they now declared, were made from airphones – or to give them their correct name, GTE Airfones.

I thought I should try to find the facts, so I made enquiries. I learned that Airfones were commonly installed on US-operated jets at the end of the 1990s. They were mounted in the back of the seat facing each passenger. I had myself seen these handsets on internal flights in the past, but I had never actually used them. They were expensive, and anyway I had no need of one.

The FBI never admitted that their earlier information was wrong – their revised assessment was announced as incontrovertibly as it had been before. Almost no one had used a mobile phone they now said. All calls had been made from Airfones.

Two years had passed and I was managing to adjust to the shock of Lil's death. The FBI revelation was an unwelcome reminder of the confusion around the attacks. Once again I could not help but wonder if one of those unidentified calls from American 77 was from Lil, intended for me. The FBI's retraction about cellphones reinforced the steady feeling of unease that what the authorities told us might be neither the whole story, nor indeed the whole truth.

FBI agents had already investigated the calls, interviewed the family members who received them, published a definitive account. The science was the same then as it was later. Why did they change the story?

I could not forget the ordinary people who had said they had spoken to their loved ones, knowing it was them, calling on their usual phones. The cellphone identity had been flagged up. Surely that was beyond question? Back then the FBI had interviewed everyone, released detailed accounts of what was said. They were in no doubt then about how the calls were made.

Nor were they in doubt now. Apart from two accepted mobile phone calls, made from United 93 at low altitude in the last desperate moments of the flight, all calls from the stricken aircraft were on Airfones.

Then the American Airlines corporation intervened. They said that before year 2000 most of their civil fleet had indeed been equipped with seat-back Airfones, but by the beginning of 2001 the devices had either been disabled or removed altogether. By September 2001, no onboard Airfones were available on American flights. Several AA cabin crew members confirmed this.

Neither passengers nor crew could have called from the AA planes. Cellphones would not work, Airfones were not available.

Jeanne

It was impossible trying to make sense of what the US author-
ities were saying. Nothing was consistent with anything else.
As soon as they tried to explain one matter, half a dozen more
anomalies appeared. I attempted once again to put it all out of
my mind and concentrate on my work.

In 2005 I began writing occasionally for an online technology
newsletter in London. I soon noticed a young Scottish woman
working in the art department, and got to know her – this was
Jeanne. We became friends, started dating, and within a few
weeks we were meeting regularly. Early in 2006 we moved
together into a small apartment in west London.

The nightmare of 9/11, the death of Lil, the maze of incon-
sistency put out by US officials, all this faded into the past. For
the first few months of our time together I barely mentioned Lil
to Jeanne, only that there was a girlfriend in the past who had
died. Then one day Jeanne noticed the little disc of jet lignite
that I still carried on my key ring, took the keys from me and
peered closely at the design: the hound, the ruined abbey, the
moon.

'Do I detect a sentimental past?' she said.

'An old girlfriend,' I said. 'I knew her years before you and I
met. Have I ever mentioned Lil?'

'Is she the one who died?'

'Yes – in fact she was killed, murdered.'

I began to describe Lil and what had happened to her, and
the way I had never been certain, still was not certain beyond
any doubt, that she was dead.

Jeanne listened in silence, then merely said: 'I knew there
was someone. You only ever mentioned someone you knew
who had died, but I always knew it was this one, that she was
special.'

'Lil was special to me,' I said. 'But she's a long way in the past.'

'I know that too.'

'Lil mattered a lot to me. I was in love with her.'

'I told you about Wolf.'

Wolfgang Franck was the German teacher Jeanne had lived with in Berlin for more than four years.

'Of course,' I said.

'It's not dissimilar. Wolf was someone I never really got over. I was madly in love with him for years, but it came to an end.'

'You never told me what happened,' I said. 'He didn't die too, did he?'

'No. For me, he might as well have died. He ran off with another woman, six years younger than me, cut me off, never explained, never tried to justify himself, never said sorry. He sent a friend round with a van to collect his stuff from our apartment. I was devastated. I was demoralized and wretched for months.'

'And deep down part of you wants to see him again?'

She briefly turned her face towards me. She was not smiling. 'Not exactly. I'll never forget him, but I'd turn my back on him and walk away if I ever saw him again.'

'Not likely, is it?'

'I can't imagine how. He's still in Germany. His new girl-friend left him a few months after he left me. He was a teacher, and so was she. He's still teaching, as far as I know. They might even still be teaching in the same school for all I care. I've no idea if he found anyone else.'

She had never told me any of this before. 'I didn't know that,' I said to her.

'Well, I realized there must be someone like that in your past. You say her name was Lil, Lilian?'

'Yes.'

'And she died in one of those planes.'

'Almost certainly. It's having to use that word *almost* that hurts. There were so many lies told about the attacks that it's impossible to know the truth. I'm not sure at all. It was nearly five years ago. But really, Jeanne, I'm long over her.'

That short exchange with Jeanne reminded me not of Lil, the woman I had lost, but of the way in which I had lost her, the manner of her being taken from me, and the impossibility of discovering the truth about it. The mystery and frustration remained, the anger about the official lies and cover-up, the refusal of the authorities to release even the simplest of evidence that would answer many questions, the lack of certainty. I was not alone – I knew there were thousands of people who were in the same position as me, all over the world.

The circling feelings of loss and despair started up once more, making me resent whoever it was that was holding back the information, making me wonder, leaving me on the precipice of hope. None of the victims or their loved ones had done anything wrong – why were we being punished like this, and for so long?

The dark mood lasted for a few days, most of a week, but then once again it slowly subsided and I felt able to live again.

THIRTEEN

then: 2006

Suburban

It was my first visit to Edinburgh – in fact, not counting a holiday with my parents when I was twelve, it was the first time I had even been in Scotland. The taxi driver brought his car to a halt in a residential road in suburban Morningside, lined on both sides with grey and substantial-looking stone-built houses. He said something, but his accent was so thick I could not follow him. I paid him the amount on the meter, handed him another pound as a gratuity, then climbed out.

I could not see the house straight away. I was looking for number 46, but none of the gateposts had numbers and the doors were set back behind their gardens. House numbers, when displayed at all, were not easily read. I was still peering uncertainly at the doors when one of them opened. A woman looked towards me.

'Are you Mr Matson?' she called.

I walked back towards the gate of that house. 'I'm looking for Mrs Glenister's house,' I said.

'Aye, this is the right one. She's waiting for you now.'

I followed her into the house, putting down my bag in the hall. The woman spoke through a doorway into a room: 'I'll be leaving you now, Lucinda. I'll call you next week.'

''Bye now, Diana.'

The woman, Diana, acknowledged me and then went past in the hallway and let herself out of the house. Jeanne's mother, Lucinda, came to meet me. We shook hands formally, as if meeting for the first time. In fact, Jeanne and I had dined with Lucinda in an expensive restaurant over a riverside pub in Chiswick about four weeks earlier, when she was on a visit to London. That evening I had felt I was on the margins of the occasion, sitting silently and apparently irrelevantly, listening with a social smile on my face as Jeanne and her mother talked intently to each other. Past friends, occasions, people they were interested in, a few polite questions to me. I had observed that they spoke alike: they had the same soft, Scottish accent, clearly enunciated and slow. I had never really noticed this in Jeanne's speech until that evening.

'Thank you for letting me stay with you, Mrs Glenister,' I said. 'I hope it will not be a nuisance for you.'

'Of course not! Jeanne told me it will be for only two or three nights. And please call me Lucinda. Should I call you Ben, or Benjamin?'

'I prefer Ben,' I said.

Making this kind of small talk we went into her spacious and tastefully furnished sitting room, where I waited alone while she was in the kitchen, running water into a kettle, getting out some cups and saucers, asking about sugar, and so on. I couldn't help noticing that Lucinda was obviously an habitual reader, with several large, glass-fronted bookcases crammed with both hardcover books and paperbacks. I peered at the titles. I glimpsed Scottish history, topography, art, folk music and natural history, European politics, craft books, autobiographies of people I had only barely heard of, serious fiction in hardcover and several paperback best-sellers with creased spines. One shelf contained a row of legal books – there were

multiple copies of two thick law titles by a writer called D. L. Glenister. Could the 'L' be Lucinda? I was about to take one down to have a look when I heard Lucinda pouring water from a kettle. I would ask her later. A large pile of magazines lay on a capacious coffee table. Another set of shelves behind the television was crammed with the plastic cases of DVDs, most of them two deep on the shelves, others piled on top of each other. I tilted my head to read the titles – they were familiar films from the last five or ten years. Jeanne and I had our own copies of many of them.

Lucinda returned, set out the cups, and enquired about my journey up from London. It had taken me all day to reach her. I told her about my friend giving me a lift in his car as far as York, a hurried lunch in a roadside restaurant, a long wait in York for the train to Edinburgh, then the ride through the north-east of England, the Scottish Borders. I had nothing much of originality to add to this account, but Lucinda listened with apparent interest.

Later she showed me to her guest bedroom. It was on the upper floor of the house, a long and narrow room under the pitch of the roof, two dormer windows facing the road outside. She told me the room had been her late husband's study – Jeanne had already told me her father had passed away. Similar houses to Lucinda's stood opposite. The sun was in the south-west, starting to cast long shadows across the roofs and the curve of the street, the multitude of parked cars.

After I had taken a shower and put on a clean shirt she produced a meal: a creamy chicken korma, with vegetables, rice and homemade chapati. While we ate, Lucinda told me a few stories about Jeanne's childhood, places she had travelled to with her husband, his long weeks away from home while working, the incidents of family life, all honest and worthwhile, touching to hear, not unusual.

I found Lucinda pleasant company. She had held a number of administrative jobs in the academic world, had travelled widely after Jeanne left home, to Germany several times to visit Jeanne in Berlin, but also to Russia, Australia, South America. She was currently on a short term admin contract with the Development & Alumni Department at Edinburgh University, only having to be in the office on alternate weeks. She was planning to take an extended vacation the following year, travelling to the USA and Canada.

I could not help speculating silently about her age. Jeanne often hinted that her mother was getting on a bit, had aged suddenly after the death of her husband, but to me Lucinda was a good-looking and fit woman, probably in her mid to late fifties. Jeanne herself was then in her mid thirties, and Lucinda had already mentioned that she and her husband were still young and recently married when Jeanne was born. There was a strong family resemblance between the two women.

She wanted to know how Jeanne and I had met, so I talked about that, and then she showed interest in how a webzine actually worked, and that led into a discussion of the internet. Social media at that time was still new, not yet a worldwide phenomenon, but Jeanne had spotted the potential early and was using it in her work.

It was getting late and I was tired after the long journey. I could not conceal it. Before I went up to the guest room I asked Lucinda if she would be able to drive me to the station in the morning.

'I can of course,' she said. 'But Jeanne said you were going to the Isle of Bute. Travelling to and fro for several days?'

'Yes I'm going to Bute. But probably not for as long as several days. There's someone I have to interview for a magazine. I've no idea how long that will take – I usually complete an

211

interview in a couple of hours, but if it goes over to the next day I'll find a cheap B&B.'

'It's a complicated journey by train,' Lucinda said.

'I can manage. There are regular trains from Glasgow, connecting with the Bute ferry.'

Lucinda pulled down a road atlas from the shelf behind her. 'Why don't you let me drive you to the island?'

'Thank you – but no. That would be kind of you, but it's a long drive.' I knew I sounded stiff and over-polite.

'It would take less than two hours to the ferry port from here. I enjoy driving, and I've never been across to Bute. This would be a chance for me to see the island. I can drop you off wherever you want to be, have a look around on my own –'

'No, Lucinda – I think I should go by train.'

'I won't hear of it.'

I argued half-heartedly for a couple more minutes, but I kept yawning and had no energy left to resist. I bade her goodnight and went up the stairs, knowing I should prefer the independence of going as planned on the train, but also thinking of the extra expenses I was running up that the magazine probably would not refund – it was a low-budget maths sheet, distributed to schools. I was going through a difficult patch financially. If Lucinda and I could share the cost of driving there –

I undressed, fell into the strange bed, slept deeply.

Car and boat

Lucinda came to the room and brought me a cup of tea as I was waking up. I then showered, put on fresh clothes and took my case downstairs, ready for the day. Lucinda was cooking me a solid Scottish breakfast, including haggis and potato scones.

The question of how I was to travel to and from Bute was apparently settled while I was asleep. She had already been out

and filled the car with fuel. We lingered over breakfast, but I was anxious to get started.

We drove away from the Edinburgh area on the motorway, an hour later we circuited Glasgow then followed the old main road alongside the River Clyde towards the coast of the firth. Lucinda was fast and effective behind the wheel, aggressive at speed but alert. She made me nervous at first but I soon realized she was a skilled driver and I began to relax. I was looking at the landscape we were passing through, a mix of post-industrial housing and vacant lots, large abandoned factory buildings, and high treeless hills.

'Who is it you are interviewing?' Lucinda asked as we drove past Port Glasgow, then towards Greenock.

'He's an American mathematician called Kyril Tatarov,' I said. 'He was born in Russia but emigrated to America when he was a child. I interviewed him about ten years ago, and I think he remembered that, because he put my name forward for this commission. I believe the whole thing was set up by him.'

'Are you a mathematician too?' Lucinda said.

'No – I can just about keep up, but I'm only a journalist. I specialize in science subjects, and maths sometimes comes into that.'

I described what I knew of Tatarov's work, his lifetime fascination with the Pèlerin Conjecture, the papers he had published, his colleagues, all fellow mathematicians competing with him but who held him in uncanny awe. They were doing their best to get a proof or a theorem completed before he did.

'He's in Scotland at the moment, on Bute,' I said. 'It's a new matter. Something about statistical control, the need for social norms and prediction of events. It's all connected somehow with the hijackings on 9/11.'

Lucinda made no reply, but she turned away from the road

and stared briefly but deliberately at me. Then she returned to her driving.

I let a few moments of silence follow – I was perplexed by her apparently negative reaction. Finally I said: 'I don't know if Jeanne has told you, but I was in America when the hijackings happened so I always take an interest in 9/11.'

'She said nothing to me. Were you affected by it?'

'No more than anyone else, at least directly. But I had a close friend who was killed.'

Again, Lucinda made no reply. I was sensing she did not want to talk about this, but already she had opened up the part of me I tried to keep closed. I began telling her how Lil and I had met, the way we had been attracted to each other. Then I told her about my being on a different flight on the day, Lil catching another plane, or maybe not that one because of her name missing from the passenger list, the doubts I had about the information given out, the misery, the lack of closure.

'You say this was before you met my daughter? What was this friend's name?'

'Lil – or Lilian.'

While I was blurting out my feelings we had reached the ferry terminal. Lucinda turned off the road and parked in one of the numbered boarding lanes. There was no sign of a ship, waiting at the ramp or even approaching the terminal. A dozen other cars and trucks stood in line ahead of us. When she turned off the car's engine I was aware of the new and sudden silence around us. A fresh wind was blowing, ferry staff in hi-vis jackets were standing near the entrance to the ramp, a prefabricated building containing the ticket office cast a shadow over the waiting area.

I realized that it was tactless to talk about a former girlfriend with my current partner's mother, and suddenly felt embarrassed. We sat in the car without saying anything.

214

A few minutes later a ship could be seen approaching, and Lucinda left the car and went to the ticket office. When she returned she tossed the printed cards on the dashboard. The ship was soon drawing up to the ramp, the helmet-visor bow already raised.

I said: 'I'm sorry. Lucinda. I've been bottling it up for years. The mystery about the way Lil died has become an obsession with me.'

'I don't mind listening to you,' she said.

The arriving vehicles were now driving off the ferry, and one by one the cars and trucks we were waiting behind moved forward to board the ship. Lucinda followed in line. When we had parked the car in the vehicle deck and locked up we climbed the stairs to the passenger saloon, queued for coffee and snacks, then found seats at a table overlooking the ship's bow.

The ship had already pulled back from the ramp, lowered the bow, turned about, and was now sailing at a steady rate into the firth. On all sides were hills and mountains, some steep and peaked, others rounded and low. To the south, the tall, jagged skyline of Arran dominated the firth and the entrance to the open sea. I stared ahead, hoping to pick out the first view of Bute, but the firth was wide and if the island lay ahead it was for the time being indistinguishable from the rest of the hilly terrain.

'Tell me more about Lilian,' Lucinda said. 'Were you married? Were you living together?'

'No, we weren't married,' I said. 'My feelings about her are no threat to Jeanne, I promise you. It was a few years ago. We probably would have married in the end, but there were problems with that, and then suddenly she was killed.'

'She still clearly matters to you.'

'She does. I wish she were not dead, I wish she had not been

215

killed. It was five years ago, and I'm more or less over her now. All I have is memories – but back then we did have plans. We had to make decisions because we lived thousands of miles apart and we wanted to be together. She was American, employed by a big corporate publisher in New York, but was able to work for part of the time in their London office. Probably not permanently, but for a few months each year.'

The ship was now passing across the widest part of the firth, the hills still clustering along the shore. Part of the town of Rothesay was in view a long way ahead. Lucinda and I were opposite each other at the table in the passenger saloon, holding our insulated styrofoam cups of coffee. I felt again a frisson of embarrassment for having opened up to this woman I hardly knew. And she was Jeanne's mother. I had said little of this to Jeanne.

'These problems you mentioned – was she married to someone else, Benjamin?'

Her directness startled me. 'Yes – but she and her husband were separated.' The urge to talk was rising again. 'There was something dark I could never fathom. It was not on the surface, I never let it come between us. Sometimes her mood would suddenly change, or she would say she needed time alone without me, or she would announce at short notice that she had to go on a publicity tour with one of the publisher's authors. At times like that I would glimpse her the way I had first seen her: sharp, slick, spouting the lines, sounding like a corporate manager. I knew by then it was a façade, a role she played, but I didn't like her playing it against me. With time of course I knew her better and better, but this ability to duck out of sight behind the shadows of her job never quite left her. We were together for about eighteen months, and ninety-nine per cent of the time we were happy. Eventually I came to believe there must be some unresolved problem, some dispute, between her and her

husband. She wouldn't tell me what it was, and I couldn't work it out. He was a senior official in Washington. He worked at the Defense Department. For all that she said about the marriage being over, they stayed married all the time I was with her. He had a hold on her and I didn't like it.'

Lucinda had been staring intently at me, but then she glanced away, through the ship's window, across the sea.

'Do you know anything about Lilian's husband?' she said. 'What he did for the government? Did you ever meet him?'

'Not until after she died.'

'My late husband was involved with the Defense Department, just before he died. He was summoned to a meeting in Washington – I never really found out why, although I had my suspicions. He often worked in Washington, but mostly to visit the Justice Department. He was a lawyer.'

'Yes,' I said, remembering seeing the legal tomes in her book-case. 'I saw the name D. L. Glenister on some of your books at home. Was that your husband?'

'He was called Dougal, but published under his initials, D. L. He was recognized as an authority in his field. He had the job of negotiating insurance losses on the Pentagon after it was damaged.'

'You mean after 9/11?' Lucinda made no answer, and continued to warm both her hands with the cup of coffee, staring down at it. 'So your husband worked in insurance?' I said.

'Mercantile law. He worked for a Lloyd's syndicate, but he was only involved in the law.'

She shook her head and smiled distantly, then turned away to look out of the saloon windows. I took it to mean she did not want to say anything more about her husband, but of course I was fascinated by the news that he had been involved in the 9/11 aftermath. I wanted to ask her about his work on the Pentagon damage, but did not.

217

After Lucinda's high-speed drive across the central belt of Scotland the saloon of the ferry was calm and calming – I was constantly aware of the beautiful scenery outside, greens and browns and patches of pale purple on the steep sides of the hills, slipping by on one side of us, reflecting upside-down on the smooth surface of the firth. Ahead was part of the Isle of Bute, houses and tenements crusting the shoreline. The island marked an escape from the tense world of my past. I no longer wanted to be defined by Lil's death, although I accepted that the complex feelings about her must still be churning away inside me.

The boat slowed as we approached Rothesay harbour, and a recorded announcement urged drivers and their passengers to go down to the car deck and return to their vehicles as soon as possible.

Tatarov displeased

We ate what I had intended should be a brief lunch in a sea-front pub in the town, but Lucinda ordered a bottle of red wine. She drank most of it herself, but made me drink more than normally I would before conducting an interview. I felt annoyed with her at first, because of this. But I was also intrigued by her behaviour, which I felt was becoming familiar, perhaps unnervingly familiar. I enjoyed being with her: she had a lively mind and an open laugh and she was fun to be with. She talked amusingly about her dead husband, not because he was dead but because of the life together they had enjoyed. She told me some more affecting stories about Jeanne as a small child, also about the sense of freedom she and Dougal had suddenly relished when Jeanne left university and found her first job in London. When she later moved to Berlin they had seen it as an opportunity to spend time in Germany.

Lucinda said she was never lonely. She had friends, and what

she called her special friends. Alarmingly, she pressed her hand against mine as she said this, then several times more in a way that I found compromising. I was beginning to wish I had not told her so much about my time with Lil, or expressed my feelings so openly. With hindsight, I realized it might have seemed like a opening of intimacy. It felt like a betrayal of Jeanne.

When Lucinda was briefly away from the table I contacted Tatarov by mobile phone. He picked up after a delay, sounding displeased. He said he had been expecting me that morning, but it was now too late in the day and anyway he was engaged in something. Tomorrow would have to do. He hung up before I could reply.

After Lucinda returned I told her this and she promptly ordered another bottle of wine.

The afternoon went by, with a familiar careless feeling that everything was slightly out of focus. As evening began we went for a walk along the sweeping curve of Rothesay sea front, rather erratically at first, gradually regaining steadiness as we breathed the clean air of the firth. Seabirds circled above us and long clumps of brown weed stirred in the shallow waves. I soaked up the serene mood of the island from the dark of the surrounding hills. The old buildings of the town, grey and rust-coloured stone-built tenements, plus many white and pastel painted Victorian villas, clustered along the road that followed the edge of the sea. It was in this pacific state of mind that I decided the Isle of Bute might one day be a place to make a permanent home. Lucinda held my arm affectionately, pulling me against her side. What was going on?

A ferry approached the harbour, gliding in on the smooth evening waters. I had been delaying thoughts of driving back to Edinburgh because of the amount of wine we had both consumed, but Lucinda appeared to have sobered up enough to drive. At least, I hoped so. I indicated the ship.

'Maybe we should drive back to your house,' I said. 'I need to be here early tomorrow. I don't want to miss another appointment.'

'There's no going to Edinburgh tonight,' Lucinda said. 'It's too far, and that's the last ferry of the day. We'll find a hotel for the night. I'll stand you the cost of the room.'

'I don't think that would be right –'

'And what's the alternative?' She squeezed my hand again. 'We can't sleep in the car – or maybe you would like to?'

She was already moving to cross the road, away from the promenade to where there were several hotels. I followed, concerned by this. I did not want to guess or imagine what Lucinda might have in mind, but I was too nervous to ask her. The first two hotels or guest houses we passed had *No Vacancies* signs hanging by the door, but the third, an imposing edifice called the Queen Victoria, had rooms to spare. To my relief Lucinda demanded from the receptionist two single rooms, with dinner that night and breakfast in the morning. When the receptionist asked if the rooms were for only one night I interceded with an emphatic Yes.

As soon as I was in my own room I called Jeanne's mobile, and told her what was happening.

'She's harmless, Ben,' she said straight away, laughing when I told her about the situation that seemed to be developing. 'She's always like that with men. She's an outrageous flirt, she's impulsive, she shows off, she wants to impress, she gets pretty emotional sometimes. Don't let her drink too much.'

'We already drank two bottles of Mâcon Rouge,' I said.

'She'll want another with dinner. Just keep your distance, and come back home as soon as you can.'

Jeanne and I chatted for a few more minutes, mostly because I started to describe the island to her enthusiastically, but Lucinda rapped on my door and said she was going down to the

bar. I joined her there a few minutes later. The truth was that whether or not she was the mother of my current girlfriend, and irrespective of the fact that she was nearly twenty years older than me, I found her company enjoyable, if somewhat unpredictable. I resolved to keep my distance, and did.

To the hydro

Tatarov answered my call on the fourth attempt.

'Come here now,' he said. 'You need the West wing. There are signs. Stay away from the other people you will see here, but one of them will meet you at the door. Be extremely careful what you say.'

'To the guy at the door, or anyone else?' I said, but Tatarov ended the call.

Lucinda was determined to take her car and start exploring the island, so she had made me call Tatarov as early as possible. She had acquired a map from hotel reception. We were still at the breakfast table, finishing our coffees. She spread the map on the table to show me where she planned to be and where everything was in relation to the hydro. The hydro, I noticed, was not marked on the map.

Twenty minutes later we were on the shore road in Port Bannatyne, close to the access drive to the hydro. After Lucinda had driven away I tried Tatarov's number again, but he was not answering. I headed on up the hill.

USA in Scotland

Long ago, Lil had shown me a blurred reproduction of a picture postcard of the hydro hotel, but it did not prepare me for the reality. The long, turreted building came into sight as soon as we were past the roadside houses – maybe in its heyday the hydro hotel had seemed an impressive pile for the moneyed classes, but to my eyes now it looked old, dilapidated, long

past its best. The gates were still in use – one was bolted into the ground, while the other had a simple latch. An American flag was depicted on a brass plate, with the familiar slogan: *E pluribus unum*.

Another sign said: *All visitors report to Border Post*. This indicated a path, one that had recently had its surface patched with tarmac filler, and been cleared of weeds. I walked on.

The border post was a recently constructed temporary building, placed across the footpath about halfway between the main gate and the building itself, with an open passage allowing access. A large Stars and Stripes flew limply from a flagpole. A US Marine in full uniform waited in the shadows, and as soon as I appeared he stepped out to intercept me.

'You have business here, sir?' he said.

'I have an appointment to see Professor Tatarov.'

The marine had a clipboard with names on it, which he checked slowly. I could see Tatarov's name upside-down even from where I was standing, but the marine read slowly through the list of names.

'Tatarov – yes, that's in order. You need to proceed to the main building, but visitors must wear this whenever moving around outside the building. This is a requirement of federal law.' He handed me a bright yellow plastic hard hat, and an identifying badge on a lanyard. This had a tiny reproduction of the US flag, and the word *Visitor*. I put on both objects.

'Are you a US citizen, sir?'

'No, I'm not.'

'Are you carrying a passport, or a visa issued by the State Department?'

'I'm British,' I said. 'A UK citizen.'

'Do you have any other form of identification? You will need to show it at the next checkpoint.'

'I have a UK driving licence,' I said.

'Sir, if you call at this establishment again, kindly clear visa requirements before attending, but we can allow a twenty-four-hour dispensation for British citizens. Your driver's licence will be sufficient. Welcome to the USA, sir.'

He stepped back and swung open the large door at the far end of the passage. I walked on through, continued towards the building. The hill, the trees, the damp and overgrown grasses, the wide view across the Kyles of Bute, all looked distinctly Scottish to me, but I was feeling bemused and passive.

I did not have much further to walk. Within about twenty more yards I came to a newly metalled track. Here the foliage had been cut back on both sides and the grasses mown down to lawn neatness. Large stones bordering the grass area were painted white. I climbed some steps and walked along a pathway against the side of the building. I noticed that this area of the old building must have been recently renovated, because the stone walls were clean and free of mosses and lichen, and the mortar between the blocks had been repointed. All the woodwork I saw was newly painted. The windows were clean and lights were on inside.

The pathway ended at a door. There was no bell-push or any other way of registering my presence. I hammered on the door with my fist. No response. I waited for another minute, then banged a second time. A young man appeared, visible through the thick glass window in the upper part of the door. He was tall and well muscled, with short hair combed up in a quiff. He was wearing a white, short-sleeved shirt, with several pens or gadgets clipped in his breast pocket.

I could see he was speaking to me, gesturing at something, but I could not hear a word. He repeated it, then held up a badge similar to the one just given to me at the border post. He gestured again, holding the badge upright and forward. I saw a black mica square inlaid in the wood, the same shape and size

as the badge, so I touched the badge against it. At once there was a mechanical noise and the door swung free. I went inside.

The young man raised his hands to halt me. He was holding a tablet computer.

'What's your name, please, sir?'

'I'm Benjamin Matson, and —'

'May I enquire about your business, Mr Matson?'

'I'm here to interview Professor Kyril Tatarov.'

'Let me see your ID.'

I found my licence and handed it to him. He scrutinized it closely, on both sides, then copied the serial number into his computer. After he gave me the licence back he peered again at his screen.

'I don't see you on the list, Mr Matson. Please say again the name of the operative you wish to visit with?'

'Tatarov, Professor Kyril Tatarov.'

'Yes, sir. But Professor Tatarov is not normally available for interviews. Just wait a moment, please, Mr Matson.'

He ran his fingers over the screen, apparently searching. His identity badge carried a colour photograph of himself, and the name *Charles K. Yalding* printed beneath.

'Mr Matson, for ten thirty. We have you. I guess you're a little early for your meeting, sir, but that's fine. If you would just let me check your passport, we can take you through.'

'I told the officer on the gate — I don't have my passport with me.'

'This is US sovereign territory, sir. You are attempting to enter a regulated outreach territory of the USA.'

'I wasn't told to bring my passport. This is Scotland, part of the United Kingdom, part of the EU.'

'Sir, with respect, you have exited Scotland and are attempting to enter the USA.'

I gestured with impatience. Why hadn't Tatarov warned

me of this? Knowing I was starting to bluster, I said: 'Look, I've travelled from London especially to interview Professor Tatarov, and at no time was I told –'

'There is a way, sir. I can issue you with a temporary visa, twenty-four hours in duration. Do you have some form of ID?'

'You've already seen my driving licence.'

'I need something more.'

My bank debit card finally satisfied him. He used his tablet to take a photograph of my face (spectacles and hard hat removed), then connected with a printer mounted in a cavity on the wall behind him, causing it to print a large card, which he pushed through a laminating device. After several minutes of this he finally presented me with my visa. He asked me to check the details. As I took it in my hand I glimpsed not just my new photograph, but a mass of extra detail, none of which I was aware I had given him: date of birth, address, employment status, nationality, the name of my doctor, the name of my dentist, tax registration number, VAT registration number, even the place of issue and the number of my absent passport. On the reverse side was printed a list of the dates, times and ports of entry of my visits to the USA in recent years. The earliest of the recorded dates was the last week of August 2001, when I had landed at JFK to visit Lil, and, as I then hoped and planned, to fly back later to London with her. My abortive flight between Charlotte and Los Angeles, via Detroit, was also listed – not, though, the enforced landing in Columbus.

Yalding indicated I should follow him. We went through an inner door into a corridor that led back into the heart of the building, or at least of that wing of the building. The door swung open automatically when he used his badge. Along the corridor there were more doorways but no doors, and as we passed I saw several people in each of the rooms. Unexceptionally, most of them were seated at desks, facing computer monitors. They

were wearing earphones with mics attached – most were in an attitude of concentration, but I saw at least three who appeared to be reading books. In another room two women were playing table-tennis. Everyone I saw was dressed casually – most were in T-shirts and jeans, or sportswear. Charles Yalding said nothing to explain or identify – in fact I had the impression he was moving me along quickly.

We came to a larger room with several long tables or desks, men and women again seated at computers. Every few moments they would speak quietly into their headsets. One of the men was rhythmically bouncing a basketball with one hand, while he typed with the other. There were cups of coffee and soft drinks everywhere.

I saw Tatarov seated at the largest of the tables. I immediately knew it was him because although he had his head bent over his work, he was wearing his invariable black NY Yankees baseball cap to shield his eyes. I also recognized the ancient loose-leaf ledger that I had seen him with at our last meeting. This, famously in the world of mathematicians, was his sole intellectual resource, his own handwritten notes, diagrams and calculations. The notes went back years and decades, scribbled in ballpoint or sometimes pencil, more or less indecipherable by anyone else, but which Tatarov himself could use for access to notes and earlier calculations with remarkable speed and ease. He told me at our last meeting that he began using the ledger before he was twelve years old, and a few years later had purchased a huge stock of the loose-leaf pages in case the manufacturers ceased to exist. (I occasionally checked them out on the internet, and they had in fact been wound up in 1991 – I still did not know if Tatarov was aware of this.) The ledger itself was now more thickly filled, but not as much more as I might have guessed. Tatarov did not strike me as someone who would remove unwanted or redundant pages.

Yalding said nothing to introduce me but passed on by, leaving me standing in front of Tatarov's table, waiting for him to notice or acknowledge me. I stood there with my hard hat in one hand, my backpack containing my digital recorder and personal stuff in the other.

Without looking up Tatarov suddenly spoke. 'You're making me nervous standing there, Matson. Sit down somewhere, please.'

'Sorry, Professor.'

'I invited you to call me Kyril at our last meeting,' he said, now looking at me. 'The invitation stands.'

'You did, sir – and I prefer to be called Ben.'

'I am Kyril. Not sir.'

'I'm sorry.'

'Have you yet learned the difference between a theorem and a conjecture?'

'I won't make that mistake again,' I said, dismayed that he remembered my gaffe.

'Nor will you. I forget nothing.'

'Professor, I mean Kyril – I am pleased to meet you again. Thank you for proposing this interview.'

It was already not going well. I offered my hand but he brushed it away. There was a spare chair behind me so I dragged it forward and sat down awkwardly. I pulled out my recorder from my backpack, a movement noticed by some of the people to the side of us. It made me aware of the lack of privacy, a condition I preferred for any interview. Tatarov also reacted to the appearance of the recorder and again made the dismissive movement of his hand.

'Not in here. Nothing like that. I will record everything now you are here and at the end I'll give you a copy. It is not wise to use an unprotected recorder.'

'Unprotected – from whom?'

227

'Although you arrived too early for this meeting, and in haste, and you did not show up as arranged yesterday, and this morning you have not given me the opportunity to prepare, we can commence immediately. If I feel tired of your questions, or enervated by your presence, we will stop. That decision will always be mine. Once we start you must stay with me and pay attention until I say otherwise. I assume you agree to that.' He stood up, picked up his thick ledger and rammed it beneath an arm. 'You are clearly ready. Say nothing now. We have a mute suite here, and I have arranged for one of the rooms to be free. We will go there directly.'

FOURTEEN

then: 2006

Muted

The mute suite consisted of two small rooms next to each other, but unconnected. They were at the far end of the corridor I had been led down when I first arrived. Unlike everywhere else I had seen, both rooms had doors with locks. Tatarov led me to the second room, used his badge to release the lock, then took me inside.

As I stood behind him for a few moments I noticed how thin his grey hair had become since our last meeting, how deeply wrinkled was the skin of his neck. He walked and moved in a hunched position. The fingers of the hand he used with the electronic key were arthritic and the joints were swollen. Thick veins stood out on the back of his hand, and on his wrist. When he turned towards me I saw his pale blue eyes looked bloodshot and watery.

He ushered me into the room and closed the door firmly. He then threw two electrical switches placed on the wall opposite the door. The Venetian blinds over the single window silently closed. I felt my inner ears change pressure, as in an aircraft descending. Steady green LEDs shone beside each of the electrical switches. The walls did not appear to be padded, but they had a sheen of plasticity, suggesting a layer

of some sort of sound-absorbent material.

Tatarov put down his ledger on the only desk in the room, then indicated a drinks vending machine standing beside the window.

'This serves four different kinds of coffee, three different blends of tea, and drinking chocolate. The coffee is undrinkable, the tea a fraction above sufficient. The drinking chocolate has no discernible taste. Do you need refreshment now?'

His voice was oddly colourless, as if the high- and low-frequency bands were being filtered out. He sounded as if he was speaking on a small speaker unit. Perhaps something like that had happened to the drinks in the machine.

'Maybe later.'

I heard the same aural neutrality of my own voice. It made me feel as if my voice were emanating from somewhere behind me.

'Let me know if you start feeling thirsty,' Tatarov said. 'I am always dry these days. How long do you intend to be here, Ben? Not all day, I hope.'

'I'll be guided by you,' I said. 'I am pleased to be here, but I have no idea what the brief is, what we will be discussing.'

'But you know of the journal we will be published in?'

'Only that it is an annual publication for high-achieving maths students, mostly teenagers still in secondary school.'

'You have no thoughts on that?'

'I assumed it was somehow connected with the Pèlerin Conjecture.' Tatarov was staring at me steadily, his expression giving nothing away. 'If that's the case,' I went on, 'I assume – I should like to believe – that you have either solved the conjecture, or are coming close to a solution.' I was unnerved not only by the tinny effect of our voices, but by his direct regard, the rheumy eyes, the sallow skin of his face. 'Is that right? Is that what this interview should be about?'

For a moment Tatarov held his regard of me, but then he turned away and placed both hands on the closed cover of the ledger.

'No, Ben – I wish I could spend all of today, all of tomorrow, perhaps all the remainder of this year, describing to you how the Pèlerin finally surrendered to me. Jean-Louis, briefly my friend and mentor but forever my adversary, conjectured that a certain fluid state might always be quantifiable in four dimensions, that it can in fact be defined and explained. It would be a culmination if I had unravelled his surmise, explained it, opened it to lucidity. Regrettably, the Pèlerin remains a conjecture for now. Time is short. A solution cannot be far away, but I no longer have enough years left in which to find it. I think M. Pèlerin will keep his secrets from me until after I am dead.'

'So have you – abandoned it?'

'I've put it aside. I never abandon a problem until it is resolved. I'll go back to it soon, directly I leave this place.'

'Should I be recording what you are saying about Pèlerin?' I said. 'I would like to include that in the interview.'

'I told you. I am recording everything. From the moment we entered this room.'

I could not see any recording device, nor even any sign of where a microphone might be concealed.

'Would you mind if I also take handwritten notes?'

'If you must.' He gestured vaguely, but not I hoped with irritation. 'Don't let your writing them interrupt what I am saying.'

'So let me begin, Professor Tatarov, by asking you why you are here working in Scotland?' I found it impossible to address him by his first name.

'We are technically within the USA.'

'The guy who opened the door said that. It sounded like

political sophistry. This is the Isle of Bute, in Scotland.'

'No – it is US federal territory. This compound has been ceded.'

'Isn't there a place within the USA where you could work?'

'Of course. But they want me here.'

'So – why?'

Tatarov was sitting across from me, with only the table between us. On it was his ledger, my unwanted recording device and my bright yellow plastic hard hat.

'They pay me money,' he said. 'Not a huge amount, but good enough. More importantly, they are presenting me with a challenge, a conjecture of immense subtlety and complexity, and of a type I would not normally encounter. It is rejuvenating my mind.'

'Do you know why they are here in Scotland?'

'I have brought you in here, to this mute room, so we may talk without being overheard. We are in what they call a federal extension of the USA, gained under a treaty that was cooked up for the purpose. They are offshore because I believe that what they are doing, what they want me to do for them, is illegal. If it's not illegal they act as if it is. They are secretive about it to what I think is a ridiculous extent. But for now I am part of them. Even to enable this interview with you, ostensibly about math, I have had to sign a disclaimer, an extract from the USA PATRIOT Act. It is therefore in my terms amoral, and probably in yours too, but not, I think, dangerous.'

He leaned back in his chair, addressed the space above the table.

He continued: 'Maybe it is dangerous in a non-physical way. No one is hurt because Scotland has been forced to sign away a parcel of territory, but it is a dangerous precedent, and probably follows similar false treaties in other parts of the world.

If I strike you so that it hurts, that is dangerous in an obvious way, but if I tell you a lie, or I threaten you, or I warn you of something, then no pain is inflicted but danger is present. It is true also of immorality.'

I listened politely as he continued with these generalizations, because I remembered from our previous meeting that it was risky to interrupt Tatarov when he was musing.

He worked by developing a chain of thought, often improvised, most usually a line of logic that ultimately would discover and reveal the beauty of mathematics. This was his habit, even when not contemplating a mathematical postulate. He was not to be interrupted when thinking.

Now he entered a long and detailed discourse on the responsibility of causing hurt, of distancing the act from the resulting pain, of scapegoating, of excusing, of finding a justification. I continued to listen, knowing that my presence in the room was for the time being unimportant.

Soon his eyes were closed, one of his ways of concentrating. His monologue continued. I did not interrupt him. Drifting mentally I suddenly remembered Lil's long-ago plan to hold or organize a vampire convention here, in the old hydro, this very place. She wanted somewhere spooky, she said, and spooks there were, although not perhaps the sort she was thinking of.

I left my chair and went quietly to the vending machine, where I selected a Caffè Americano – a suitable choice, I thought. The machine whirred and clunked and gurgled, and the paper cup filled with hot brown liquid. It smelled like real coffee to me. I picked up a sachet of sugar and a plastic spoon, and returned to my seat.

'– it is therefore a question of judgement, of the exercise of personal taste, the result of an assessment of the hurt or damage that might be caused. I trust you are following this?'

'Yes, Professor.'

Without opening his eyes, he said: 'I am always thirsty these days. The tea is adequate. No milk or sugar.'

While I returned to the vending machine Tatarov did not change position. I went back to the table, setting the paper cup in front of him.

'So please continue, Professor,' I said.

'I am waiting for your next question.'

'What is your function as a mathematician in this place?' I said.

'The function of all mathematical research is the quest for beauty, for perfection, for the absolute rightness of a clear proof. That is why I am here, why also I work at the Courant Institute. I am a differential topologist, and I am fascinated by manifolds, shapes and solids. Shapes have a quantum state of uncertainty, what we call equivalences and deformations. A shape might change but the space containing it remains the same –'

His soliloquy continued. While he delivered it, and without opening his eyes, he reached forward gently with one hand and found the cup of tea. In mid-sentence he paused to sip it, billow it around his teeth and gums, then swallowed. He returned to his sentence, still holding the paper cup.

My thoughts drifted away but I stayed alert to the general shape of his argument. Tatarov was being recorded. I could concentrate later. I glanced around, wondering why this featureless room existed in an enclave of the USA, on a hill overlooking a Scottish firth. Why did they need a place where secrets could be discussed?

Who might they be? Superficially, the people I had seen looked like almost any group of people you could see in a modern firm or organization, young, casually but smartly dressed, absorbed in their work on computers. No sign of anything unusual, so

why the need to set it up as a territorial entity, a part of the USA? Presumably there would have been some kind of legal framework – Tatarov said there had been a cession, presumably with the collaboration of either the devolved Scottish parliament, or the UK government in London. Why had it not been made public, though?

There were precedents – for instance, there was a court set up in 2001 in the Netherlands under the adjudication of Scottish law. This enabled the trial of the alleged terrorist saboteurs of PanAm Flight 103 over Lockerbie, in 1988. There was also the US Navy base at Guantánamo Bay, a federal territory on the south coast of Cuba. And there were the USAF bomber and drone bases in Britain, ostensibly part of the Royal Air Force and called RAF bases, but in reality the RAF presence and therefore national identity was vested in a single appointed RAF liaison officer. Everything else about the bases was exclusively American in method, military strategy, governance, responsibility.

If there was any equivalence with those, then the purpose and activities of this place must be managed at the highest level. I felt uneasy with the thought. I had no information about this, no advance sense of what Tatarov might be doing here.

Tatarov was approaching the end of his argument, abstruse and convoluted: '– solitude leads to completion. The "seriousness" of a mathematical theorem lies not in its practical consequence, which is usually insignificant, but in the importance of the mathematical ideas it summons. A mathematical theorem is therefore one which connects significant ideas, and has a reference of some kind to the real world of physical existence. It is likely to lead on to an important advance in mathematics itself and even in other sciences. Overall, it justifies the behaviour of the mathematician, who in this respect is similar to a poet. We do not look for results in a poem, but

poetry means nothing unless it correlates to recognizable reality.'

Tatarov opened his eyes, looked into the paper cup, saw that he had already emptied it of its contents, and put it to one side.

'Are you still following me?' he said. 'I realize that my answers to your questions are complex, but I know you are capable of interpreting the arguments.'

'Yes, Professor. If I am in any doubt I will refer to the recording.'

'So – next?'

I had allowed my concentration to wander and I was not ready with another question. I glanced at my handwritten notes. My gaze touched on a couple of words I had underlined, ringed and followed with two question marks. I seized on them and in my confusion I blurted out: 'Professor, when we last met you introduced me to the Thomas Theorem. Does this have any reference to the work you are doing at present?'

'Now you are interesting me. Of course – that is why I am here.'

'Would you explain?'

Slowly, he leaned back in his chair again. Although he fell into physical repose, at the same time he seemed to come truly alive, fully functioning in the only way he knew.

'Thomas – yes, of course. I am pleased you remember that. This place, this enclave in Scotland, is an embodiment of the Thomas Theorem. Here it is happening. The Thomas Theorem is what mathematicians call a conditional theorem, so it is similar to much quantization work I have been doing for years. It is, however, not itself mathematical. I have already explained this to you. Because it is a social theorem, dealing with real people in familiar situations, it has been largely unexplored by other mathematicians. The Thomas Theorem deals with consequences. It therefore has an application in the real world. To return

briefly to my earlier analogy, the Thomas Theorem is like concrete poetry. It has a use, a tangible form. It was formulated in the 1920s by sociologists concerned with the consequences of human behaviour and human beliefs –'

Again, I found myself starting to drift away, but I was now alert to the risks of Tatarov realizing I was not concentrating, so I prepared the next question I would ask.

Tatarov was thinking and speaking with speed and clarity. He was returning to conjectures. I paid attention. He said that to him a non-mathematical conjecture could be treated as a real-world dilemma or enigma. It arose not from some abstract quantum concept, but from the lives and actions of real people.

He gave one illustration after another – there were certain unhappy or vulnerable people who sought psychological treatment. He had analysed their case histories. Sometimes the intense examination of criminals with deviant or anti-social motives became a possibility. What was the story a sociopath or psychopath believed in, that allowed the breaking of all social values? Tatarov added that he had interested himself in despotic leaders, whose decisions were often made without considering the consequences: he had taken particular interest in the decision by Hitler to invade the Soviet Union in 1941.

In the terms Tatarov said he was developing, any social change that affected millions would be logically a conjecture leading to the Thomas Theorem. He suggested any of a number of terrible events: natural disasters, crimes, civil unrest, any upheaval sufficiently serious that it created a global reaction. These events could be interpreted as conjectures, and the consequences of them were similar to theorems that resolved them.

I was beginning to lose his train of argument again. He was

difficult. Time was passing and I was in need of a comfort break, a chance perhaps to get outside and breathe some fresh air, assemble my thoughts so that I could ask more questions, perhaps to tease greater clarity from him. Tatarov seemed unstoppable, though, so I sat tight, waiting, holding on, hoping for a natural pause.

Finally it came. He tipped slowly forward in his chair, opened his eyes – he would have found me staring directly at him. He removed his baseball cap and scratched the top of his head. What was left of his hair was thinly spread, standing wild.

'Time for a rest, I think.' he said. 'If you come with me I will show you a part of this building you would not normally be allowed to enter.'

He touched something under the rim of his desk, and the weird acoustic of the room changed.

'Will I need this?' I said, meaning my hard hat. The normality of my own voice briefly surprised me. My inner ears had popped again.

'No – so long as we stay within the building. But bring it anyway. Nothing is safe outside these offices.'

I wondered if he meant the likelihood of parts of the old building falling on me, or the company he was keeping.

The water treatment

We used the modern toilets located within the renovated suite of offices, then Tatarov led me away through a side passage. We had to pass through one of the hydro hotel's original doors, for which Tatarov produced an ancient iron key, tarnished by use and age. On the other side we were immediately surrounded by neglect and dilapidation – all the paint, wallpaper and in many places the plaster itself had disappeared, leaving dark and broken patches of bare wall brickwork, with wooden laths and

studs visibly decaying and detaching themselves. The ceilings hung loose in many places.

I put on the hard hat.

After descending a short flight of steps we came to a wide hall with a high ceiling, lined on both sides with about two dozen deep sinks and bathing troughs. This had been the main faucet area for drawing water from the source. The troughs and basins stood against two walls. Every one of them was either broken, chipped, falling away or at least crazed with the brittleness of old age. A discoloured tap was mounted above each of them. The mineral-rich water had been leaking for years, spreading green and brown and yellow stains beneath the leaks in the pipes, and over the crazed surfaces of the old porcelain units.

Some modern plastic cups were arranged on a shelf. Tatarov took down two of them and ripped off the translucent plastic covers.

'You must try the waters while you are here,' he said. With difficulty he cranked one of the faucets around. Cloudy water trickled into his cup.

'I'd rather not,' I said, aware of the filthy surroundings.

'You must. It is entirely hygienic. Remember this is the source. We are directly above the spring. The water is as good now as it was a century ago. Wealthy people would pay hundreds of dollars for the privilege of coming to this hotel and drinking this.' He raised his cup in a brief, mocking toast. 'Zdoroviye!'

I hesitated a few moments longer, then drew off half a cupful. I raised it towards him. It looked like a weak mixture of water and milk. I drank it in one. It was extremely cold, salty in flavour and left a metallic aftertaste.

'These young Americans I have to work with here — they will not come to take the waters. They open their blue plastic

bottles, drink the water made in factories. This is purity and health!'

He drank the rest of his water, then ran off another cupful. He took it with him as we returned to the office area. I did not. In this I was at one with his young American colleagues.

The purpose of it all

We returned to the mute suite and closed the door firmly – Tatarov put back on his NYC Yankees cap, and I removed my plastic head protector. I had had plenty of time to prepare for another question. Our voices were synthetically neutralized once again.

The one question rapidly became a series. I said: 'Professor – who are these people? What are they doing? Why is this sovereign American territory? What exactly is going on here?'

'Exactly? That is an interesting concept, and how would you arrange it so that every fact might be exactly established? How long, exactly, is the coast of Australia? How big, exactly, is a cloud? You know chaos theory, of course. Exactitude is relative and therefore not significant until it can be quantified. As to what is going on here, as you put it. Well, for example I know of a number of relationships that have started between some of these people while I have been here. Are human relationships exact? Two people were suddenly given leave of absence, for reasons I never exactly discovered, but were probably because of something going on, in your imprecise phrase. What you mean is that you wish to know what they are actually aiming to achieve, what methods and procedures they are using –'

He slowly began to tip back to his preferred position for thinking aloud. His eyelids drooped. His voice remained clear, steady and fast moving. I relaxed, knowing that the answer would be buried somewhere in all his reflections, and that I

would probably not grasp it now, nor even soon after, but that I should have to make a close study of the recording and use my own intuition.

This time I did pay attention to what he was saying, hoping for clues. And I did not want to be caught out by my lack of concentration again.

The minutes passed, the words ran on. It was intriguing and challenging to be there, to listen to a brilliant if quirky mind in full flow. His discourse meandered through ten or twelve subjects, all seeming adjacent, one leading to the next, none of the connections obvious to me until I heard him make them.

Then I was suddenly alert.

He said: '– for this reason the internet is inherently uncontrollable, which is the key to its strength, and explains its appeal. I naturally have to remind you of the Platonic Dilemma, which concerned universal literacy. Plato's dilemma then is the same as our dilemma now. The analogy is close – the internet is, or will be, universal. In particular the people here are concerned with the social media software which I had predicted and warned against some years ago and which we are now seeing emerge.

'More than two thousand years ago Plato argued that literacy would change the way people think, would weaken memory and judgement, shift power from an enlightened elite to the populist mass, and consequently have a negative effect on the social order. His mentor Socrates feared universal literacy would promote the appearance of wisdom among people who were not wise, but who merely had information. Plato was further concerned with the social effects – what might then be written and what people would do with the written information they read. Both cognitive and social effects, he argued, would alter the social status quo ante and could give power to those without the wisdom to rule. This is the exact,

241

to use your word, the *exact* problem of a burgeoning internet, open to all.

'Social media on the internet now exist as semi-hidden but ever-present layers of society. Social media therefore have genuine social value and genuine appeal. Already hundreds of thousands of equal voices are in open dialogue. By this time next year the number of people using social media will be in their millions. Eventually, I assume, most of the people in the world will be communicating with each other. This is to me a profoundly important social development. Free expression is being democratized.

'However, the people I am working with see it differently. To them, dialogue between voices of equal, untested value constitutes a fundamental shift in the nature and use of facts, and the weight we should give to an alleged fact. Opinion is clearly more attractive to ordinary people than the reporting of facts, and contains its own dynamic.'

I started scribbling notes while Tatarov was speaking. When I came to analyse the recording I would need headwords. His words were speeding up, fleeing past me.

'Before the real world was affected by the introduction of social media, qualities such as ideas, prejudices, coercions, theories, analysis, messages of love, contradictions, jokes, threats, insults, promises, and so on, were monologic. That is to say that until now relatively few people, a self-appointed but intelligent elite, have had access to the means of distribution. These were the artists, writers, journalists, philosophers, academics, politicians, and so on. The few spoke to the many. In doing so they helped shape the society in which the many lived. Now because of the internet, the many speak freely to the many. Facts have been replaced by opinions. They are unmediated and are therefore malleable, changeable.

'This is what the people here say. To them it is an opportunity

to take control of opinion, to discard facts, to question and therefore change memories. I am answering your question. This is what they are doing, exactly. They are changing what many people remember as the past with the intention of influencing the future. I am speaking for them, you understand, not for myself. I am not one of them. All I am here to do is to solve the conjecture. It is an abstract challenge to me, although abhorrent to consider.'

'So you are saying?'

He opened his eyes, sat forward. He took off his baseball cap.

'I will say more. First we have lunch.'

Questions reversed

We walked together to the refectory. Several of the young operatives I had seen earlier were already there. Some stood at the food selection bays, others were already seated at the small tables with their meals. The hubbub of conversation died as Tatarov and I entered, but immediately resumed. Tatarov and I went to the selection bays, waited for them to come free. Soon, he and I were the only two people there. The bays were automated. Tatarov dialled for a cheeseburger, relish, bacon on the side, fries, salad, Thousand Island dressing and, after some thought, a Diet Pepsi. I looked at the part of the menu that alleged itself to be French, and I punched in the numbers for *côte de porc, salade sans vinaigrette,* fries, corn bread and a Fanta Orange. There was nothing to pay. Everything was delivered with astonishing speed and accuracy. Steam rose from our main dishes.

I looked around for a vacant table.

Tatarov said: 'We'll eat in the mute suite. You want to talk.'

'I do.'

We walked back through the offices. Once we were in the mute room we started eating straight away. I was not intending

243

to resume the interview until we had both had a break, but we were still only halfway through eating when Tatarov picked up his baseball cap and placed it on his head. He turned the switches – the room's acoustics were neutralized again.

'You were in the USA on the day of the 9/11 attacks,' he said. 'That's correct?'

'Correct, yes, but how –?'

'Were you in New York City?'

'First tell me how you knew I was in the States, and why you want me to confirm that.'

'You must have been in New York, then. I was there too.'

I cleared my mouth of the food I had been chewing. 'No – that morning I was in Charlotte, North Carolina. I was in fact on a plane that had just taken off.' I briefly described the short but worrying flight to Columbus, Ohio.

'I see – I understood you saw some of the attacks taking place.'

'Understood from whom?'

'The people here, who are spending so much money to employ me, the ones you are so curious about.'

'What do they know about me?'

'It would surprise you to find out. Their intelligence is good. Intelligence, of course, with the special meaning that they are able find out what they wish to know. They are intelligent in the other sense too, although after consideration of their general awareness of the world's realities I must say –'

Sensing that another lengthy Tatarov side-issue discourse was about to begin, I said: 'But what is it they know about me, or think they know?'

'Allow me to ask you some questions myself. Did you witness any of the events of that day?'

'I saw them on television,' I said. 'Like everybody else in the world.'

244

'You were never in New York City?'

'Yes, I was – immediately before 9/11, and a few days afterwards. But I was not there on the day.'

'That might be what they meant. They are usually right about these things, but the day itself was full of confusion. So you watched the events on television. Were you satisfied with the television coverage? With the way the events were reported?'

'Satisfied? I was appalled and horrified.'

'Naturally so. But as you watched did you accept that what you were seeing was verifiably true?'

I stared down at my half-finished lunch. Suddenly I wanted no more of it.

'I believed it then,' I said. 'There was no reason not to. But now – I'm not so sure.'

'That is right,' Tatarov said. 'You were with someone, I believe – a woman named Lilian Viklund.'

'How do you know about her?'

'The people here told me. What they do not know about the events of 9/11, and those who were involved, is negligible. It is where this project began. 9/11 is why they are here, why I am here with them, why you are here with me. It is predominantly an attempt by the authorities to maintain and consolidate what is known about the facts of the event. At least, they wish to consolidate what is *remembered* of the facts. So, let us be clear: it's true that you were with this woman? Was Lilian Viklund with you on the plane that flew to Columbus?'

I said: 'No. She was a passenger on American 77, the aircraft –'

'Yes, the Pentagon. I know, of course. But I did not realize she was one of those aboard. I don't recall seeing her name. I would have noticed had it been there.'

245

'I believe she was on the plane, but I haven't been able to find absolute proof. There is no other explanation for her disappearance.'

'She was not named on the passenger list.'

'I know.'

'Do you know why?'

'Her husband told me she was flying in a seat reserved by his Department.'

'So you know who her husband was?'

'His name is Martin Viklund.'

'Are you aware of what position Viklund holds now?'

'When I met him he was in the Pentagon, the Defense Department.'

'In 2001, at the time of the attacks, he was working for the US Northern Command, as a senior Deputy Secretary of the Army,' Tatarov said. 'It was a position that placed him approximately third or fourth in line of strategic decision making, after the President. But he's moved on. Two years ago he was re-appointed to Homeland Security.'

'And now?'

'Officially he's still with Homeland Security, but that's just his office base. He does this and that.' Tatarov gestured with a wave of an arm, to suggest the room we were in, to include the building we were in, to include the US enclave we were in. 'At present, what he mostly does is this.'

I stared in surprise at Tatarov.

'You mean he runs this place?'

'I do. He does.'

'Is he here now?'

'Not at the moment. He is in Washington this week. I do not know when he will return. Some of the people here say he is grooming himself for greater things. He intends to run for President one day.'

The three Objects

We cleared away the remains of our meals, finished our soft drinks. Tatarov placed the recyclable plates and cutlery in a bin, then went to visit the toilet. When he returned he found the plastic cup of cloudy spa water he had drawn off earlier and stood it on the table in front of him. He settled the baseball cap on his head.

'You have more questions for me?' he said.

'Only one.' I was remembering that the reason for the interview was a short profile of Tatarov for a schools magazine. Most of what we had discussed so far was unsuitable for that. 'I'd like to ask, Professor, what are you doing here? You appear to have abandoned the challenge of the conjecture which has inspired you throughout your life. It cannot be simply the money. You have always lived on a higher plane. What is your role here, and what are you contributing to this project?'

'I have exchanged one conjecture for another. Pèlerin is enduring, immanent.' Tatarov pressed his hand lightly against the faded, timeworn cover of his ledger. 'The Pèlerin Conjecture will survive me, but I can never abandon my old adversary and soon my work here will be finished. Then I will return to my small, overheated office at the Courant, and resume.

'So what, you ask, with your zeal for exactness, am I achieving? The conjecture they are struggling with here is a societal one. They wish to change the reality of events they do not agree with by surrounding them with false facts that they prefer. My work is to derive a theorem that proves the conjecture is sound – I have almost completed that. We have discussed the Thomas Theorem, which is what I am using as a template –'

It was an effort for me to keep up, but at last I was growing accustomed to his digressions, his discursive approach to everything, his distracting manner. I tried to stay tuned, to let

his notions slide past me and make a general impression, get an understanding of sorts of what was behind it all. At last it began to cohere.

He said: '— I am writing code for their computers, devising algorithms, setting out in machine code what they seek to make of the world. I am constantly aware of their shortcomings — they are concerned with reality, but they do not see the difference between a bottle of manufactured mineral water and the flow from a centuries-old spring. Which is the real thing, which is the imitation? Which do we prefer? They see the new social media spreading throughout the world, and they will use the programs opportunistically to create what they see as controllable new reality. They believe in interpretations, not reporting. They praise opinions, but they despise facts. They talk of actions, whereas they are merely noticing the consequences of other people's actions. A false reality, they believe, has consequences just as tangible as the truth, no better, no worse — what's the difference? they seem to be asking. The two Thomases identified these people a hundred years ago. *If people define situations as real, they are real in their consequences. In other words, the interpretation of a situation causes the action.* You understand?'

'Yes,' I said, but I added silently to myself: better, but not entirely.

'Because these people care nothing for facts, only consequences, let me illustrate the difference.

'Assume for the sake of this example the existence of an object, a real thing. I will call it Object A. When we see it or hold it or examine it, we instantly create two alternative realities. There is the original, Object A, and our perception of it, which I call Object B. The two might be very alike, depending on how well or accurately we perceive it, or how accurately we interpret what we have seen. Now: add a second observer.

If more than one person observes Object A, and they have the means to discuss it, a consensus comes into being. Object A is unchanged, but Object B seems more real, more dimensional, more subtle. It becomes more credible. As the number increases of people who see it or hold it or examine it the more powerful the consensus about it becomes. The greater are the assumptions made about it, and therefore the more unstoppable are the consequences of it. Objects A and B still seem much alike, but they are already beginning to diverge from one another.

'Now let us turn to the subject that interests me most: what happened to America on September 11, five years ago. Both of these Objects are involved.

'Object A is the series of events everybody saw on that terrible day five years ago. Some of us were close enough, as I happened to be, to witness some of it before our own eyes. The building where I work is only a short distance from the World Trade Center. Everyone else, the overwhelming majority, such as yourself, saw it at a remove: a television broadcast, or perhaps video footage online later. Either way, these events can be described as Object A.

'Object B is closely similar, but it consists of our individual interpretation of what we saw, enhanced by the views of other people with the same experience. For a long time there was only one topic of conversation in New York, and around the world. This was further enhanced by the speculation and explanation that quickly came from several sources: the media, the commentators, the aviation and terrorism experts, but most of all by the actions and statements of the US authorities. Object B is the narrative about 9/11, the story of 9/11, the one with which we are all familiar. It involves hijackers from the Middle East who travelled to the USA to learn to fly big jets, who then boarded and violently seized four aircraft full of innocent passengers and crew. Some of those people who were trapped

were able to make phone calls to their loved ones. The hijackers crashed three of the planes into important buildings in New York and Washington, but lost control of one of them when the passengers and crew valiantly fought back. Even before these appalling events were concluded, al-Qaeda, a terrorist organization based in Afghanistan, had been named as the perpetrators. A war on terror was almost immediately declared. That is the story.

'Every violent or terrible thing that has happened since that day in the world outside the USA, and some of it within, can be traced directly or indirectly back to that theory, that explanation, that consequence.

'Because Object A and Object B of 9/11 are so alike, most people accept that B accounts for A. The story ends because there is no more story to come. Objects A and B seem to match each other. They take comfort from the fact that there is an explanation for the traumatic events they saw occurring, events they know for certain actually did occur. People really died, planes really collided with buildings, three huge buildings really did collapse and a fourth was seriously damaged.

'But then there is Object C. We have not mentioned Object C before. This is made up of the inexplicable irregularities in the story of 9/11, the inconsistencies, the unsolved mysteries, the glib lies, the missing or faulty evidence, the breaking of physical scientific principles, the refusal to discuss a matter after it has been arbitrarily declared closed.

'There are too many of these inconsistencies to be ignored. At every step of the 9/11 story there is doubt, or there are unanswered questions, or simple logical gaps. You have noticed most of them yourself. So much doubt means, unarguably, that Object B can no longer be a valid explanation of Object A. The two do not after all match. What we saw for ourselves can not be explained, unless we are prepared to rethink everything we

take for granted about a democratically elected government running an advanced and civilized nation.

'For most people that is a revision of reality that they are not prepared to make. So the story of 9/11 that everyone knows, Object B, remains for them as the reality, or as good as. Object C, for all its plausible argument by experts and examination by specialists of engineering, aviation, psychology, evidence, demolition methods, and much more, is discredited by the authorities.

'These authorities claim that the story they have told, Object B, is not only true but it has been fully investigated by them and is now final. The case is closed, because they closed it. Most people accept that. However, Object C continues to stand up to calm and logical examination, the science is good, the arguments are compelling, it fits the evidence. But because of the doubts it raises, it no longer resembles Object A at all. Object B stands undamaged by facts, because it is not about facts at all. Object B is a myth but it is all most people have, all most of the world wants to have. The false has replaced the real, and we are living now with the consequences.'

Tatarov sat forward suddenly, his chair legs clunking down to the floor. He surprised me.

'That is what I wish to say,' he said.

With an air of finality he went quickly across the room and switched off the muting device, reverting our voices to normal. He opened a drawer on his side of the table, reached inside, tugged at something and after a moment produced a USB memory stick.

'Here is the promised recording of what we have discussed today. Transcribing it will be your responsibility, but I know because of what you said that you will be exact. I will not need to check or approve it. But I must tell you plainly that if you quote, in your magazine article or anywhere else, what I have

said about the present work in this place, I will deny every single thing about it. You would also find yourself in personal jeopardy. Not from me, of course. The people who are behind this endeavour are dangerous and ruthless. Perhaps you already realize that is true of Mr Viklund. Therefore you should treat everything about this meeting with the utmost confidence. It is best that you do not even mention to anyone that we have met here. Is that clear?'

I said: 'It is, of course. Thank you, Professor Tatarov.'

'Do not thank me. Do what I say. Good day to you.'

FIFTEEN

now

London in London

I was in London again, feeling more alienated than ever by the
city where I and both my parents had been born, where I went
to school, where I had found my first jobs, where I had met my
first girlfriends, and where I eventually met Jeanne, now my
life partner.

I had always felt I knew London well, but of course it must
have changed as I grew up and I accepted that. Changes in a
place only become obvious when you move away and return
at intervals. That is how I saw London after living in Scotland
for a few years.

Now every street in the centre of the London I used to know
had traffic-calming stanchions and humps, lanes narrowed to
make cars, taxis and buses drive more slowly. Large or im-
portant buildings had immense concrete or steel blocks placed
between them and the road – one or two even had sandbag
emplacements as well, as if an aerial bombardment or a sudden
flood were expected. All the traffic bridges across the Thames
had barriers to separate vehicles from pedestrians. There were
armed security guards at or behind the entrance to every large
office building, their Metropolitan Police licences bright on
their chests and backs, standing prominently and deliberately

with automatic weapons cradled in their arms. These guards were clad in bulletproof vests, helmets and goggles, with extra deterrents – body cams, chemical sprays and night-sticks, and unidentifiable electronic aids hanging blackly on their belts.

No police officers were visible on London's streets, but their armoured vehicles patrolled slowly in the main areas of the West End, the City and Dockland. CCTV cameras were everywhere, in the concourse and public areas of office buildings, in every hotel, in the big stores, on every floor and in every department of smaller shops, on street corners, high on buildings, studded against transit tunnel walls in the Underground stations, hidden inside discreet dark-glass domes in buses, taxicabs and train carriages. The quasi-comforting feeling that they were there to protect me, that they were not aimed at me, was one that had worn off twenty-five years earlier – the cameras and guns were indeed aimed at me because they were aimed at everybody and, like me, everybody had something to hide, however small or innocent.

For this latest trip to London I had arranged with the company to put me up in a hotel rather than the apartment – they found me a room in a recently opened hotel near Camden Town. I went there by taxi straight from the airport. I found my room, dumped my bag, freshened up speedily then set off across inner London to be at the office by mid-afternoon.

Miranda Hamid, still my commissioning editor, had told me she had a new job for me, one with cash bonuses for prompt delivery and a decent travel and accommodation package, but one which would require me to be out of the country for a few days. I checked with Jeanne, and packed my bag.

TELL ME MORE ABOUT THE JOB? I texted Miranda while I was still travelling to London.

254

Her immediate reply: OFF THE RECORD FOR NOW. BRING YOUR PASSPORT.

I typed: ALWAYS DO.

That was the end of the exchange.

Much was unchanged at the office itself, although this time I had to identify myself and register at the main entrance to the building. Their security measure was an ID procedure involving a blood sample from my thumb, which I thought intrusive, but pragmatically accepted it. The guy on the door recognized me and addressed me by my first name, as he had for many years, but the test went ahead anyway. At the end he handed me a laminated card, same size and dimensions as a credit card, with an electronic swipe and a machine readable code.

He said: 'That's good now for clearing border controls anywhere outside the EU.'

'But I live in the EU.'

'Nobody's perfect.'

From the unsmiling manner in which he muttered this I realized it was not a joke. I pocketed the card and moved on.

On the fifteenth floor everything seemed to be in the usual familiar chaos. I went along to the meeting room where an editorial conference was winding up. A few of my colleagues nodded to me in recognition as I entered, but I sat in a chair at the back, taking no part. They were discussing a special issue for three months ahead, to coincide with a futures conference and accompanying science expo in Pretoria. That was not going to involve me, otherwise Miranda would have made sure I was there for the whole session.

She signalled to me to stay put as the other writers and subs dispersed.

'Here are the briefing documents,' she said without preamble, handing me a stiff card folder with shiny covers. There were only about five sheets of paper inside, but each of them was

255

printed with several readable codes, linking me to whatever it was.

'Miranda, where are you sending me, and what do I need to know before I get there?'

'Download the flight info and boarding passes from the file,' she said. 'You'll be going to Philadelphia. Have you kept up with energy storage capacitors? Superfast materials?'

'No – but I can find out.'

'As you do. The downloads are all about it. Your contact at Prestell University is a Dr Rufus Schlaben, in Materials and Science Engineering. He's a metallurgist, apparently one of the best in the USA. You won't meet him but he has arranged for you to visit the site. Someone else will take you there. You will need to collect a letter of endorsement from his department. We don't know the whole story yet, but there's been a break-through in fast discharge supercapacitors.'

'You mentioned a site. Is it away from the university?'

'You'll be going outside Philadelphia, to a US Navy base. There's an Alamo car rental voucher included.'

'Is it a security zone?'

'Not that I know of. Are you concerned about security?'

'Why is the US Navy involved?'

'There's a ship – perhaps they've been running tests. We'll carry the story next week, so if you can email it to us that would be great, but we can wait until you're back if there's more to it than we know at the moment.'

'Thanks, Miranda.'

'Don't mention it.'

I took the folder and left. While I was still inside the building I wandered across to the directory board beside the elevators and located the name and floor of the film company Jaye said she had worked for. They were on the twelfth floor, so I rode down the three levels and went in search. I saw the entrance

to the reception area straight away, but wooden battens had been placed in front of the doorway. The office was closed and locked. I found a member of the building staff and asked what had happened. They had gone out of business, she told me. They were shut down. Last month.

I went to my hotel.

Texas in London

Many years ago, when I was still in my early twenties, I went on a vacation tour of the USA. I travelled on trains and rode in cars, sometimes alone, sometimes with friends, sometimes with people I happened to meet on the road. I was away from home for about six weeks, but being in the States stimulated and energized me. I loved everything about America: the people and their astonishing range of attitudes, the scenery, the feeling of freedom, the sense that anything was possible. It was the best time of my life.

At some point towards the middle of the final week, when I was already starting to think of home, I was with a young woman I had met, in a car crossing west Texas from the border with New Mexico through blistering heat towards the state capital, Austin. There were still more than three hundred miles ahead. The highway was straight, the landscape grey and gravelly, broken by huge buttes rising bleakly on both sides. The hot wind was lifting dust devils. At regular intervals, donkey pumpers were visible, sometimes alone, sometimes in groups, sucking up the oil, dark heads slowly dipping and raising. The rest of the long journey was a grim prospect, and the sun was going down. We came to a small town called Pecos, where we saw there was a motel with a steak house attached. We pulled over, took a room.

The restaurant was a cheerful, noisy place, traditional country music piped nonstop through loudspeakers. Steel guitars,

electric fiddles and folksy voices. About half the tables and booths were occupied. The one next to ours had six young people enjoying their dinner. The women were pretty and happy, laughing together. The three guys looked pleased to be there, smiled a lot but said little. All three men were wearing work clothes, kerchiefs around their throats, dusty jeans and heeled leather boots, cowboy hats tipped back on their heads. The women were dressed for an evening out. I had already been in Texas for nearly a week before this, and there was nothing unusual about these people. The long car ride had induced a feeling of physical stasis in me, and I was soon staring blankly across at this table. I wondered about their lives, what they hoped for, where they lived and worked, how they knew each other, what their future lives were going to be like. It was a glimpse of a world in which I would never play a part, however much I might want to – which for a few moments I did, attracted by their good nature, their easy manners.

Back in the motel room with the air conditioner on full we watched TV for a while, read for a while, talked for a while. We were trapped in the room by the oppressive night heat outside. The evening passed slowly. Out on the highway the traffic was intermittent, but noisily disruptive whenever a large rig went through. Cars came and went in the parking lot. Music briefly flared as doors were opened and closed.

I relaxed for a few minutes by lying on the floor, the coolest part of the room. I closed my eyes and imagined the fabulous American continent stretching away from me in all directions, mysterious to me, strange, full of places I would never visit or even hear about, the greatest of countries, idealistic, free, a country of opportunity and hope. I felt keenly, then, the narrow expectations of my own life in Britain, the close horizons, the old traditions, the hidebound culture. I was tempted

258

to stay longer in the US, see more of the country while I still had the chance.

Late in the evening I went to the bathroom at the back. The window could be opened, so I leaned out to the rich smell of cedar pollen, the frantic stridulation of hidden insects. I looked across the area behind the motel. Deep night had fallen but the unmoving summer humidity of the Texan high plains lay like swamp water between the stunted, misshapen bushes growing behind the building. The stillness drew me. Lights on the main building, somewhere to the side of me, partly illuminated the area. I saw a long row of trash cans, some with the lids lifted permanently open by the pressures of overfilling, an abandoned car with rusted bodywork, no wheels and the windows knocked out, behind it an even more ruined truck, rust-brown in colour, filthy, unusable, unmovable, some wooden staves tossed in an uneven pile, a roll of barbed wire, a scattering of broken glass. It looked as if no one had been out there for weeks, a deserted, forgotten zone.

For the first time in my life I felt an acute sense of culture shock. This was not my world at all. No more than I could understand or ever share the lives of those young Texans in the steak house, I was surrounded by an immense bare landscape of similar alienation, one where my only escape was the car and the presence of the person I was travelling with. Moving on was for me a fragile link to normality, a path of comprehensible reality through a burning land of foreign assumptions.

Decades later – now, in the present day – I was in the modern high-rise hotel in Camden Town, chosen for me by Miranda's PA, less than half a mile from where I was born. The room was clean and fresh and smelled faintly of polish and new sheets. It had recessed lights that I could program to respond to my movements from one area to another, and an air blower that I could turn up or down, but not off, and

which would send either warm or cool air into the room, as I chose. It was furnished with lightweight, ergonomic Scandinavian chairs, a desk designed to take a laptop computer or a tablet, a phone charging point. There was a minibar with beer and whisky and gin, bottled water and packets of mixed nuts, and some Swiss chocolate. A nosegay of flowers was next to the bed, together with three pieces of wrapped candy. A handwritten note from someone calling herself my maid asked me to contact her or her supervisor if I had any complaint. I had none. The room was perfect. My maid's name was Tala.

I called Jeanne and we spoke for several minutes while I sat on the edge of my bed. After this I turned on my laptop, connected it to the hotel wifi, checked my email and the online news and science sites I regularly visited. Then I went to the window.

The curtains were made of heavy material, and although they could with difficulty be opened there was an arrangement of pull-strings and tags that I had to work out how to use. I gained the feeling that opening the curtains was discouraged. The window itself was metal framed and double glazed – it could be opened to a narrow gap, but intentionally not wide enough to allow anyone to clamber through. I felt the cool air drifting in past my face, heard the familiar London roar of traffic. I pressed forward, looking down towards the ground – my room was on the third floor at the back of the building, so I had a high view of what was below. It was an inner yard or well, surrounded by the bulk of the hotel and the other buildings beside and behind it. The only lighting came from a few of the rooms overlooking the well. There was a row of large horizontal fans, mounted in brick vents, turning with a constant sound. A grey metal duct emerged from one wall and led upwards into the darkness. A wheeled trolley of some kind was pressed at an

angle against the wall where my room was situated. A tangle of wires and cables someone had left in a heap. Something large was covered by a tarpaulin. I could see a wide entrance arch with a steel gate, presently closed to make a barrier. It looked as if when opened it would allow access for service vehicles. A row of industrial waste hoppers stood in a group – many flattened cardboard cartons were strewn on the ground around them.

I felt again the sense of isolation I had experienced years before, standing in the same way at a window in the back of the motel in Texas. What was there below was hidden from the world, hidden even from most people inside the building. Who would choose to look, who cared about such places? It was an alien space, a glimpse of a lower, utilitarian world of abandoned junk or things left lying around to be picked up by vehicles. I felt repelled by its emptiness and darkness, positioned there at the centre of the hotel, but it also made me feel that I too had a void in my heart, that I came from nowhere, belonged to nowhere, that wherever I was at that moment I was not a part of it.

I drew back from the window, pulled it hard to shut it (resistance from the hinge released a small drift of dust and grit), wrangled the curtains closed, then stepped back into the modernist anonymity of the hotel room. In this place I was only a short distance from my parents' former home, where my brother Saul and I had been born. If there was anywhere on the planet I could truly call home this part of London was it. If I left the hotel and walked there I should be standing outside the house within ten minutes – another five minutes and I would see the first school I went to when I was five. I knew both buildings were still there because on another trip to London a couple of years ago I had checked, and they were more or less as I remembered them. Yet the feeling of alienation was real,

with the same psychic barrenness as there had been that time in Pecos, west Texas.

The next day I flew from London Heathrow to Philadelphia.

SIXTEEN

then: 2006–2011

Reality

Nobody interrogated me as I left the mute suite in the hydro building, demanded to check my passport, see my visa, hear my intentions, anything. They barely glanced up to see me go. There was no sign of Charles K. Yalding. I reached the door by which I had entered and remembered to use the badge to open it. My ears were still popping, adjusting to normality. I tensed my jaw to try to ease the feeling. Wind blew from the direction of the Cowal peninsula. I walked down the path, passed unchallenged through the border post, headed for the village. I felt dazed, was preoccupied with much of what Tatarov had been saying.

When I reached the coast road by the old quay I realized I was still holding the yellow hard hat by its elasticated chin strap. It took me a moment to remember why I was carrying it.

I found a litter bin and dumped the hat. I kept the visitor's badge.

I called Lucinda's mobile. Twenty minutes later she picked me up in her car. It was still only mid-afternoon so we drove to the ferry terminal and waited for the next sailing. We were back in Edinburgh by the early evening. I stayed the night in her spare bedroom, and was home in London by the end of the following day.

The interview with Tatarov took place in the late summer of 2006. There were still slightly more than two years of George W. Bush's second term of presidency to run. It was five years since the 9/11 attacks. In terms of America's direct reaction to 9/11, and the consequences that followed, it was a relatively uneventful year. The disaster was in the past, the discussion was over, controversy was not welcome.

In January 2002, President Bush, in his State of the Union speech, had described Iraq as part of what he called the 'axis of evil'. US troops were by then already fighting in Afghanistan, which was said to be part of the same alleged axis. The official story of 9/11 was accepted by almost everyone, and American fears of terrorism and aggression were high. In particular there was a persistent belief in the West that the Iraqi régime was stockpiling weapons of mass destruction. This belief gradually became more entrenched as time passed, in spite of an almost complete lack of evidence. Iraq was invaded in 2003, and Britain, under Tony Blair, was complicit, faking the evidence of the weapons to show solidarity with the US.

Saddam Hussein was soon overthrown, went into hiding, was eventually caught and later executed. No weapons of mass destruction were ever found.

Three scenarios (1)

I was a writer. Bryan Claremont offered to pay me a more than respectable sum of money to write a screenplay because of my two short interviews with Tatarov. I wrote it and he paid me. I rewrote it, then rewrote it, and then made corrections and additions to the text for another three months at least.

All through this work I could not forget the reality of Tatarov and what we had discussed: his interesting, opaque, apparently digressive rambles through the fascinating complexities of his mind.

Perhaps for the sake of this first scenario I should identify that discussion with Tatarov as Object A.

Because he hoped to raise his profile as a film-maker, and go on to make another film about the tragedy of 9/11, Claremont wanted the Tatarov-based film to be one he could sell to a mainstream distributor, and therefore to a popular audience. That is more or less what he paid for in the bland romantic comedy he received from me. However, he and I ran out of belief in each other, and Claremont commissioned new revisions from other writers, in the end getting the screenplay he wanted.

The film made from that script could be described as Object B.

However, there was a subtext. Somewhere in the space between Claremont and myself, above us, around us, were many unvoiced thoughts. Prime amongst them were my suspicions about what was really being worked on by those young operatives in the US enclave on the Isle of Bute.

In a way that was oddly parallel to my writing of Claremont's screenplay, the realities of war, aggression, memory, political ambition, as they related to 9/11, which in general I thought I understood, were being subjected to revision by other people. There were deletions, changes, new emphasis, extra material, all being put in by people of whom I knew nothing. With Tatarov's collaboration, the power of the populist internet was being deployed to falsify history. The vernacular became pre-eminent.

This undeclared knowledge, which Claremont and myself shared, was Object C.

Three scenarios (2)

Within three days of returning from Scotland I was supposed to submit my profile of Tatarov to *Pi and Maths*, the magazine that had commissioned me. My mind was still turning over

what Tatarov had said at such length and in so much detail that I found it difficult to filter it out and concentrate on what I should be doing.

I looked back over the four recent issues of the magazine the editor had sent me as samples. I admired the candid, good-humoured approach of many of the contributors. Every issue contained a range of mathematical problems and challenges. The questions varied in their difficulty so that there were suitable starting points for all ages of student. The editors knew, as I did, that most of the young people who were given copies by their teachers would not have a natural aptitude for maths, but the witty style and the clever demonstration of mathematical concepts gave the whole thing an attractive flavour. At the same time, the casual knowingness would have an obvious appeal to the young people who loved and were fascinated by mathematics.

I made my article into a personal profile of Tatarov, depicting him as one of mathematics' living masters, drawing on odd fragments of ideas he had expressed that I came across on the recording. Mainly, though, I worked into this new article some of the material from my earlier meeting with him. Everything could be given natural immediacy by the fact I had spent so much time with him in person. I made gentle fun of his baseball cap, the way he drank tea, and so on.

Although *Pi and Maths* was written and edited by members of the Mathematics Society, based in Derby, it was actually published by a corporate producer of scientific and business journals in London. A few weeks after I sent in my Tatarov profile I was approached by one of the editors there, and for a long time afterwards I received regular commissions for more articles. These opened up several other doors in my career. One more matter for which I have to thank Professor Tatarov.

Three scenarios (3)

This was the longest and hardest of the three scenarios which Tatarov led me to. The main difficulty was to be certain that Tatarov, for all his digressions, was saying what I believed he was.

I studied the recordings, first listening two or three times to the whole session (in which, incidentally, the neutralizing effect of the mute suite disappeared, and our voices sounded normal), then carefully transcribing everything and reading the text through repeatedly.

I discovered that Tatarov had given several clues, before coming to his peroration about the 9/11 attacks.

The US territory in an enclave in Scotland. Tatarov referred to what he saw as the illegality and amorality of what was taking place at the hydro. Later he mentioned the USA PATRIOT Act. This should have no legal force outside the US, unless of course you happened to be a victim of the intrusive processes it legitimized. By attributing to the old hydro building the condition of US territory, a state of affairs to which the British government must have consented, US federal laws would apply.

The USA PATRIOT Act. This law was introduced to Congress six weeks after 9/11. It was a vast and complicated document, and was presented with almost no time for careful advance reading. The sheer size and complexity of the document gave rise to the suspicion that it must have been in preparation for many months before 9/11. It was passed by both houses within the next three days, without serious or critical examination, and by a huge majority – when it came before the Senate only one senator voted against it. It was signed into law by the President on October 26, 2001.

The name of the Act is an acronym, and is usually printed in capital letters. Its full title is: *Uniting and Strengthening*

America by Providing Appropriate Tools Required to Intercept and Obstruct Terrorism. It granted to the authorities extensive and wide-ranging powers of investigation, surveillance and intervention. The range of new powers included the monitoring of telephone and email communication, and the collection and examination of bank and credit records. The FBI was authorized by the Act to issue National Security Letters (NSLs) without the approval of a judge. Someone receiving an NSL was prohibited by the Act from telling anyone else that it had been sent. In the first four years after the USA PATRIOT Act came into force, approximately four hundred thousand NSLs were issued – only one terrorism-related conviction was achieved as a result. Most Americans appeared to support the Act because it was represented to them as an anti-terror law which would not impact the lives of ordinary people. In reality, the Act enabled powers of intrusion, search and arrest at least comparable to those of any extremist police state in, say, the former Soviet Union.

In his soliloquies describing what was going on at the hydro, Tatarov mentioned the USA PATRIOT Act several times. I took this to mean that the enclave itself had been enabled by the Act, and once the zone containing the hydro had been delegated by the UK as American soil the federal agents I saw in the place had the same sweeping powers outside the USA as they would have had within it. In other words, they would be enabled to exercise intrusive powers against non-US citizens, and in particular against areas of the internet not based in the USA. Presumably there would be legal safeguards for non-Americans, but they would have to be tested in a court, the outcome postponed by the process of a new kind of international law.

Exact. Why did Tatarov deride my interest in exactness? My discipline is science, where exactitude is a quality to be sought. Mathematicians are not scientists and are wont to describe the higher reaches of maths in organic terms: beauty, perfection,

grace, poetry. This is not over-weening aggrandisement. The concepts of higher mathematics are frequently evanescent, intangible, evasive – they are inexpressible except in terms of other mathematical ideas or existing theorems, themselves based on the vapour trails of solved conjectures.

Hurt and damage. Tatarov went into some detail about the distinction between being hurt and being damaged. In everyday life this is something most people would instinctively understand.

I suddenly remembered, for instance, the feeling of acute hurt I unexpectedly experienced when I discovered that the data and voice recorders on most of the 9/11 aircraft had either not been found, or were damaged beyond retrieval. It was a personal blow, the end of a hope I had managed to keep hidden until then. I knew that there were virtually no air crashes in the past in which the data recorders had either not been found, or if found had been damaged beyond recovery. The collisions with the buildings had been catastrophic – massive impact, huge explosions, fire apparently hot enough to make steel glow cherry red – but in terms of aviation crashes they had no extra features of destructiveness. Many dozens of other crashes, just as terrifyingly destructive, had yielded black box data. The physical tolerances of the data recorders were designed to be well above the stresses of that sort of crash.

(The passport of one of the hijackers was said to have been found in the rubble of the twin towers, treated as incriminating evidence. This booklet made of card and paper, carried on the plane by its user, had somehow miraculously survived the impact, explosion and heat, while the reinforced, heatproof metal shells of the data recorders allegedly had not.)

The whole subject of the 9/11 data recorders was clearly a lie – someone cooked the evidence, falsified the story. There

was something so blatant and offensive about that lie that I felt maligned by it, damaged, in Tatarov's terms.

Social media. In 2006, when I met Tatarov at the hydro, the social media phenomenon was a minor feature of the internet. Twitter was created in March of that year; Facebook was experiencing its first period of expansion, after having been previously used only in universities. Other interactive forums were rapidly springing up. The exponential growth that was to follow was neither inevitable nor obvious, but the concept was clear from the start. Tatarov and the people he was involved with had accurately realized the potential for social revolution.

Social media are merely part of a communication process, thus inherently harmless, but because they cannot be easily controlled by governments they can be perceived by rogue régimes, or rogue elements within them, to be a threat. When authorities crave control they are motivated by the wish not to answer for their actions. It moves them into dark areas. Taking control, or trying to, leads inevitably to censorship, which in turn leads to the temptations of manipulation. When the motive is malign, facts and known events are no longer empirical. They can be downgraded into theories, suspicions, lies, alleged conspiracies. They can be redacted. History itself falls into doubt. Excuses for the mistakes or misjudgments of those in power can be made, cover-ups for their wrong-doing can be spread, prejudices can be sanctioned, imagined threats can be treated as real, wars can be started.

Everything Tatarov said or implied here related directly to the consequences of 9/11.

War was the result. No war is ever started for high motives, whatever the sophistry that attends it. War is the lowest, the most disgraceful of human activities. War is always about disputes over land and property, shortage of water, lack of food, need for mineral resources, antagonistic political theory,

religious bigotry, race prejudice, sheer bloody-mindedness.

Lil and me. They knew about us. Our names were linked. We were involved in 9/11. All this was true, but they were wrong in detail. They thought they knew everything but they did not. They said we were in New York on the day. Or that we were together on another plane. They did not know that Lil was aboard one of the planes that was destroyed, the one on which her husband, deeply involved in whatever was happening, had arranged for her to be that day. This was the plane they claimed to know most about, the one with a phoney flight data record, they one they allowed to enter the closed skies above Washington DC, the most fiercely controlled and defended airspace in the world.

That proved their intelligence was not so good. They did not know everything about me or Lil. They were not good at detail. They fucked up. Facts eluded them. Reality was something they thought they could change, but they should know they could not.

The rationale. Those young people at the hydro were intensely interested in the 9/11 attacks, Tatarov said. What they did not know about the events of 9/11 was negligible, he said. It was the rationale for their presence on the island. But even Tatarov himself did not know everything. What he called negligible were the omissions where the lives of real people existed, where hearts were broken, lives were lost.

The interview between us took place about five years after 9/11, a time when although public concern about the attacks had largely ceased and the media no longer pressed for explanations or evidence, certain parties began to form interest-groups to question the official story. These were airline pilots, structural engineers, architects, scientists, air traffic controllers, demolition experts, scholars, psychologists, academics, medical workers, victims' families.

Enquiries under the US Freedom of Information Act were being lodged in increasing numbers with the authorities, and a few previously unknown matters were coming to light, often with seeming reluctance on the part of those in charge. Invariably, once they had made an official disclosure under the Act, the relevant authority or government department, when queried, refused to engage further. No questions would be answered, no anomalies would be clarified, no obvious errors would be corrected, no explanation would be offered for why certain crucial facts were omitted. Or why, under the professed freedom of information, so much had been redacted with impenetrably thick black lines.

In the real world, where freedom was a daily assumption, the events of 9/11 were already history. Because of the taint of conspiracy theory, mainstream publishers tended to stay away from the subject, forcing the many books that were being written into the hands of underfunded fringe or independent publishers, who lacked the distribution power and credibility of the larger imprints. The same was true of films: no mainstream distributor would touch the material. Meanwhile, the number of online forums and amateur videos steadily proliferated.

Sidelining the subject like this had the effect of driving the argument underground, where it looked less confident and made it easier for detractors to denigrate what was said. Many of the books I came across were badly written, incompetently argued, and usually both. The homemade videos were even worse, with the same footage endlessly recycled, and fallacious arguments mixed in with the serious ones. It became too easy to dismiss as a conspiracy theorist anyone who argued with the official story, to treat valid work and unformed supposition with equal contempt.

Five years after my interview with Tatarov, on the tenth anniversary of the attacks, interest in 9/11 was naturally

renewed. The National Memorial on the site of the World Trade Center was officially opened in New York City, and work was well advanced on reconstructing or replacing the buildings that had been destroyed or damaged. By 2011 there were many more books in print from fringe publishers, hundreds of online videos and thousands of blog pages rehearsing the events of September 11, 2001. What many of these productions lacked in professional skill they made up for with passion, persistence and (in some cases) a disregard for possible reprisals against themselves.

In 2011 anyone with a computer and an open mind could explore this radical material, watch again the familiar video footage of the aircraft crashing into the twin towers, go carefully over the alleged events, learn about the mysteries, the lies, the cover-ups. Briefly, and in some cases memorably, the subject became public property once again.

But the official account remained essentially intact. Those who actively supported it set themselves against those who questioned it. Many of these detractors were persuasive and usually powerful. Facts became debatable, just as Tatarov had predicted. The sheer mass of material made serious research all but impossible.

Life went on somehow, although not for the many thousands who suffered and died in the military chaos that gripped the Middle East. The spread of religious fundamentalism led to terrorist attacks in major cities around the world. These were the consequences of 9/11 that we were having to come to terms with, just as the Thomas Theorem declared.

Those who were alive on the day were steadily growing older. Time would eventually remove them. Every year that passed pushed the story into greater seeming irrelevance for the modern world, set it further into the past, made the arguments more remote, made the truth harder to prove. What was

needed was the revelation of some hitherto unsuspected secret, or an extra event on that terrible day that had slipped past unnoticed. New light had to be shone, real facts found, new evidence produced, something that exposed the official story for what it was.

'9/11 is why these people are here at the hydro,' Tatarov said to me at the end of our interview. 'It is why I am here with them, and why you are here with me.'

SEVENTEEN

now

USA in USA

I took a seven-hour Delta Airlines flight, nothing unusual or alarming about it, efficiently crewed and smoothly flown. It took off from London on schedule, landed in Philadelphia on time – not much to remember of the journey as soon as it was over, but even so I was glad to be back on the ground. There was no interest in my border-enabling blood test card as I went through security at Heathrow, and no one asked to see it, nor was there any scanning device compatible with it, at Philadelphia International.

I arrived in the evening, local time, so I rented a car at the Alamo desk and drove it the short distance to the airport hotel, funded by Miranda on behalf of the magazine company. I hooked up the car to the battery charging point. The eleventh-floor room I was given had a densely curtained window that faced the rear of the hotel, but I did not look out.

I ate in the 'Freedom Grill' on the mezzanine floor, and began remembering how much I enjoyed American things, and the generous and open way most Americans acted and behaved towards visitors.

I had spent so much time fretting over the 9/11 story that I had started to forget a basic truth – that there is a huge

difference between the way a country works and the way it is run. This was a glimpse of America working as normal: people with friends and family, enjoying food and a feeling of easeful comfort, well-being and a civilized way of life.

I was in that weird physical condition that sometimes follows a long flight: a sense of elation, physical tiredness, a general vagueness of purpose and mind. It was probably not a reliable state for inner reflection, and I well knew that this restaurant in this hotel was in no sense typical of everything about the USA, that the immense, diverse and complex American society existed in thousands of shades of difference. The people I was seeing around me were relatively well off, travellers mostly, or aircrew on hold between flights, passing through. They did not represent a generality of the USA any more than I represented the Scottish way of life, or Britain, or the European Community, but even so we were all real. We had no agenda beyond the immediate needs and plans of whatever our lives were as we sat there enjoying dinner.

My argument about 9/11 was with a nebulous, distant group I thought of as 'officials' or 'the authorities', whatever those terms might mean and whoever might be the actual people concealed within the metonymy. Loosely, I supposed them to include senior members of government departments, maybe the President and the Vice President, maybe also the teams of aides, advisers and consultants in the White House administration, representatives and senators in Congress, business leaders perhaps, or the FBI, the CIA, the NSA and the Secret Service. In this sense I never specified who I thought they might be as individuals, even in my frequent inner brooding about what might have happened.

Or they might be of a darker, more secretive stripe – for example the neo-conservative think-tank *Project for a New American Century*, whose stated goal was to defend the homeland, to

secure unquestioned American military supremacy abroad and to promote American leadership worldwide. Although PNAC had ceased to exist in the second term of the George W. Bush administration, it was formed in 1997 and its most active period of lobbying and planning had been during the months leading up to 9/11. Of the twenty-five people who signed the founding statement of PNAC principles ten served in the Bush administration, including Vice President Dick Cheney and the Secretary of Defense Donald Rumsfeld.

Then there were the many different lobbyists, interest groups, campaigners, conservatives, liberal activists, cadres of the armed forces, managers of the intelligence services – and whoever it was, for a further instance, who had created an enclave of US territory, a so-called outreach establishment, on a hillside of a small Scottish island. Professor Tatarov had said without evidence, but so casually it sounded true, that it was Martin Viklund – I wanted both to believe and disbelieve that.

Somehow the falsity of 9/11 evidence had been put together – the story had not created itself, but maybe it had accrued around itself, rather than being deliberately plotted. I still believed the 9/11 deception began as an attempt to cover up something the authorities found embarrassing, but which had gone quickly out of control. Unable to restrain them, the lies grew wider, deeper, more elaborate. So there would have been no intention at first, for all I knew, but soon there were decisions taken and actions carried out that enabled the story to take hold.

Who was it who changed the passenger lists handed out to the press? Who had arranged the demolition of the three skyscrapers in New York City, and how did they do it? How were the phone calls from the hijacked planes actually made? Who had forged the flight data of the plane my lover was on?

The questions remained. But as I sat there in the well lit, tastefully decorated hotel restaurant, eating a perfectly cooked and attractively presented meal of pan-fried diver scallops, a plateful of food and extras far more generous than I could ever realistically eat, served by attentive and friendly staff, and surrounded on all sides by other diners, relaxed, seemingly contented Americans enjoying themselves – I found it difficult to connect the wilful malignity of the false 9/11 story with what I saw around me.

Maybe some of these people, if only it were possible for me to know, would be supporters of powerful lobbies like PNAC, maybe they too believed a strong and militarily supreme USA could benefit the world by dominating it with force of arms. They would feel no need to question the 9/11 story because it matched their own worldview, and they continued with their lives, untroubled.

Then again, maybe like me they questioned and doubted the official story, were troubled by its lack of truth, were not sure what they could do about it, but because there was no alternative they too went on with their lives.

Or, most likely of all, they had seen the events taking place on television two decades earlier, heard the authorities' explanation and accepted it. They too believed that something definitely had to be done as a response to this unprovoked attack, lived with the consequences of deploying military supremacy abroad, and did their best not to dwell too heavily on its implications.

The next morning I was awake early with the effects of jetlag. After breakfast I drove to the Prestell University on the west bank of the Schuylgill River, and found a recharging space in a parking lot close to the main entrance to the building that housed the Materials Science and Engineering Department.

Highway through the trees

Two and a half hours later I was in another parking lot, this one outside a strip mall located just off the highway in wooded country in the state of Delaware. At the university I had collected my letter of endorsement from Dr Schlaben's office (in which Dr Schlaben warmly introduced me as a close and trusted colleague – this from someone I had never met), and for the last two hours had been following a car driven extremely slowly by a young man called Bud, who had introduced himself as Dr Schlaben's senior research assistant. The highway ran south through thick forest.

We finally parked next to each other and climbed out of our cars.

'OK, here's the score, Mr Matson,' Bud said. 'I can't go with you any further because I need a pass to enter a military base.'

'Then I would too.'

'No – Dr Schlaben has entered you as a party to a Freedom of Information enquiry. Give them the letter you have at the gate, and some other form of ID. Let me show you how to find where you need to be.'

Bud produced a large-scale map he had downloaded from the internet, and pointed out the way to the base from where we were at that moment. We were standing less than half a mile before the turn-off I would need to take.

I said: 'Bud – what is all this about? I came to discuss superconductors.'

'Yeah, I know. Dr Schlaben felt this would interest you as much, probably more. He said to tell you that until shortly before Professor Tatarov died earlier this year, they were working closely together. You and Dr Schlaben have interests in common with Tatarov, whom I met several times and liked. He spoke well of you.'

'So am I going to meet Dr Schlaben?'

'Not this time – he has been called away to Washington.'

Bud then apologized for having driven us so slowly to this point, but explained that our Freedom of Information enquiry was time-stamped. He said I should now drive directly to the base, as the others were about to arrive.

'Others?'

'You are not alone in your interest.'

We shook hands and returned to our separate cars. I waited until he had driven back through the trees towards the highway, then went after him, his computer-printed map resting on the dash as I drove. I noticed that the dashboard read-out on the level of battery charge had entered the amber zone.

Once I turned off the highway towards the coast the forest started to thin out, and soon I could see a glimpse of Delaware Bay ahead of me. I passed several large and beautiful houses, but not long afterwards I was driving across low-lying land with shallow pools and swampy areas, an undeveloped zone that continued for about five miles.

I had no idea what to expect of my destination – perhaps a vast naval yard, where aircraft carriers and missile launchers and nuclear-powered submarines were built or repaired in dry dock, with barracks and training areas and deep-sea wharves, and swarms of personnel moving about. That was not what I found. The road came up to and then ran alongside a heavy fence, twelve or fifteen feet high, and of course endless coils of razor wire wound into the top and sides. The ground beyond was mostly bare.

I came to the gate suddenly: there was a gap in the fence where the road turned in. Two white-painted guard booths stood on each side – a woman officer wearing a white and orange hi-vis jacket over her smartly tailored uniform held out a white-gloved hand to halt my car. A large US flag fluttered in

the breeze. Above the gate was a painted sign, which I glimpsed as I brought the car to a halt: *Cape Henlopen Naval Base, Repairs and Provisioning, West Gate*. I triggered the window, which wound down smoothly.

The interrogation that followed was thankfully brief. I handed over Dr Schlaben's letter. My name was indeed on the guardpost list, and when the officer asked for more identification I played a hunch and presented the blood-test card I had been given in London. To my surprise it worked first time. She handed me a badge on a lanyard, which I looped around my neck.

The officer said, leaning down by my car window and pointing ahead, a droning prepared speech: 'You are expected in Facility 2, Mr Matson. You will follow the route to the right, and Facility 2 is the first building you come to. You are entering a US Navy Activity Base under the Freedom of Information Act. You are therefore required to abide by the lawful conditions of that Act. Your entry is permitted for a maximum of twelve hours, at the end of which you must leave. If you wish to return at a later date you must re-apply for entry.'

She moved back one step. I drove slowly away from her. As I did so the amber warning light on the dash began blinking bright red. Fortunately, Facility 2 was a short distance from the gate, and its wide parking lot had several unoccupied recharging bays.

I halted in the nearest one and set about hooking up the car. My credit card would not register on the first attempt, so I tried waving the badge I had just been given in front of an optical reader – after that the credit card was accepted and the recharging process began.

While I was concentrating on this, with the midday sun beating down on me, I was aware that someone was walking

281

across the lot in my direction. When I turned around I saw it was Jaye.

Her hair was no longer orange, and it had grown since the last time I saw her. She was wearing khaki shorts and a white T-shirt, and semi-silvered shades pushed up into her pale brown hair. She was smiling.

'Welcome to the land of free information, Ben,' she said.

There was a ship

We greeted each other informally, as if we had last seen each other only a couple of days before. The casual response made us both laugh. I was astonished to see her – here we were in a place I had not even known existed that morning, a parking lot on a remote coastline of one of the smallest states in the USA. For a few moments it seemed like an inexplicable coincidence.

'Why are you here?' I said at last.

'Same reason as you. We arrived about twenty minutes before you. Bud called to say you were on your way.'

'You know Bud?'

'And Rufus Schlaben. I've known Rufus for years. He's one of the people I make sure I see whenever I'm in the US. He was one of the team who discovered traces of nanothermite in the dust from the twin towers. He made the FoIA application for today.' She glanced up at the sun, then dropped her sunglasses down over her eyes. 'Let's get out of this heat.'

We set off across the blistering tarmac of the parking lot, heading for a small door set in the side of the immense, hangar-like building ahead of us.

'You'll meet some officials in a moment,' she said. 'Watch out for them. They're always around, but because we have Freedom of Information rights they can't stop us examining what's here. They obviously don't want us, though. I think they are recording us, tracking us electronically.'

'This is a Navy base. I'd expect them to be wary of visitors.'

'These aren't Navy people. The Navy is incidental to this. It's their facility, their maintenance hangar, but the guys I'm talking about are from Washington.'

'Federal agents?'

'US Coast Guard. That's the logo they have on the backs of their jackets. But they also have a logo saying FoIA stitched on their breasts. They don't want to let us any nearer the displayed evidence than they have to. One of them takes pictures of us through a long lens. It makes me nervy. Say yes to everything they want.' We were almost at the closed door. She was carrying several sheets of paper clipped together, and now she passed them to me. 'You need to have these. You are named as a co-applicant.'

I glimpsed five sheets of densely printed text. A long letter, another letter, some bullet-pointed paragraphs, many items with boxes waiting to be ticked..

'I can't read this now. How long would it take?'

'All you need to do is be seen holding it. The people I'm here with are filming, which in the end might provide us with a clear record of what's actually going on.'

'Jaye – as a matter of interest, what *is* going on here?'

Her fingers were already on the metal bar that released the door catch. The bar lay in direct sunlight, and she snatched her hand back, wincing. The silver rings on her fingers glinted.

'This is where the Navy brought the wreckage of the ship they pulled out of the sea. You know, the one they originally said was a plane, the one they didn't want on the news. We've applied to examine it and photograph it. That's the right they've granted – within certain restrictions. It took a long time to get this far, but they did finally agree. We haven't begun yet – it takes a while to set up camera and lights. But I've already had

a quick look, and there's one piece of the wreckage you should see too.'

'What is it?'

'You should make up your own mind. And in a separate area there's a small collection of personal items that were found – mostly coins, metal buttons and dogtags, I believe. I only caught a quick glimpse of them. Check them out while you're here.'

She touched her hand to the metal bar again, this time more gingerly, and pushed open the door. We moved from the late summer heat and glare into cool semi-darkness. She pushed up her sunglasses into her hair. A second door led to the main part of the building. This was a vast enclosed space under a high, glass-panelled roof. There were many hoists, cranes and gantries, fenced off working areas. At least half the space at one end was filled with roof-high stacking shelves crammed with stuff. Several fork-lift trucks were in sight, none of them in use. I took in all this at a glance – the overall impression was one of emptiness, a lack of human activity. There was the sound of a huge ventilator running constantly. The air was cool.

I saw Jaye's film crew on the far side of the space. They were all women, working to get their equipment set up.

As soon as we were inside the main area, three young men wearing dark blue or black tracksuits stepped out to intercept us.

Ignoring Jaye, one of them said: 'Sir, I understand you are Benjamin Matson, a Scottish citizen, co-applicant under the 1967 Freedom of Information Act to examine the remains of the US armed merchant ship, the *Edward B. Hawley*. Is this you, sir?'

'Yes, it is.'

'You may not touch the exhibit or go any nearer to it than the barrier allows. Your co-applicants have permission to film, also without making physical contact. Here is a copy of the

metallurgical report which was the basis for your application.'

He handed me a sheet of paper, which was printed with the Prestell University letterhead. Even while I was glancing at it the three young men moved away. I noticed, as Jaye had said, that the front of their jackets carried the FoIA logo. There was a glassed-in cabin or office close to the door where we had entered, and they went inside. They stood against the windowed wall from which they could look out into the body of the hangar. One of them took up a camera with a telephoto lens.

Jaye led me across the floor to where the film crew were setting up three portable camera lights. I was greeted by them and we all shook hands, but I was distracted by the sight of the exhibit laid out for inspection on the hangar floor. There was a long assemblage of broken and twisted metal, most of it filthy, smeared with the remains of seaweed or algae growth. It was encrusted with shells, deep gouges, jagged edges. There were several large pieces of steel, bent or broken, twisted and warped. One sheet had petal-like curves punched out of it. There was a stench of sea, of decay, rust, oil. I could not really tell what it was – I had never smelled anything like it before.

Alloy 7075

I was still staring around at the wreckage when Jaye turned and stood beside me.

'Have you read Rufus's report?' She indicated the Prestell letter, which the official had handed me.

'Not yet. I haven't had a chance.'

'Just read it, Ben.'

'Tell me what I need to know,' I said. 'I'm suffering information overload.'

Jaye moved close to me, so that our shoulders touched and we both had our backs towards the office space. She reached over to where I was holding the letter from the university.

Speaking softly, she said: 'OK, but we have to be careful. I think they have directional mics – keep facing away from them. Through his university, Rufus was commissioned to carry out a metallurgical assay of this wreckage.' Her finger ran across a short list: several different kinds of steel, copper, brass, a number of alloys – about fifteen items in all. 'This is the one we're interested in,' Jaye said, pointing at the last item on the list, identified as Alloy 7075. 'Rufus found several pieces of it. He said he saw about twelve or fifteen large sections, but they've nearly all been removed since. There's only one piece left in the exhibit, and as Rufus told me last week, it's still here. Presumably no one recognized it. 7075 is a modern alloy of aluminium and zinc, plus some other metals in smaller quantities. It can't belong to the ship. The alloy was developed in Japan during the Second World War – this ship, the *Edward B. Hawley*, was a Liberty Ship, built in New Jersey during 1940. She was torpedoed in 1941. Alloy 7075 is a superstrength lightweight alloy, rarely found on ships, certainly not on ships of this age. These days the alloy is used to build aircraft wings and fuselages. After Rufus had filed his report he immediately started the application for an examination under Freedom of Information.'

'Why isn't he here himself?'

'We don't know for sure. Two nights ago he was taken to Washington – they said he had to give evidence at a Senate committee investigation. He couldn't get out of it.' Jaye was looking uneasy. She said: 'Look, if we stand here too long they'll get interested in what we're talking about. We're supposed simply to walk along and look at the wreckage.'

'Without touching it.'

'Without any visible reaction at all,' she said. 'Don't give anything away.'

We started by the end of the heaped metal wreckage. Closer

to, the smell was even more overpowering, as if releasing the remains of this ship from the grip of the seabed had accelerated its decay. Every piece of broken metal laid out for us to examine was torn or corroded. I suddenly felt gloomily overwhelmed by the sour smell of the ocean, the association of death by violence, death by drowning, the chaos of this killing by submarine – so long ago, in a war fought and finished two decades before I was born. I could easily imagine the violence of the torpedo, slamming in and exploding against the hull. Men were inside the ship, some instantly killed, others thrown into the sea, all eventually dead one way or another. I imagined the slow end of the crippled ship, sinking through the peaceful shallows, the greenish light from above fading, the final descent to the darkness below.

We walked side by side, slowly. Jaye stayed on my left, placing herself between me and the men monitoring us, so her head was turned away from them. We passed one monstrous tangle of rusting, broken steel after another. Everything was corroded, but some pieces had lighter patches, inexplicably clean, while many others had deep holes or gashes.

Jaye stopped walking.

'This is it,' she said quietly, a whisper, almost inaudible. 'In front of us now. Slightly to the left. This was one of the pieces Rufus identified.'

Superficially, the piece of metal she was indicating looked little different from the rest of the wreckage, but allowing for the encrustation and stains, the stress of being under the sea for so long, it appeared to be more or less flat. Then I saw it was actually smoothly curved – not bent or pressured, but made that way. It had a shape, an intent, like the side of a large jet's fuselage, or the upper surface of a wing? The edge of it closest to us had been torn away from something else, so it was jagged. We could see how thin it was.

'That's not steel, Ben.'

'It looks much the same as everything else.'

'Only on the surface. It's thinner, shallower, it doesn't have the weighty look of steel plate. It's different.'

I saw what she meant. All the other wreckage looked bulky, heavy. The piece she was indicating looked unlike the rest – it appeared lighter, manufactured with more engineering.

Jaye suddenly reacted, turning away from me in surprise. In the same instant one of the Coast Guard men took hold of my elbow from behind. He had come up behind us silently. The grip was painfully tight. I curled away from Jaye, trying to defend myself, raise my arm.

'We require you to keep moving, sir.'

He was somehow pressing on or activating a nerve. It was excruciating. I managed to turn strenuously enough to make him release my elbow. The papers I had been clutching fluttered to the floor, one of them beyond the barrier I had been instructed never to cross. I backed away from the man, my painful arm pressed against my stomach. I bent forward over it, protecting it. I was gasping in agony.

'You appear to have dropped your papers, sir. Let me help you.'

As he bent down to scoop up what I had dropped, Jaye said: 'We have the right to examine this evidence.'

'That right is unchallenged. You must continue at a normal walking pace. You must not interfere with the wreckage.'

'We were just looking.'

'Move on.'

The pain was starting to subside, and my focus returned. I took a breath and was able to say:'There's a piece there that does not appear to be ship steel –'

'All the evidence is as you see it. Keep moving.'

We stepped away from the man. I was furious at what had

happened and was ready to confront him with what I thought our rights were, but Jaye briefly took hold of my good arm and we went on. The man remained by the low barrier, standing in the place where we had been closest to the sheet of alloy.

Jaye suddenly turned back to him.

'There's a display here of personal effects found with the wreck. We have been granted permission to examine them too.'

'Correct,' he said.

'Where is the display? Is it still in that office?'

'You have the permission document. That states the evidence is displayed separately.'

He vaguely indicated the office area where his two colleagues were still in sight.

We left him, continuing the weird, leisured stroll past the wreckage of many human lives. My arm was throbbing from where the man had pinched my nerve, and I was still seething.

I gestured angrily at the corroded metal dumped beyond the barrier.

'If that sheet of metal is part of an aircraft – what's this heap of ship wreckage about? Was the sunken ship in the same part of the sea? Did they actually find it there, next to the remains of the aircraft? What sort of coincidence is that? Or did they already have a wreck of a ship on hand, ready for use as a decoy?'

'Ben, it doesn't matter where this wreckage came from. A lot of shipping was lost along this coast during the war. It's false evidence. The key information is that the presence of the alloy here proves an aircraft went down in the sea at that position. Rufus said he was certain the sheet was part of a wing panel from American 77.'

'But if the alloy was in general use it could be from any other aircraft, not just that one.'

'No other aircraft is missing. American 77 is the only crashed US commercial plane that's never been found.'

'So is that it, or part of it? It's from the actual plane – the one they claimed crashed into the Pentagon, but which couldn't have?'

'Seems that way.'

We continued our self-conscious amble beside the barrier, turning back so that we might pass the piece of wing alloy again. The man from the Coast Guard had walked away. Another glimpse of the fragment of wing. I was in awe of it, the immense significance of it as a relic, a surviving piece of the real American 77, an icon of modern history, final proof that what we had been told about the Pentagon attack was untrue.

On this second pass the difference between it and the rest of the wreckage seemed obvious. It radiated its singularity, the only fragment of reality in an exhibition of deception.

'But why is it still here, Jaye? These Coast Guard people clearly know something about it. Dr Schlaben's report was explicit about his findings. Surely someone read it, understood it? If they were cheating with this display, why didn't they just dump everything that might have been part of the aircraft?'

'They probably meant to. But the guys here today – they're too junior to have been involved with any decision to falsify the evidence. They weren't the people who raised the wreckage from the sea – they weren't even the ones who brought it here for storage. They are here to keep an eye on us, according to the book. To them, 9/11 is something that happened back in their childhood – look how young they are.'

One of the women from the film crew was walking quickly towards us.

'Jaye, we have a bit of a problem,' she said. 'We need you.'

Looking back I saw that the three Coast Guards had turned their attention to the crew. The woman operating the camera was being held back from the dolly where she had been mounting

it, and she was struggling to keep hold of it. Another of the men stood in front of her spreading his arms. A light stand fell over as one of the men tried to move it.

I stayed where I was, knowing Jaye could deal with it.

I flexed my sore elbow, feeling another twinge of pain. My anger about that was fading, but my arm still hurt.

I took the opportunity to take another long look at the sheet of lightweight alloy. Now that I was sure what it was, its difference from the rest of the wreckage seemed beyond question. Under the corrosion and encrustation, the steel plates from the old ship's hull had a darkness, a crude hard look of heavyweight purpose. Strength in mass. The sheet of alloy had been fashioned, crafted, manufactured to a precise specification, for an exact purpose.

Beneath its own layers of sea-change I glimpsed lightness, a silvery surface. Perhaps I was imagining it, willing it to be that way, but clarity comes with understanding.

It was yet another strand to the string of old lies, the long and familiar story.

The closed case

I walked back to where Jaye was standing with the film crew. The Coast Guard men had backed off again. Two of the women were packing up – they were coiling the power leads, disconnecting the lights, putting away the camera.

Jaye walked across to meet me. 'We're going to close down. There's nothing here we can film that would add to what we've seen. It was probably a mistake to try, but we didn't know what we were going to find. Rufus's metallurgical report is really all the evidence we need. You've seen the actual sheet of alloy, I've seen it. We're getting negative shit from these guys, and we don't need the footage. We have several close-up shots of the alloy – that's enough.'

The Coast Guards were returning to the office area where they had been earlier.

'Before I leave I think I should take a look at the personal stuff the divers brought up.'

'It's all back there.' She pointed across to where the Coast Guards had gone.

'If those guys are in there maybe I'll give it a miss.'

'No, you should see it — there might be something I didn't notice. I'm going to have to help get this gear back to our truck.'

I had come to this place without expectation — but everything had been changed by meeting Jaye again, by the grim sight of that ancient steel wreckage and its images of destruction and death, but above all by the realization that maybe there had in fact been a plane lost at sea. I suddenly remembered seeing the snatch of newsreel I found on the Canadian website: Helena McCardle and her crew, filming perhaps by chance something lightweight and silvery as it was lifted from the sea. Helena and her crew were then precipitately bundled out of the USA on the next plane to Glasgow. If that was not the piece of alloy that was lying there now, ten metres from where I was standing, then it was another part of the same plane, another fragment of evidence. I was realizing the truth of what had happened to Lil's plane. I should examine everything there was to see while I had the opportunity.

'Wait for me in the parking lot,' I said.

The atmosphere in the immense hangar was alien and disturbing. I was anxious to be through with the whole thing. I disliked the idea of being watched and challenged, and, of course, suffering another physical assault. What secret was so great as to justify these elaborate arrangements, almost obsessive in preparation? We were entitled to know the truth, and this charade about freedom of information was an affront to the idea it implicitly contained.

292

I walked across to the office. The Coast Guards were standing by the windows, surveilling the interior space of the hangar as Jaye and her colleagues started removing the camera gear. I went in.

'Personal effects,' I said without preamble. 'Where are they?'

'In here, sir.' The man who spoke pointed to a small wooden box, which had been placed on one of the working surfaces close to where they were standing.

'I should like to examine them.'

'Go ahead.'

'I should like to examine them without you three standing here.'

'We have to make sure you will not touch any of the items. We are authorized under the 1967 Freedom of Information Act —'

'I've no intention of touching them,' I said. 'I have authority too. Get out of here. I'll tell you when I've finished. Just leave. When I'm gone you can check the items against your inventory.'

'Sir, there is no inventory.'

'That's your problem, not mine. Get out of this room now.'

There was a moment's further hesitation, then without another word the three of them left. The door closed behind them: not a slam, a gentle clicking of the catch. Two of them walked away, but the third stayed beyond the glass panelled door, standing there to watch me. I went straight across to him, pulled the door open again angrily.

'Get the hell out of my face,' I said.

He backed off.

Finally I was alone. I imagined the telephoto camera lens was going to be pointed at me, but at least those bastards were no longer around me. While I stood watching, making sure the last of the Coast Guard men was well away from me, I saw Jaye

and another woman carrying one of the light mounts towards the exit.

I raised the lid of the box.

Jaye had warned me there was not much to see, and she was right. Almost everything inside was as corroded as the main wreckage, and as I raised the lid the now familiar sour smell of salt water and old decay rose around me.

The first thing I could identify was what looked to me like half of an expandable metal wristwatch strap. It had fused into an immovable strip.

A ball of unidentifiably dirty and degraded fabric, half rotted into itself, presumably all that remained of garments that had somehow survived, if only to an extent.

Tarnished cutlery, bent and distorted to an almost unrecognizable degree: spoons, a fork, a long knife with a bent blade and no handle.

Dogtags normally worn by US servicemen – I counted fifteen of these, placed neatly in a boxed section at the bottom of the case. They were indecipherably twisted and corroded, and any identifying impressions on them had long ago worn away.

A buckle. A chunk of slimy-looking rubber or plastic, or something that had rotted down to that appearance, roughly in the shape of a shoe. The flint wheel and shield of a cigarette lighter. Three glass bottles, unbroken but crazed and clouded, unidentifiably. Many small pieces of metal, with no hint of what they might once have been: parts of pocket knives, parts of pens, pieces of jewellery?

In a plastic bowl placed at the bottom of the case were many coins, a thick soup of old metal, too many to count. I leaned closer to try to identify them, but because they were corroded, and had been swept by the undersea tidal friction of sand and grit, it was almost impossible to see what they had once been. I assumed they were mostly American coins – the size of them

looked about right. I stared down at them all, trying to pick out details. I wondered if there was a date still visible anywhere, as anything marked later than 1941 would be corroboration of a sort.

I moved back from the case, then went to the office door and looked out into the main area. Jaye's crew had almost finished packing their equipment. The three Coast Guard men were observing what the women were doing, standing near them.

I returned to the case and reached down into the bowl. I fingered aside many of the coins near the top, to try to find some that were less obscured by the action of the sea. I turned several of them over, looking for the dates. The movement unexpectedly released another wave of the unpleasant smell of decay.

Mixed in with the coins were a few tiny objects, flat and circular, carelessly mixed up. I felt and pushed aside about a dozen buttons, a yellow plastic counter, several small glass slivers, a medallion of some kind.

And a little black disc, with a hole punched into a tab that stuck out from the perimeter. It was still intact. It had a design etched into the surface – I could feel the relief against my fingertips. It was jet black, a piece of mineral jet lignite, unharmed by two decades immersed in deep sea water.

I held it under one of the lights. I saw the large, slavering jaws of a hound. Behind, I could just make out the masts and tattered sails of a merchantman, wrecked on a sandbar. The last time I had seen this charm was when Lil and I were kissing as we separated in New York City, September 9, 2001. I remembered hearing her bangle bracelet clattering lightly against the side of my face as she reached up to stroke my hair. I had taken her hand, looked at the charms, repeated needlessly our plans to meet in two days' time in Los Angeles. I had moved the charms around, found the Dracula icon, made some joke about it, kissed her again. Then we parted.

I should have rejoiced with the feeling, at last, of closure. Two decades of uncertainty were at an end. Instead, I felt the rage in me redoubling.

But for me at last, it was over. Now I knew how Lil had been killed – American 77 had been flown out to sea, where it crashed or was deliberately ditched.

I slipped the charm into my shirt pocket, where it rested thinly and invisibly. I closed the lid of the case. I stepped back. The Coast Guards were coming towards me.

I ignored them, walked past them and away, went to the door that I knew led to the outside. I could see the sunlight limned around the edge of the outer door. I pushed it open and strode into the parking lot, felt the heat of the early afternoon swelling around me, a glare of white sunlight, a feeling of dust and dryness, the smell of trees, of tarmac and cars under the sun.

A short distance from where I was standing was a truck I had not noticed on arrival, while walking with Jaye. Painted on the side was a name: *Astra*, a women's media collective based in Philadelphia. The women were still pushing their camera gear into the rear of the truck, with the tailgate down.

Between them and me stood three black cars. They were not parked: they had come to a halt at an angle across the white lines of the designated bays. The front and rear vehicles were both SUVs, polished to a high shine. A woman in a business suit stood beside the first car – a man in a business suit stood against the third. They were bracketing another car, a longer, lower saloon, heavy on its wheels, window glass half-silvered.

I came to a halt. I had nothing in my hands apart from the papers Jaye had given me earlier. I raised both hands to reveal this, then let the pages slip away, spinning down to the ground. I walked quickly towards the car in the centre, and before either of the two security people could stop me I had seized the

handle of one of the passenger doors, trying to wrench it open. It was immovable. A moment later they were on me, throwing me violently to the ground, slamming my head against the hard surface of the parking lot. My already tender elbow took my weight as I fell. I shrieked with pain, but also with anger and humiliation. A knee pressed hard on my back, pushing me against the ground. A hand shoved my head down, jamming it immovably against the hot tarmac. One of the men knelt beside me, very close indeed. His knee pressed against my nose. He moved a gun barrel to where I could see it.

I was facing the wrong way – I could not turn my head. I heard a car door open behind me, probably the one I had tried a few seconds before. I could not see who was there.

His voice said: 'His name is Matson – I know who he is. He can be released. Frisk him first.'

'Yes, sir!'

They still held me, though, and I heard the man who had spoken moving back to his car, his long low saloon with the armour plating and the silvered windows.

I shouted: 'Why don't you look at what you've pulled out of the sea, Viklund!' But I could hardly draw breath. That was all I could say. I felt as if my words were released into the windless space around the hangar, lost in the hot air.

Three car engines started. Then I was released, hauled to my feet, thrown hard against the side of one of the SUVs, briefly but thoroughly frisked, pushed roughly aside and abandoned. All doors slammed.

As the cars swept away I pressed my hand to the breast pocket of my shirt. Lil's charm was still safely hidden inside.

EIGHTEEN

ahead: 2024

The Democrat conceded

Jeanne and I stayed up most of the night to watch the results coming in on television. It was Tuesday, November 5, 2024, and the USA was electing its 47th President.

We sat side by side on the rug in front of the television, the volume low so as not to wake the boys. The curtains in our living room were open, but the town and the sea road were silent in the darkness. A thick cloud layer obscured the moon. The waters of the firth were still and black, the street-lights on the far side of the bay reflecting on the surface. It was uncanny how normal and familiar it looked, while the election of the new President was fraught with the possibilities of change and upheaval, and much danger in a destabilized world.

At around four in the morning, Scottish time, the Democrat candidate finally conceded defeat. The Republican candidate, now President-elect, delivered a gracious acceptance speech in the hotel in Washington DC where he had made his temporary headquarters. A huge crowd of supporters were jammed into the lobby, cheering and waving banners. His wife and two of their adult children were there to support him. His running mate, now Vice President-elect, stood beside him. The scene

was a dazzle of American flags, drifting tinsel, with blue, white and red balloons floating down from above.

The speech included an announcement of the executive orders he would sign as soon as he moved into the Oval Office in January. Most of these were based on pledges he had made during the election campaign.

For the last few months, Jeanne and I had been following the primaries, then the campaign itself. At first we were aware only of headlines on television news, or on the political pages of the online newspapers, and for that short period the distant feeling of unreality and dread felt slight. American elections always concerned us, because like everyone in the world who was not an American we had no vote but were always affected by the outcome. As the season of primaries continued, though, and front-runners emerged, we felt resigned to the result. Only when the Republican convention was held in Chicago, and the winning candidate announced his running mate, did we at last take real notice.

The Republican nominee for Vice President was Martin Oliver Viklund.

At the end of his short acceptance speech, gracious to his opponent, healing to the nation as a whole, the President-elect said this:

'I intend at last to put right one of the worst mistakes this great nation of ours has ever made. It was one for which I have personally suffered for nearly a quarter of a century. Twenty-three years ago, my oldest son Daniel was tragically killed while on duty in New York City. Danny was a firefighter. On September 11, 2001, he was called upon to try to rescue the people who were trapped on the upper levels of the north tower of the World Trade Center. He and three other brave young men managed to climb to the eighty-ninth floor, carrying their fire-fighter's apparatus, in itself a massive achievement on foot. His

last radio contact with the ground was one minute before the tower collapsed. He was still inside. His body has never been found and identified, nor have I ever received any satisfactory explanation of what actually happened on that terrible day. I know that my son Danny was a victim of the worst terrorist attack this country has ever known, along with at least three thousand other innocent Americans. However, the real truth of that day has never been revealed. On September 11, 2001, America lost its innocence –'

Beside him, Vice President-elect Martin Viklund stood proudly, the smile of electoral success spreading across his face.

Then the President-elect said:

'– Soon after I take office next year, I plan to set up a Commission for 9/11 Truth and Forgiveness. It will have the full authority of the office of President. Every man and women who had official contact with the events of 9/11 will be expected to come forward, first to tell the truth about what they know, then to be granted forgiveness and amnesty, should they have made mistakes, or in any way, large or small, done wrong. At last this great nation shall be told exactly what was suffered and lost during that day of tragedy and mystery.'

Martin Viklund's smile did not fade. He applauded his new boss vigorously, as the crowd roared enthusiastic support. He was still smiling as the President-elect raised his hand in thanks and farewell, put his arm around his wife, and left the lobby. Viklund's own arm was still held high as he passed out of sight.

The truth

When the speech was over we turned off the TV and went to bed. I could not sleep, and although she was lying still beside me I suspected that Jeanne was also awake. My thoughts circled, as they often do when sleep is not possible.

I thought about Martin Viklund, everything I knew of him, everything I knew or believed he had done, and everything I thought he might be capable of doing during the years ahead. What truths did he actually know? Would he own up to them? Could his word be trusted? Would he somehow manipulate the terms of the commission so that his role in 9/11 would never be known? The memory of his smiling face haunted me, his arm raised in triumph as he turned away from the cameras. Would he seek or receive forgiveness?

Soon after seven o'clock Jeanne and I dressed and hung around the house together, waiting for the moment when we could rouse the boys, prepare them for another ordinary day at school. Lucinda appeared in her robe at around eight o'clock, smiled at both of us, then went to make herself some tea. She walked unsteadily. Physically, she was frail, but for at least the last twelve months she had remained lucid. We said nothing to her about what had happened in the USA.

Two hours later, with the boys at school, and with Lucinda dressed and sitting in her customary armchair in our living room, Jeanne said: 'I need a walk. We should both get some fresh air.'

I moved the car from the garage and we drove along the coast road to Port Bannatyne. I parked on the sea front and for twenty minutes we walked beside the sea wall, feeling the wind curling in from the Kyles. It was still too early in the winter for snowfall, even on the mountains around us, but the wind was icily cold.

At the edge of the village we reached the gate where we could join the West Island Way, a path for walkers that climbed the hills of the interior. We were not dressed for a long hike, but we were restless and not yet ready to return home. We decided to ascend the first hill, where the path ran alongside the boundary of the former hydro hotel grounds.

We climbed as far as the place where the treeline began, which also marked the upper border of the old hydro grounds. I had been here many times before, Jeanne less often. While we caught our breath we looked across at the stunning scenery, sharp and clear in the winter light, but with the trees bare and the fields lying fallow the view was bleaker, starker than it looked when the summer visitors were on the island. Woodsmoke rose from chimneys along the village road. One of the ferries, small and distant, was chugging across the bay, breaking the waves, heading for the mainland.

I noticed Jeanne was shivering. She huddled down inside her fleece, lowering her chin, pulling the hood down over her forehead.

'Let's go back,' I said. 'We shouldn't leave Lucinda alone too long.'

'She's OK. She often naps at this time of day.'

We started walking down the uneven track, back towards the village. I could not help glancing across at where the hydro had once been. That patch of territory ceded to a foreign power. Why and how it had been done I never knew for sure, but it must have been ceded back since. It had become a vacant site. There was talk in the town of a business group with plans to build a luxury hotel on the hill, with a conference suite and sports club, and an extended marina along the shore.

'You're not saying anything,' Jeanne said.

'About Viklund? There's nothing left I want to say about him.'

'What's going to happen?'

'A Truth and Forgiveness enquiry into 9/11?' I said. 'I cannot believe they mean that. Viklund knows the truth already.'

'You still believe he was involved?'

'I don't doubt it for a moment. But as for what he will do next, I have no idea.'

I was approaching my sixtieth birthday – I was with Jeanne and the boys, living in the part of the world where I was most happy. I was given strength by the airs of Scotland, the sublime scenery, the love of this good woman, our shared love of the children. These were the only truths that counted. I had fought for another kind of truth, but I no longer had the appetite for the fight.

And forgiveness?

We drove home. My keys dangled from the ignition as usual. The two little discs of jet were almost out of sight behind the leather fob. When we were back in the house I brought in some extra logs for the stove in our living room, and set about lighting a fire. Although the central heating was switched on, the room was chilly, and Lucinda, curled up on her armchair with a small blanket, looked as if she had been trying to keep warm. Her eyes were closed. She must have heard me clattering and banging around as I cleaned out the ashes, placed kindling and logs in the fire basket, started the fire, but she did not rouse. As I sometimes did I stared at her long enough to be certain she was breathing steadily.

Afterwards I went to my basement study. I caught up with emails, read my regular choice of internet news pages. I sent an enquiry to one of the magazines I was hoping to sell some work to, and a suggestion for a story about a radical new surgical procedure that was being pioneered in a hospital in the Far East. A normal day – only the knowledge of the new American President and his choice of Vice President was lurking obstinately at the back of my conscious mind.

At midday I returned to the living room, now warm and snug. I threw on two more logs, then went to the window to look at

the weather. The wind was sending low clouds scudding across the firth, and a drifting, misty rain fell unrelentingly.

I turned on the STV news from Edinburgh – the main story was of course the new President in the USA. It was an emphatic electoral win, with a clear majority of the popular vote as well as the electoral college. It seemed to many commentators a good result – a great number of governments around the world had sent congratulatory messages to the next president, although the Scottish government had not.

The news programme re-ran the recording of the final part of the President-elect's acceptance speech, then showed reactions to the announcement about his planned 9/11 commission. Some senior American political figures were brought out of retirement to be asked for their views: they all said it astonished and concerned them that the coals of a long-past event should now be raked over.

At the end of the story, the TV news returned to Viklund's fixed smile, his triumphantly raised arm. They froze the image, made no comment. Why should they concentrate on him? A silent image is sometimes more powerful than one that is described.

Lucinda roused, turned in her seat so that she could see the screen. She leaned forward, staring at the President-elect.

'That's Viklund,' she said. 'Did he win?'

'His party won – he'll be the new Vice President.'

'Viklund was the man Dougal had been summoned to see, the next day, the day they found him in his room. He phoned me the evening before – I had already gone to bed, but his call woke me up.'

'You've known about Viklund?' I said.

'Only his name. Only that Dougal had been told to go and see him.'

She continued staring at the screen after the film finished.

A political commentator was in the studio, and began a brief assessment of the new president's likely impact in the White House.

Talking over the broadcast, I said to Lucinda: 'Why did Dougal phone you that night? He must have known he would get you out of bed, because of the time difference.'

'I don't know. He wanted me to know the name of the man and remember it. The line wasn't very good – it had an echo on it. I knew he was worried, but I kept thinking someone was listening in. We didn't talk long. He told me to search through his papers, his notes – he said he had kept a copy of his manuscript. In the basement, hidden away. And he said to be careful. He didn't say which book – just the book, the book. He made me say I knew which book he meant. Of course I knew exactly what he was talking about, but I was sure there was someone else on the line. I told him I would do what he wanted. Then we hung up. That was the last time I spoke to him.'

'Did you find his papers?'

'Not then. I wasn't able to search for them until a few weeks later. The news that he had died came through the next day, and nothing else mattered. Jeanne – you must remember that day.'

Jeanne crossed the room and went to her mother's chair. They held hands, a quick movement, a tight squeeze of their fingers.

'I was still living in Berlin,' she said. 'It was already evening when I heard, so I couldn't get a flight until the next day. Even then, I wasn't back in Edinburgh until nearly midnight. I'll never forget that.'

I said to Lucinda: 'So you found Dougal's papers later. Are they still there, where he had left them?'

'They're in the same box,' Lucinda said.

'Did you read them?'

'I read his manuscript, or some of it. By then I loathed everything to do with the hijackings. I didn't want to be reminded. I was curious, but in my heart I didn't want to know.'

'Can you remember if Viklund was mentioned in it?'

'I only skimmed, but if his name was there I would have noticed. I didn't see anything about him.'

'But since then, since Dougal died, you've found out more about Viklund?' I said.

'Until today, still only his name.'

'Are you suggesting that he had something to do with Dougal's death?'

'No. Dougal had a heart attack. That's what they said, that's what they certified.'

'Then what's the connection with Viklund?'

'There's a difference between what I accept as true and what I believe might really have happened. But I've seen what Viklund looks like now. I'll never forget his face. Why was he smiling like that?'

'He had just won the election.'

'Well, I'll never forgive him, whatever they say now at their investigation.' She shook her shoulders in an irritated way. 'He'll go on doing what he does, no matter what we think. He's everyone's problem now.'

The television was showing old footage of him, his past career, an extract from one of his speeches during the campaign. This was followed by an oddly disturbing shot I had never seen before: Viklund, walking with other suited officials on the lawn of the Pentagon, the building still on fire behind them. He was holding a piece of white-painted metal wreckage.

Then Lucinda said: 'Your friend Lilian was married to him, wasn't she?'

'How do you know that?'

'I worked it out. I have time to think these days, time to listen. What happened back then is all of a pattern, everything connects. Or do you believe in coincidences, Ben?'

Lucinda rested her head on the cushion behind her, turned her face to the side.

I tried to concentrate on what they were talking about on the news broadcast. The political commentator was discussing the new President's promise of a thorough investigation into 9/11. She was saying: 'Although the facts of this story were exhaustively investigated years ago, and made public, there are many people in America who maintain that crucial information is still being withheld. Whether the new President's initiative will ever be enough to satisfy the conspiracy theorists remains to be seen.'

Lucinda had closed her eyes, and was wrapped up beneath her blanket. She was soon breathing steadily, calmly. Jeanne sat down beside me.

'Has she ever said anything about Viklund before?' I asked her.

'Not to me.'

'Nor to me.'

The logs settled in the woodburner – sparks spat and flew. I heard the arriving note of the ferry whistle as the ship headed slowly for the quay. I left the sofa and went to the window, always liking to watch the ships as they docked. Their crossings to and from the mainland were like the island's slow heartbeat, regular and reliable, keeping the place alive. The fine cold rain was falling insistently, like a mist, hiding the hills, blending the sea with the sky so that there was no visible horizon. Jeanne had followed, and stood beside me.

'Are you going to look for Dad's papers?' she said quietly, a whisper.

'I don't know,' I said. 'Do you want me to?'

I reached into my pocket, felt down with my fingertips to my key ring, touched the two little discs of jet lignite. After I found the one that had been Lil's I had hoped they would be all that remained of the story, but now I was no longer sure.

Author's Note and Acknowledgements

An American Story is of course fiction, a novel. It is not investigative journalism. However, the narrator is a journalist and he does investigate. Ben Matson's views are not necessarily mine, but we did much the same research.

Some readers I imagine will be interested in following Matson's trail of evidence, and of course the world of the internet lies waiting to help out. Leaving aside social media (which for a serious researcher must always remain a total no-go zone) there are literally thousands of websites and blogs which carry evidence, arguments, interviews, opinions, theories, videos and much else about the 9/11 attacks on the USA. A lot of it is crackpot conspiracy stuff, and much of the rest is amateurishly made and argued – but some of the material is undeniably intriguing, and a certain number of sites offer plausible, disturbing and in many cases convincing arguments against the officially accepted explanation. The best of these are based on intelligent reasoning, scientific fact or engineering knowhow and a forensic thoroughness in sorting evidence.

Here then are a few words as a brief guide to the best sources of responsible argument. Links to internet sites are not shown – this is because the printed word has a long shelf-life, and internet conventions constantly change. In my direct experience,

printed URLs are often out of date, or lead to closed or expired sites, or in some cases ones which are not safe to explore. A search engine will of course lead you to the most recent versions of any sites I mention here.

The best all-round site for clear, calm and well supported argument against the official version is **Consensus 9/11: The 9/11 Best Evidence Panel**. This is kept up to date, it is available in many languages, and will lead the serious researcher to fully indexed and cross-referenced material, some of it video evidence not easily found elsewhere.

Then there are the loosely connected professional websites which remain sceptical about the official account through their own specialist area of knowledge or experience. These are often scathingly referred to as 'truthers' or 'conspiracy theorists', as if a concern with truth or fact were somehow disreputable or irrational. Wikipedia has a long and reasonably balanced entry under **9/11 Truth Movement**, with links to the various professional groups who insist on raising awkward questions. These include **Architects and Engineers for 9/11 Truth, Scholars for 9/11 Truth, Pilots for 9/11 Truth, Firefighters for 9/11 Truth** – the headings alone should give an immediate idea of the range of professionals who do not accept the official explanation of what happened that terrible day.

In book form, I recommend *9/11: The Simple Facts*, by Arthur Naiman (Softskull Press). This is short, succinct and full of common sense, argued plausibly and persuasively. It concentrates entirely on facts and undisputed evidence, and is free of theories. It is available both in paperback and as an ebook.

In the interests of balance and fairness I should add that the American magazine *Practical Mechanics* published a wide-ranging debunking exercise of what they call 'conspiracy theories'. Summaries of their work (as well as the full text) can be found online.

Finally, the official account is available in paperback and online, and copies are kept in most public libraries. The epigraph to the novel is an excerpt from the report, technically from: 'Afterword: The Twilight War' by Philip Zelikow. Copyright © 2011 by W. W. Norton & Company, Inc., from *The 9/11 Commission Report: the Attack From Planning to Aftermath by National Commission on Terrorist Attacks*. Used by permission of W. W. Norton & Company, Inc.

Christopher Priest
Isle of Bute, 2018